CRITICAL PRAISE FOR *SEE JANE DATE* BY

Melissa Senate

"You could almost imagine a star like Renée Zellweger being interested in playing a character like this."
—*Entertainment Weekly*

"*See Jane Date* tells the tale of a smart, funny 28-year-old editor at a Manhattan publishing house who has been trapped in a 2-year date drought. Alas, she must dig up a presentable boyfriend to accompany her to her cousin's fancy wedding. The mad date dash is on."
—*USA TODAY*

"...a refreshing change of pace..."
—*Publishers Weekly*

"It's fun to watch Jane bumble her way through the singles scene and find out that sometimes people aren't what they first appear. Senate's debut is both witty and snappy."
—*Booklist*

"The story unfolds like a brightly wrapped bonbon. It's tantalizing and tasty...."
—*Sacramento Bee*

"This Cinderella story provides plot and dramatic tension, but what makes it more than a fairytale is that Jane's daily life...captures the very real loneliness of being a contemporary, urban single."
—*The Washington Monthly*

MELISSA SENATE

Thirtysomething Melissa Senate lives in New York City with her husband, Adam, their son, Max, and their four cats, Pierre, Pandora, Thisbe and Blue. She has a bachelor's degree in creative writing and is halfway through a master's degree in English literature. A former book editor (women's fiction and young adult), Melissa is now a full-time writer. Her debut novel, the bestselling *See Jane Date,* has been translated into over ten languages, is the subject of an answer to a question in the 20th Anniversary Edition of Trivial Pursuit and was adapted for an ABC Family telefilm. *The Solomon Sisters Wise Up* is Melissa's second novel. Her third novel, featuring the character Eloise Manfred from *See Jane Date,* will be published in 2004. Visit Melissa's Web site at www.melissasenate.com.

Melissa Senate

The Solomon Sisters Wise Up

RED DRESS INK™

First edition December 2003

THE SOLOMON SISTERS WISE UP

A Red Dress Ink novel

ISBN 0-373-25041-X

Visit Red Dress Ink at www.reddressink.com

Printed in U.S.A.

For the two great loves of my life, Adam Kempler
and our baby son, Max.

1

Sarah

Between the reality of being six weeks pregnant by a guy I'd been dating for two months and the fantasy of pushing a baby stroller down Columbus Avenue with a wedding ring on my finger were a lot of possibilities. All having much to do with Griffen Maxwell's reaction to the news.

The Ideal Conversation:

Me: "Griffen, I'm pregnant!"

Him: "You've made me the happiest guy in the world." (Drops down on one knee.) "Will you marry me?"

The problem with that scenario was that Griffen had yet to throw around words like *exclusivity,* let alone phrases like *I love you.* And according to my older sister, Ally, that was a good thing; it meant he was normal. *"You can't love someone you've known for eight weeks,"* she'd told me.

But you could.

Ally saw things going more like this:

The Realistic Conversation:

Me: "Griffen, I'm pregnant!"

Him: "Waiter—check, please!" (Runs out of restaurant, never to be seen or heard from again.)

I wanted to have more faith in Griffen than that, but as my sister had pointed out with another piece of unsolicited Ally-wisdom, I didn't really *know-know* the guy. Not in the way you knew your husband, she'd said, or someone you'd been with a long time. *"Ordering in Chow Fun for two and tipsily watching* Fear Factor *or a Yankees game before sex one night during the week and one night of the weekend does not knowing a man make, Sarah."*

Which explained why I'd been stalling for the past half hour. At this very moment, the man in question was sitting across from me in Julien's Brasserie, where he'd taken me to celebrate my twenty-ninth birthday. But instead of my throwing around words like *zygote* and phrases like *Diaphragms aren't one hundred percent effective,* I was talking about the food.

The Actual Conversation:

Me: "Griffen, how's your salmon?"

Him: "Delicious." *(Forks a bite and leans across the table to slip it between my lips. Smiles that amazing smile.)* "Aren't you going to try the champagne, birthday girl?"

There was my in. He'd unwittingly provided me with my segue into why—despite our knowing each other for only eight weeks—he would be tied to me for the rest of his life.

"What makes you think he wouldn't want to be?" friend and co-worker Lisa had asked a few days ago on our lunch hour as we sat on a park bench, staring at pigeons and tossing them most of our sandwiches. "Maybe he's more crazy about you than you think."

Ah, the support of a best friend.

"Sarah doesn't need bullshit," our friend Sabrina had

cut in. "He hasn't exactly been acting like a guy who's madly in love."

I repeat: Ah, the support of a best friend. In Lisa and Sabrina, I had exactly what I needed: one who coddled and one who told the truth.

"Mmm..." Griffen murmured as he sipped his champagne, closing his eyes for a moment. "Good stuff."

Tell him, I ordered myself. Tell him!

Wish I could chug the entire bottle, Griffen, but, alas, no bubbly for me for the next seven and a half months—I'm pregnant!

Thing was, as Griffen Maxwell of the dimples and pale brown eyes went on to tell me a funny story about an idiot news anchor (he's a television news producer)—"She forgot to say *allegedly* murdered and now the station and network are being sued for millions!"—and stabbed his spinach salad and sipped his champagne and grimaced at the escargots I thought I had a craving for but now couldn't bear the smell of, I wasn't quite ready to change his entire life.

Which was exactly what one quarter-inch, horizontal pink line on the stick of a home pregnancy test did to me four mornings ago in a bathroom stall at work on an ordinary October Monday. Before that pink line, I was the usual me, fretting over whether my story ideas for *Wow Woman* magazine—where I was a junior editor—were good enough for the weekly staff meeting and my boss's overplucked eyebrow, which rose whenever she liked an idea, as though she couldn't believe a member of the underappreciated junior editorial staff had thought of it. I'd spent the previous evening coming up with five good concepts, including "Thirty Things To Do Before

You're Thirty." I'd been particularly attached to that one, since I was about to turn twenty-nine and had done absolutely nothing on my list. But I could…take that solo trip to Paris! Go to a movie alone on a Saturday night! Read *Middlemarch!* Open a Roth IRA! Have sex in a naughty locale!

What wasn't on the list? Have a baby!

Because five nights ago, when I made up that list, I couldn't have a baby. I couldn't even fathom it, not even in the abstract—not yet, anyway. My salary, my roommate, my penchant for vodka and cranberry juice every Thursday, Friday and Saturday night, my lack of a serious relationship, let alone a husband, my distaste for milk, green vegetables, flabby abs, doctors with rubber gloves, pain and the unknown all negated the concept of baby.

"Jesus, Sarah, ever heard of birth control? What the hell is wrong with you? What are you, seventeen? If you need money, just ask, okay? Where would you put a crib in that shoebox of an apartment—in the kitchen next to the litter box? Do you want to move in with me and Andrew? How could you be so careless? What did your gyno say? Is she an OB too? Do you feel pregnant? How come you're so goddamned fertile, anyway?"

Those were my sister Ally's rush of questions, which followed a long silence when I told her the news at three o'clock this morning. I hadn't meant to call Ally, hadn't meant to tell her at all, at least not right away, not before I had a handle on it myself. But after tossing and turning for hours last night, with Griffen's potential reactions getting scarier and scarier, I'd grabbed the phone and sobbed into it. After two hours, Ally had gotten me to stop crying and extracted a promise to call her the minute I decided what I was going to do. I knew what I was going to do, but you didn't tell a lawyer that. You told a lawyer, one like Ally, anyway, that you'd think over your options very carefully.

And yes, I had been using birth control. I'd been fitted for a diaphragm a few years ago that hadn't seen the light of day in a year and a half, until Griffen. I used it every time we made love. Fifteen times, to be exact. Griffen and I had settled into a twice-a-week pattern, on Tuesday or Wednesday night and either Friday or Saturday night. And during our second week of dating, when I didn't even know if he had a middle name, we'd gone back to my apartment for a nightcap and unknowingly made a child.

I was amazed that no one could tell. Moments after the pink line changed everything, I'd stared at myself under the fluorescent lights in *Wow*'s bathroom mirror for ten minutes, puzzled that I looked and felt exactly as I had before the pink line. Same blue eyes. Same dark brown, just-past-the-shoulders straight hair. Same teeny-tiny scar above my lip. You couldn't tell. Couldn't see it. Everything was the same.

"Your boobs are bigger," Lisa had said, staring at my reflection.

"And your feet are gonna grow half a size," Sabrina had added later.

But I looked the same. I felt the same. Just as I had when I'd gotten my period for the first time at twelve and lost my virginity at nineteen. I'd been walking around pregnant for six weeks and didn't know it. Miracles big and small were in the making in my own body, and I'd been eating bagels and taking the subway and having sex and complaining about work and my sisters as though nothing out of the ordinary were happening.

It never occurred to me that I might be pregnant. The only reason I even took the pregnancy test was because Lisa, who got pregnant once and lived in fear of it ever happening again, insisted. Lisa always kept a kit in her bathroom medicine cabinet and her desk drawer at work. She was on the pill and made her live-in boyfriend use condoms during ovulation days, but if her period was even a half hour late, she took a home pregnancy test for peace of mind. So when I'd whispered in the elevator on our way up to *Wow*'s offices that I thought my period, which I rarely kept track of, was late, but that I wasn't worried because I had wicked PMS, Lisa looked at me very closely.

"Are you tired?" she asked. "I mean, *really* tired? That's a surefire symptom of pregnancy."

Of course I was tired. Who wasn't? I worked ten-hour days at *Wow Woman,* trying to outdo my rival for a promotion and impress our boss and come up with story ideas such as "What Your Eye Shadow Says About You" and "Is She Really Your Friend?" and assigning and editing those pieces (and sometimes writing them myself). Two weeks ago, the senior features editor had gotten herself a job at *Elle,* so there was an opening. My competition for the promotion and I both had four years at the magazine (we'd started as editorial assistants the same month), but until this past Monday, I'd thought the job was mine-all-mine. Danielle Ann (yes, that was her last name) was seven months pregnant, and our boss, editor-in-chief Astrid O'Connor, wasn't exactly sympathetic to exhaustion, bathroom breaks, doctor appointments during work hours or maternity leave.

Note to self: reveal pregnancy to boss at last possible moment.

"And has your appetite increased?" Lisa had wanted to know as we walked into *Wow*'s loftlike office. "And are your breasts rock-hard yet really sore?"

"Yeah, and it's called PMS," I'd said on my way to the

bathroom to make sure that my makeup, shirt, skirt, tights and shoes were Astrid-proof.

Astrid O'Connor knew that *Wow*'s staff made crap money, but she expected you to dress creatively-stylishly-on-a-budget if you worked for a women's magazine. If she didn't approve of your skirt or your lipstick, she'd stare at the offending item for a full ten seconds (which felt like an eternity), then turn her back and walk away. Before Danielle announced her pregnancy, Astrid had assigned her the "How To Dress Stylishly on a Budget" piece, since Danielle was the most stylish of all the junior staff. After the big announcement, Astrid glanced at Danielle's maternity shirts, elastic waistbands and comfortable shoes with the word *sloth* in her eyes.

Self-Astrid-proofed, I'd disappeared into a stall only to find Lisa handing me a *Know Now* home pregnancy test under the door.

"For *me,*" Lisa said. "For *my* peace of mind, okay?"

If you want to waste the eleven bucks, I thought as she whispered the instructions. I did as she said, then placed the stick on top of the toilet paper dispenser.

Lisa squeezed into the stall with me and stared at her watch. "Have you been super moody lately?" she asked.

"I'm not pregnant, Lisa. What you're describing is called PMS, and I've got it big-time."

"Okay, okay," she said, eyes on her watch. "Ding. Time."

"Be my guest," I told her, gesturing at the stick.

Lisa picked it up and stared at it, her eyes wide. "Um, it doesn't look *exactly* like the one on the back of the box."

I elbowed her in the ribs with a "shut up."

"Sarah—" She held out the stick to me.

I unlocked the stall door. "C'mon, we're going to be late for the staff meeting."

Lisa pulled me back and latched the stall and I expected her to shout out, *April Fools!* even though it was October. But she didn't. She stared at me, then started gnawing on her lower lip. When her hand began trembling, I took the stick and looked in the little square.

And there was one life-changing quarter-inch, horizontal pink line, a bit fainter than the one on the test box, but there nonetheless.

I grabbed the box and read the bold print. *The appearance of a pink line, no matter how faint or broken, indicates pregnancy. See your doctor...*

And then I dropped down on the toilet bowl, staring at the pink line that wasn't supposed to be there.

With a very serious "I'll be right back," Lisa went to tell Astrid's assistant that I'd gotten violently ill in the bathroom after eating a bad scrambled-eggs-and-bacon sandwich from the deli on the corner and that she was taking me home in a taxi. Five minutes later, the two of us were sitting on a bench in Union Square Park, where we didn't move for two hours, except to get up to hug Sabrina, who came rushing over the moment Lisa called her with the news that I was pregnant with Griffen Maxwell's baby.

"Embryo!" Sabrina corrected. "It's not a baby, it's an *embryo!* And after it's an embryo, it'll be a *fetus!* It's not a baby!"

Even in my state of numbed *I'm-pregnant* shock, I understood that my dear friend Sabrina was telling me that I had options to consider. Choices.

The only choices running through my mind on that park bench were nature's: Would the baby god pick Griffen's wavy blond hair or my poker-straight dark brown?

Griffen's light brown eyes, or my blue ones? His dimples, or my lack of them? The Solomon aquiline nose or Griffen's Roman one?

"Embryos don't have hair or eye colors!" Sabrina practically shouted when I wondered those thoughts aloud.

But they sort of did, and that was when I burst into tears and wished more than ever that my mother was alive, so I could run straight into her arms and *be* the baby. Was *I* going to *have* a baby? I *was* going to have a baby. *I'm pregnant,* I thought over and over and over. *I'm pregnant. Pregnant. Pregnant. Pregnant.*

"I guess we can't go to Princess for their killer margaritas," Lisa said, and we all turned to look across the park at our favorite trendy bar.

"We can if she's going to have an abortion," Sabrina pointed out.

And then they both looked at me, and I bit my lip and shook my head.

"Earth to Sarah. Earth to Sarah."

I glanced up from my picked-at filet mignon in béarnaise sauce to find Griffen Maxwell smiling that smile, the one that had led to sex on our second date.

"You were a million miles away," he said, taking another sip of the champagne that I wanted to chug. "Trying to figure out what I got you for your birthday?" He eyed the bright red gift bag next to him. Silver tissue paper puffed over the top. "It's something you hinted you wanted," he added, surprising me even more than he had by getting me a gift in the first place.

That reminded me of the "Is He Your Boyfriend or Just a Guy You're Dating?" quiz that Lisa had written for *Wow* a couple of years ago:

Q: You've been dating for six weeks, but aren't exclusive. For your birthday, he gives you:

A) Nothing.

B) A gold bracelet.

C) Dinner and a movie.

D) A book.

I'd given it my best guess, *C*, which turned out to be the *He's on the Way To Becoming Your Boyfriend* answer. Answer *A* meant he was a jerk. *D* depended on the book. *The History of Western Civilization* from the bargain bin meant he didn't care about you but knew no present meant no sex. The hardcover you'd mentioned you wanted to read when you were browsing Barnes & Noble together meant that he not only liked you but was a good listener (not that Griffen and I had ever browsed a bookstore together). *B* meant he was a potential stalker.

I'd been right about *C*, except for the movie part, but Griffen *had* also gotten me a present.

Maybe Lisa was right. Maybe he was more committed to the relationship than I thought.

Tell him, I ordered myself. *Tell him right now.*

I opened my mouth, but slid in a forkful of steak.

I opened my mouth again, but the waiter came over, granting me a twelve-second reprieve. And while Griffen ordered another bottle of Pellegrino, I stared at his Roman nose and hoped the baby inherited it.

My stomach churned. How *would* he react? Unlike Ally, I didn't think Griffen would run screaming out of the restaurant, never to be seen or heard from again. I also didn't think he'd drop down on one knee and offer me the ring of my choice in Tiffany's (I rented *Sweet Home Alabama* a few nights ago).

I had no idea what he'd say. I knew only that as he sat across from me, I had visions of the two of us in the nursery of our Upper West Side brownstone or Upper East Side two-bedroom prewar high-rise on the twenty-something floor, deciding on a *Where the Wild Things Are* or *Peter Pan* mural and registering for essential items like musical mobiles and bouncy seats.

Tell him! Tell him!

"I'm *dying* to know what's in that bag," I said.

Chicken shit.

With that sex-inducing smile, Griffen slid the red bag across the table.

Inside all that passionate red and silver puffing was a thick paperback biography of Theodore Roosevelt, which was right up there with *The History of Western Civilization.*

"Griffen, are you seeing anyone else?" I blurted out.

We both froze, his fork in midair, midway to his mouth, my mind in midthought. I hadn't meant to ask that question; it was way too loaded for what I really had to blurt out tonight.

He took the bite of herb-encrusted salmon. "Uh-oh, you don't like the book," he said, coy smile on those lips. "I should have gotten you the scarf. I knew it."

A scarf would have been better. A biography of *Eleanor* Roosevelt would have been better.

Damn. Damn. Damn. There was no denying that Griffen Maxwell wasn't in love with me. You knew when a guy really liked you and when he just *liked* you and liked having sex with you. You knew. From date one, I'd figured Griffen was somewhere in between. But I still thought there was potential. After all, as article after *Wow* article said, you weren't supposed to have expectations. You were supposed to *have fun while leading your busy life!*

"He'll never marry you," Ally had said two minutes into our phone conversation last night. *"Signs, Sarah,"* she said.

"You have to pay attention to the signs. A guy in love doesn't leave your apartment at three in the morning. A guy in love doesn't play racquetball on Sunday mornings when he should be having lox and bagels and the Times *in bed with you. It's like that Fleetwood Mac song says—if he doesn't love you now, he'll never love you again."*

I told her I thought that was the most depressing thing I'd ever heard, that we *had* been dating for only two months.

"Duh!" and *"Stop living in a fucking fairy tale already"* were among just a few of her responses. *"The guy doesn't even sleep over, Sarah. He's not going to pass out cigars when you tell him you're pregnant."*

I wasn't sure why Ally, who married her smarmy husband right out of law school at age twenty-three, thought she knew anything about men or dating. That expertise had been bestowed on my half sister, Zoe, who at twenty-six somehow managed to make a very good living as a relationship guru by critiquing people's dates. I would have hired Zoe myself during my early dates with Griffen, but she lived in L.A. and we weren't exactly close on sisterly terms.

Griffen was flipping through my birthday present. "I think you'll really like the book," he said. "Teddy Roosevelt's one of my heroes. The station's doing a segment on him next week. I'll set up your VCR to tape it."

Before the pink line, a statement like that would have gotten me very excited. I would have read into it, extrapolating: 1) I want to see you again. 2) I want to be inside your apartment. 3) I want to do things for you. 4) I want to share my work with you. 5) This relationship is definitely going somewhere.

Now, though, all I heard was exactly what he said.

I took a sip of my Pellegrino and wondered if he'd still

come over to tape it for me after running screaming out of the restaurant. "Great! Thanks," I told him.

"So you *do* like the present," he said. "Whew! It's not easy buying a birthday present for someone you haven't been seeing that long."

Bad sign number two.

He then rushed into a monologue about Teddy Roosevelt and the turn of the last century. As he talked on and on about old New York and corruption and poverty and the Lower East Side, I realized that he knew I wanted an answer to The Question and that he was hoping I'd either back down or be bored to death.

"Um, Griffen?"

He paused, busying himself with the saltshaker, sipping his champagne, slicing, dabbing.

"I was serious back there," I said. "I really need to know if you're dating anyone else."

"Sarah..." He smiled a bit tightly and suddenly took both my hands across the table. "You know what *I* really need to know? If you're finished with your dinner so that I can propose a toast." He didn't wait or even take a breath. He raised his champagne glass. "To you, on your twenty-ninth birthday."

The words *so that I can propose* echoed in my head. *So that I can propose. So that I can propose. Propose. Propose. Propose.*

I didn't lift my glass. He eyed me, then took a sip of his champagne.

"Griffen?"

Blank stare. Slight tinge of annoyance on his face.

"Sa-rah..."

I could feel my cheeks turning red. "Look, Griffen, we've been seeing each other for two months, and I'd like to know where we stand. It's not so out of line for me to ask."

Screw how loaded the question was, given what I had to tell him. I wanted to know. I had to know.

He sighed. "Okay. You're right. It's not out of line at all."

I waited.

He took another sip of champagne, then leaned across the table, took both my hands again and smiled. "Sarah, I really like you and we have a good time together. How about if we leave it at that for now and just enjoy ourselves?"

Why did guys always say that? Why? It meant *Yes, I am seeing other people,* or *Not necessarily, but I want to reserve the right because I don't really feel that way about you, even though I like you fine and enjoy your company.*

Tears pricked the backs of my eyes, and I blinked them back hard.

He squinted across the table at me in the candlelight. "Oh shit, are you crying?" He sat back.

"I just want to know if we're headed anywhere," I said, my voice squeaking.

Groan of frustration. "Honestly, Sarah, I don't know. I like you a lot. I really enjoy your company. That's what I know."

A small sob escaped me.

He took a deep breath. "Okay. For starters, I think you're taking this a lot more seriously than I am. I'm not really looking for anything serious right now. If you want the truth, that's it."

That's when the tears came, fast and furious.

And that was also when I heard the faint beginning of someone singing "Happy Birthday To You." The song got louder, closer. I looked up to find our waiter finishing, "Happy birthday, dear Sarah, Happy birthday to you," and setting down a cupcake with a tiny lit candle in the center.

"Make a wish!" Griffen said. He smiled and was looking at me with the expression of a guy who was under the impression that a thoughtful gesture would allow us to kiss and make up—or at least get me to shut up. I was tempted to conk him over the head with the bottle of Pellegrino. Was he a jerk or just clueless? "It's chocolate with white icing," he added. "I remembered when we passed Veniero's on our first date, you looked at all the desserts in the window and said that with all the amazing treats to choose from, your favorite was still a plain old chocolate cupcake with white icing."

He couldn't be a jerk. Jerks didn't remember things like that. Or say things like that. Right?

He stared at me for a second, clearly waiting for a smile or a *You're right, we're enjoying ourselves! Let's just have a good time!* When I hung my head so low that I almost got frosting on my chin, he said, "Look, Sarah, I feel like I should just come right out and say what's on my mind."

I'm in love with you, Sarah. I'm in love with you. I'm in love with you.

He cleared his throat. "I really like you, but I don't want to lead you on. Maybe we should just be friends."

What, and be a single mother? I thought numbly, per that old joke.

But it wasn't a joke.

I was only supposed to be pregnant. That was enough to contend with. For the past week, I'd been slowly accepting that word as applicable to myself. *I am pregnant. I am a pregnant woman. I take prenatal vitamins and don't drink coffee or alcoholic beverages. If I have a cold or a sore throat, I brave it out. I am a pregnant person.*

The concept of single motherhood hadn't really registered on my radar.

I stared down at my cupcake and cried. The man and woman at the table to our right were glancing at me.

"Sarah," Griffen said through gritted teeth, "why don't you have some champagne? It'll help you calm down."

"I can't have any champagne," I muttered.

"Have some," he said as though I hadn't spoken, his eyes darting around in embarrassment. "You'll feel better, trust me."

"I can't have any alcohol, you asshole! I'm pregnant!"

Griffen didn't signal the waiter and ask for the check and go running out of the restaurant, the way my sister thought he might.

He just sat there, looking as though someone had just kicked him very hard in the stomach.

"Congratulations, honey," the elderly woman at the next table whispered to me.

It was a good thing I didn't know until three o'clock this morning that Sarah was pregnant, or I would have ended up driving back into the city last night to drag Andrew away from his shareholders' dinner meeting and into the bathroom of the Palm steakhouse for a quickie against the sink.

I was ovulating.

And my sister, my *younger* sister, was pregnant.

I was ovulating, my younger sister was pregnant, and where was my husband? He was working late, meeting clients early, researching something online, going for a jog. He was anywhere but in bed with me.

And as my eggs were at this very moment aging in unbearable bumper-to-bumper traffic on the Cross Island Expressway—I slammed down on the horn with a *honnnnnk!*—I had to concede that my marriage wasn't what it used to be.

"Whose is?" my friend Kristina had said earlier this afternoon during lunch-hour Botox injections in a small spa near our midtown law offices. "It stops being about sex after the second year."

I would have shaken my head, but a woman in a white lab coat was aiming a needle at the "angry spot" between my eyes. "Andrew and I had good sex for longer than two years," I countered. "We still have decent sex. Well, sometimes."

Kristina snort-laughed. "Yeah, because you're having it once a month, Ally. Of course it's good. And trust me, if you two weren't trying to get pregnant, you'd have sex once every three months."

I didn't know about that. Andrew and I had been trying in earnest to have a baby for only the past five years. We'd been married eleven. That left six years. Take away the first two, and that left four years in between of good, more-than-once-every-month sex.

"Anyway, Kris, what man would willingly go without sex for three months?"

She sat up and looked at me as if I'd just sprung down from Planet Naive. "No man would. It's called a little harmless nookie on the side."

I sat up and looked at her as if she'd just sprung down from Planet Are You Kidding Me? "Since when is 'nooky on the side' little or harmless?" I asked, grabbing a mirror and admiring the newly plump bridge of my nose. "Wait a minute—are you saying you know that Jack is cheating on you and you don't care?"

She rolled her eyes. "It's not that I don't *care,* it's that I don't care to know *for sure.* We have a good, solid marriage, we love our little Ben, we have history. That's what I care about."

Kristina had been married for two years. Two. She'd given her longtime boyfriend (of seven years) an ultimatum three times over the course of six months, and the third time had been the charm.

She got pregnant on her honeymoon.

We freshened our lipsticks and fluffed our hair in the large, round mirror on the wall. "Trust me, Kris, if Andrew were even thinking about cheating on me, I'd know it. We've been married for eleven years, and we dated for two years before that. I *know* the man."

"Okay, okay," she said. "There's another category, then. Husbands like Andrew in their late thirties, early forties, who don't need it like they used to. Sex is available every night, right there in their own bed, but they're too tired, like us. We all work twelve-hour days, commute three hours round trip, spend our lunch hours getting Botox and facials or running a few miles at the track at the gym. Who has time or energy for sex? Married couples want to come home, eat dinner, read a chapter or two in a book, watch a little TV and kiss their spouse goodnight. Lights out. A little dull, but comfortable. You get through the seven-year-itch, your marriage is stronger for it. And then one day you realize you're your parents."

How romantic. And that didn't describe my parents' marriage. The seven-year-itch hadn't destroyed my parents' marriage—another woman had.

But it did describe my own marriage.

Which was why I was reading an asinine book called *How To Spice Up Your Marriage* by the equally asinine and ridiculously popular married marriage therapists, Doctor Joan and Doctor Jake. I was on chapter four, which was about the importance of oral sex in bringing back the sparks. *Ladies, when was the last time you performed oral sex on your husband?* Doctor Jake asked in his section of the chapter. *Hit the video stores and rent the classic* Deep Throat. *That's all the education you need, ladies!*

Idiot.

Dr. Joan had then chastised her husband and colleague in her section (that was their schtick), then gave step-by-step instructions on how to give a proper blow job. *And you've gotta swallow, girls!*

Sexual intercourse didn't always interest Andrew. But if I put my mouth anywhere near the region of his penis, he began to pant. And then I'd get what I wanted. Sperm inside me. And, sorry, Dr. Jake and Dr. Joan, but I wasn't referring to my throat. I needed the sperm to fertilize my eggs—not to make me gag and run to the bathroom.

Honkkkkkkkkkkkkkkk!

"Move, goddammit!" I screamed at the traffic.

Calm down. Calm down. Calm down. Remember what the gynecologist said. *Stress is not good for making a baby.*

Still, I didn't have time for rush-hour traffic. My eggs didn't have time for rush-hour traffic.

It was five-thirty, and I wanted to be home by six-thirty to have a good hour to prepare for Andrew, who, according to his snotty little priss of a secretary, would be stopping home for a half hour or so at seven-thirty before a tennis match with a client at the club.

I had thirty minutes of Andrew Sharp's precious time. All I needed was thirty seconds.

For those precious thirty seconds, for my surging luteinizing hormone, I'd gone shopping. I'd left work at five o'clock, the earliest in the history of my law career (and that was after taking the two-hour lunch with Kristina for Botox) so I could nip up to Victoria's Secret. I eyed the pink shopping bag on the passenger seat of my car. *I* could have written the chapter on sex accessories in *How To Spice Up Your Marriage.* Inside that bag was a short, sheer, lacy, low-cut red teddy, matching thong and a grocery bag containing a can of fat-free Cool Whip. I had enough slutty nighties, edible underwear, Kama Sutra body oil and paraphernalia from Come Again, an "adult toy store," to interest my husband in the process of making a thousand babies.

I only wanted one.

"You're going to be thirty-five next month, Ally," my gynecologist had said at my last checkup. *"You can get pregnant through your early forties.* Can. *Maybe. But the odds are very slim. Your best time to conceive was when you were twenty-seven. Your eggs aren't what they used to be. Off the record, Al, either get pregnant now, or start putting yourself on adoption waiting lists."*

For the past five years, my doctor had assured me there was absolutely nothing wrong with me, and Andrew's doctor had assured him his sperm count was just fine.

"All you have to do to get pregnant," my gynecologist had said, *"is make love with your husband. Have lots of sex, regularly. Oh, and decrease your level of stress. Your blood pressure is at the high range of normal."*

Decrease my level of stress. Okay, Doc.

What was making my blood pressure rise to the high range of normal? How about the sixty-hour work week, the quota of two hundred and fifty billable hours a month, and the five male idiots I had to work with at my law firm? If it weren't for Kristina and a female associate and a favorite paralegal, I'd have quit Funwell, Funwell and Logsworth a long time ago—eleven years ago.

And how about the very fancy envelope that arrived in my mailbox two weeks ago, alerting me to the fact that my father and his girlfriend were engaged? (Had my father called to tell me the news himself? Of course not.) Also included was a little card inviting me to participate in "Archweller-Solomon Wedding Fest," the wedding-planning extravaganza to which my father and Wife No. 3-to-be were subjecting their immediate family. Invited were the three Solomon daughters, the fiancée's toddler (oh, she'd be a big help) and the fiancée's mother. The invitation included days and times (starting late October and continuing through after New Year's) for visiting venues, caterers, florists, harpists, photographers, dress boutiques, et cetera, conveniently after work hours and on weekends so that the Solomon sisters and their patriarch, all of whom actually worked for a living (except for Zoe—sorry, half sis, but I wouldn't call being the "Dating Diva of L.A." a *job*) could attend all or some events.

Then again, given that Zoe's own ex-friend had stolen Daddy Dearest away from Zoe's mother, I doubted Zoe would be flying anywhere near New York City to smell floral arrangements and taste rubber chicken.

My father was out of his mind. Had been for as long as I'd known him. And my stepmother-to-be was twenty-five.

That reminded me. Also added to my list of stressors was the fact that said stepmother-to-be was younger than myself and my younger sisters.

And one of those sisters was pregnant. Without trying. With trying *not* to get pregnant.

It was so goddamned fucking unfair!

I've learned a lot from Ally, but she curses excessively in the office, and I don't think it's professional….

Ally has screamed at me four times in the past month over minor errors in minor briefs. I've documented every instance….

Ally, the senior partners and I commend you on another stellar performance review. However, several of the male associates have commented that your management style is a bit emasculating….

Yeah, because I don't have a penis, you wuss! I'd wanted to yell at Funwell number two this morning. (Funwell number one was long dead.)

That was one more thing to add to my list. Not the penis, but the double standard. Why were the male senior attorneys allowed to yell their heads off and bully the associates, but I wasn't? Because I was a woman, that's why.

"Why would you want to bully anyone?" my sister Sarah had asked last week—pre-knowledge of pregnancy—when we'd met for lunch to discuss how many Wedding Fest "events" we'd really have to attend. Sarah thought three, tops. I thought one. We both thought Princess Zoe should have to pick up the slack since she had always been our father's favorite, but Sarah also doubted Zoe would make an appearance. "My boss is a bully," Sarah continued, "and all it does is alienate people."

"No, Sarah," I told her, pointing a bread stick at her. "Intimidating people, especially in the workplace, is a *good* thing. It gets things accomplished and gets you what you want, what you need. If you weren't so nicey-nicey, you'd probably be a senior editor by now."

She rolled her eyes and sipped her Coke (would she *ever* learn to order iced tea in a real restaurant?). "I'd rather be a nice junior editor than a bitchy senior editor."

"And what do you have for being so nice?" I demanded.

"I have good friends," Sarah said. "I have a job I'm very happy with, thank you very much. I have a new black leather jacket from you. If I weren't so nice, you wouldn't have gotten me such a great birthday present, and a whole week early."

"You're wrong," I told her. "I didn't get the jacket for you because you're nice. I got it for you because you *need* it. And you need it *now,* not a week from now. That ratty sweater-coat you've been wearing is three seasons ago and covered with your roommate's cat fur. You'll never get promoted if you show up for work at a women's magazine in that thing."

"Now who's nice?" she singsonged.

I pointed the bread stick at her again. "*Nice* has nothing to do with why people do things for you. Last year, you waited in line for two hours in the freezing cold to get me tickets to the Rockettes' Christmas show for my birthday. You didn't do it because I'm nice."

"You're right. I did it because *I'm* nice," she countered, grabbing the bread stick. She tore off a piece and popped it into her mouth. "And, anyway, Mom was nice."

I held my tongue. I wasn't sure whether Sarah brought up our mother because she knew it would always shut me up or because she didn't understand *why* it always shut me up.

My mother had been nice. And it had cost her.

Sarah was nice and she was pregnant.

So which was it? My mother was nice and had ended up with nothing. My sister was nice and had ended up with what I wanted more than anything.

Was I being denied a baby because I was a little bitchy?

Bitchy. Ten years ago, when Andrew and I were barely out of the newlywed stage (and having sex three times a day), Sarah had called me a bitch over something I'd said to Zoe during a tense Thanksgiving dinner, the last Solomon Thanksgiving I attended. The verbal slap hurt. Our mother had died several months earlier, and there Sarah and I were—sitting like Cinderellas at the Solomon dinner table two thousand miles away in bizarrely warm Los Angeles with our father, our crazy stepmother, Judith, their Princess Zoe, who at the time was sixteen, her anorexic aunt and pontificating uncle, their rude kid and

Zoe's shedding Persian cat, which kept rubbing up against my new black pants—celebrating Thanksgiving without our mother for the first time in our lives. Our father was our only connection to that table, to the holiday, and that wasn't saying much. Sarah was all I had. And she'd called me a bitch.

Had I said a mean thing? Yes. Had I deserved to be called a bitch? Probably. But not by Sarah, not by my own sister, my only ally left in the world. And that night, in one of my father's guest bedrooms, after Andrew and I had made love, when we were entwined in each other's arms and legs, my head on his chest and his hands in my hair, my greatest pleasure listening to the gradual slowing of his racing heartbeat, I asked him, hiding the tears in my eyes and the pain in my voice, if he thought I was a bitch.

He'd kissed the top of my head and said, "You're quite possibly the sweetest person I've ever known, Allison Solomon Sharp." And then he drifted off to sleep, and so did I, and I'd woken up okay.

I'd also woken up with one of those personal paradigm shifts from seeing what I didn't have to seeing what I did. When had I reverted back?

Honk!!! Honk!!! Honnnnnnnnnnnnnnnnnnnnnnnk!

Only one of those honks was mine—but it was the long one. Traffic was crawling! *Honk!!!*

Calm down. Calm down. Calm down. Stress is not good for making a baby.

Soon I'd be luxuriating in a lavender-scented bath, reading the new *In Style,* slipping into the new nightie and doing my hair—about which Andrew had commented last week he liked longer and less red-red, though according to me and the *Vogue* page I'd handed the stylist, my newly short tresses and You Rock Red color were superhip.

We'd have some wine, nibble on some cheese and crackers and make love. In under twenty-five minutes.

And (please God) maybe we'd make a baby.

As the traffic moved at a two-miles-an-hour pace, I stared at the Baby On Board sign in the back window of the SUV in front of me and wondered why I had allowed Andrew to put me off for those first five years of our marriage—the years my eggs were at their peak!

"We're too young," Andrew had said. *"I want to spend time with my beautiful wife for a while. I want to make love to you at two in the morning, not change diapers or feed a screaming baby. I want to travel the world with you. Ally, we make a fortune. We're young and ambitious. We have a great social life. Let's enjoy our lives for a few years, and then start a family. What's the rush?"*

The rush turned out to be time itself. Yes, we'd enjoyed our lives. Yes, we lived very well. We had an amazing house in Great Neck, Long Island. We took vacations. I had expensive facials; Andrew bought pricey golf clubs. We had a Jaguar, a Mercedes SUV and a Volvo for crappy weather.

But we had lived well for a long time.

And the nursery in our house, all set up for its tiny occupant, remained empty.

Sigh. The day after I returned from my honeymoon (Greek islands), I'd driven straight to Baby Central and spent over three thousand dollars outfitting the nursery. I had the Italian crib, the Diaper Genie, twelve receiving blankets—including one made out of cashmere that I'd bought in Greece—diapers in two sizes, just in case I had a particularly large baby (Andrew was six-two and very muscular). I had the mobiles, the car seat, the stroller. The bouncy seat, the breast pump, the changing table.

I had everything I could possibly need or want, except the baby.

That shopping trip had been eleven years ago.

Which meant I'd been through changes in safety regulations, recalls and my own taste. Back went the Italian pecan-colored crib for a white sleigh model from Pottery Barn Kids. Back went the car seat with a three-point harness for one with a five-point harness. Back went the brightly colored mobile when I read an article stating that infants prefer black-and-white.

Lately, I'd started giving some things in the nursery to Allison, the six-month-old who lived two houses down. I wasn't particularly close with Allison's mother and barely knew her father, but the couple had named their baby girl Allison, and I'd felt particularly close to my tiny namesake (despite the fact that they refused to call her Ally and chastised anyone who did. "Her name is Alli-*son,*" they'd snap.). She was a colicky little thing, constantly crying, her skinny legs stiff, her tiny fists balled, that newborn face red and scrunched. A week after her mother, Tara, had brought her home from the hospital, I'd gone over with a Baby Gap gift to get a peek, and Tara, close to tears of frustration and exhaustion, had asked me if I'd hold Allison for just five minutes while she washed her face and took a breath.

Thrilled, I sent Tara off to the sofa for as long a nap as she wanted. And while she snored, I walked that little swaddled bundle up and down the length of the house for an hour. I sang nursery rhymes to her, I fed her a bottle of formula, I rocked her, I nuzzled her cheek.

I fell in love with that screaming thing before I'd even laid eyes on her.

Tara and I hadn't become friends over the months; we were too different (she was the Earth mother type), but we had become friendly enough, and she had taken me up on my offer to baby-sit many times. One Saturday afternoon, Andrew had come home to find me trying to calm Allison, my ivory Donna Karan suit jacket soaked with projectile-vomited formula and drool, and he'd stared at us with an expression I couldn't name. It wasn't the expression of a man touched by the sight of his wife holding an infant. And it wasn't horror, exactly. It was fear, maybe.

And it was fear that had kept me from asking him about it. If he had any hesitations about having a baby, I didn't want to know about them.

And so I'd continued to baby-sit Allison, showing her the nursery in my house that her new little friend-to-be would live in, letting her play with the colorful, squishy Lamaze toys, watching her eyes follow the hanging animals on the activity gym, calming her in the vibrating bouncy seat.

I planned to name my baby after my mother, Leah. Leigh for a girl and Lee for a boy.

"Ally, you can't get desperate," my gynecologist had said. *"You have to relax to make a baby. You hear all the time about women who spend a fortune on fertility drugs and don't conceive, only to eventually conceive on their own when they stop trying so hard...."*

I *was* desperate.

And desperate was exactly how I felt when I finally pulled in to my driveway at six-thirty. The path to the house was pitch-dark, and I almost tripped on a branch that had fallen during Wednesday's near-monsoon. I craned my neck around the huge oak tree in the front yard to see if Tara and Allison were home, but the lights were out at their house.

Allison had outgrown her colic but was now beginning to teethe, and I'd picked up a cute teething ring for her in the drugstore when I'd been restocking my supply of Tums. It was probably a good thing that the lights were off at Allison's; if I stopped by, I wouldn't be able to resist fussing over her, and I had only a half hour to get ready for Andrew.

Get ready for Andrew. There had been a time when all I had to do was appear. Sweatpants or naked, it hadn't mattered. Now, I had to work hard. Fifty minutes of Pilates twice a week. Kundalini yoga three times a week. Three-mile run four days a week. And the hard work paid off—at thirty-five-to-be, I had the body of a woman in her twenties. A killer body, Andrew used to say.

When? Up until six months ago? A year ago? Two years? Five? When had Andrew Sharp stopped salivating over me?

"You're such a goddamned bitch sometimes, Ally," he'd said a few times this year.

Maybe that was when he'd stopped. Somehow I'd gone from being the sweetest person he'd ever met to being a goddamned bitch.

Why? Because I asked for what I wanted? Because I didn't let him get away with crap?

I was back to my original question. Why was I a bitch for *wanting?*

Bark! Bark-bark!

The moment I opened the front door, Mary Jane, my Maltese terrier, tried to jump up into my arms.

"Hello, precious," I cooed. I threw my briefcase, keys and suit jacket on the back of the couch, then scooped up Mary Jane and nuzzled her soft white fur. She licked my chin (*"And you expect me to kiss you?"* Andrew liked to ask when he witnessed Mary Jane's affection for me), then she flew out of my arms for the doggie door leading to the backyard. I heard her scamper on the pile of dry leaves that Andrew had raked last Sunday. Great. He'd have a fit. He hated Mary Jane as it was.

"What the fu—" I heard my husband yell.

Andrew was home?

I walked to the door that led to the deck. And there, barely visible in the gathering darkness, was Mary Jane on the hammock between the two evergreens. She was sitting on Andrew's bare back.

I was about to call out to ask him what the hell he was doing taking a nap naked on the hammock (it was unseasonably warm for late October but it wasn't *that* warm), when I noticed one long, slender leg shoot up around his.

As I stood there squinting to see, Andrew tried to shoo Mary Jane off him, and he raised himself up so that his penis was dangling.

Someone was underneath him.

"Forget the stupid dog," said a woman's voice, a familiar voice I couldn't place, and then she grabbed Andrew's ass and pulled him against her. In seconds, his ass was bobbing up and down, accompanied by grunts.

A ponytail of long, thick blond hair was tossed over the side of the hammock, and Andrew fisted it. The woman let out a series of sounds I hadn't made in years.

I knew that hair. Very well. Twice a week well. My husband was screwing my Pilates instructor.

As the old grandfather clock tick-tocked, I stood there and watched Andrew's ass bob up and down, listened to him and Marnie moan, listened to Andrew say, *Shush, the neighbors might hear,* listened to Mary Jane kicking up leaves under the hammock.

And I was still standing there when the two of them got up, bare naked, and came through the door into the living room.

At the sight of me, Andrew's eyes went wide and he froze.

Marnie gasped, said, "Oh, shit!" and ran for the couch, where she threw on her jacket and bolted out the door.

Andrew's expression went from nervousness to anger back to nervousness.

We stared at each other for a good half minute.

"I didn't think you'd be home until at least seven-thirty," he said, raking a hand through his thick, chestnut-colored hair. "You're never home before seven-thirty."

"That's what you have to say?" I asked.

The spots of red on his cheeks flamed in and out the way they did when he was flustered and trying to get himself out a mess. "I just mean that I wouldn't have— If I knew you were coming home early, I never would have—"

"So you didn't plan on getting caught," I said. "Is that it?"

Those shrewd green eyes were measuring me, taking stock of my expression, of whether I was more hurt or angry. I always could tell when Andrew was trying to figure out how to play me. "I just meant that— Ally, hurting you is the last thing I'd want. Of course I wouldn't want—" He paused, taking in the fury sparking off me. Even I could feel it. "Al, it was just sex," he said, reaching for his underwear, which I hadn't noticed, on the floor next to Mary Jane's pet bed. "It didn't mean anything."

He put on his underwear and his pants and then stepped closer to me.

I stepped back.

"Ally, you know it didn't mean anything. I love you."

Was he kidding?

"Ally, I'm sorry. I'm really sorry. It didn't mean anything. I swear."

A little harmless nooky...

I slid down on my butt and covered my face with my hands. This was happening. This was really happening.

"Al, sweetie," he said, kneeling down next to me. I smelled the familiar scent of Marnie's sweat and perfume on his body. "Come on, Al. It doesn't mean anything."

"Of course it means something!" I screamed. "Get the hell away from me!"

He didn't move. "Ally, it's just sex. Sex. No emotion attached to it. It never means anything. I come home to you every night, don't I?"

My head shot up. This wasn't the first time?

"Look, Ally, I know we need to talk. I know things between us haven't been so great lately. We've just both been so busy that we haven't had time to even sit down and have a conversation. We just need to get back on track."

"You mean, back on track in our new open marriage?" I asked, springing up.

He chuckled as though I'd said something truly amusing and also stood. "Ally, it was just a fuck. No big deal. You know I love you." He slipped his hand under my chin and caressed my cheek, then brushed my hair behind my ear. "I do love you. You know that, right?"

I scooped up Mary Jane, slapped Andrew across the face and ran out the door.

Zoe

"I think my biggest problem with men is that I tend to sleep with them too soon," my client said to her date, an attractive man in his mid-thirties. "My shrink says I do it because I'm really seeking intimacy—not sex."

The moment the words *sleep with them too soon* came out of her glossed mouth, her date's eyes traveled south from her eyes to her cleavage and remained there.

What she said next wasn't important; her date was no longer listening to her. He was fantasizing about sex.

From my perch at the bar two feet from their table, where I could hear every word and monitor their body language, I added these thoughts to the three pages I'd already filled up about my client's dating style. In the two statements she'd just uttered, she'd used four words on the first date no-no list: problem, shrink, intimacy and sex.

"Don't you just love L.A.?" my client asked her date. "I used to live in Chicago, but I followed some loser boyfriend out here and ended up staying when I met some other guy. Everything's so free and easy in L.A."

Especially you, the man was most likely thinking.

I jotted down that thought and closed the notebook with a sigh. When I had a client like this one, I felt I was earning my money, which was $225 for a first date, and $175 for subsequent dates.

I critiqued dates for a living. And both unfortunately and fortunately, what a good living it was. Like most of my clients, Amber had hired me to help her figure out why she rarely got a second date. She was especially perplexed because her dates seemed to like her so much when they were having sex with her at the close of the first date.

Earlier this afternoon I had a client whose money I'd tried to refund, but she wouldn't take it. Her problem was a bad case of shyness. She didn't giggle on her date, she didn't lean over and flash her cleavage, she didn't drink too much, she didn't talk about sex, politics, psychologists, religion or her mother. She simply didn't talk. Her date had tried to bring her out of her shell, but she could only nod and occasionally agree with him about something. By the end of the date, which had lasted twenty-five minutes before he'd made an excuse to leave, she had uttered exactly four sentences.

She didn't need me to tell her that the reason he and previous dates never called was because she came across devoid of personality and opinions, despite the fact that she was probably quite interesting. Shy people knew they were shy, which was why I felt she deserved her money back. I'd given her some conversation tips for basic first-date questions, open-ended answers about where she was from and her job as a court stenographer that she could easily remember and that would lead her date to respond and ask more questions. Hopefully, in time that would help her begin to open up.

Amber, however, did need me to tell her why her dates never called. Although, I had a feeling she knew exactly what she was doing. Knew that her coy act would result in interesting the man in sex. But what she was forgetting was that it didn't interest the man in *her.* And that was what she wanted.

"Give it to me straight, Zoe," Amber had said when she'd called to arrange for my services a few days ago. "Be brutal. Not even gently brutal."

Gently brutal was how *L.A. Magazine* had described my advice to the "lovelorn" in the profile they did on me last year, in which they'd dubbed me "the Dating Diva of L.A."

> Zoe Solomon is a relationship guru whom desperate singletons hire to spy on their dates from a nearby table and take notes on everything they do and say wrong so that they can work on all their defenses, bad habits, tics and annoying qualities, such as interrupting, twirling the ends of their hair, crossing their arms, talking too much about themselves, acting like an idiot, drinking too much, talking sex, politics, or past relationships and any other date destroyers. She offers gently brutal advice to the lovelorn and often receives cards and letters from former clients who've transformed from dating disasters to dating divas themselves....

The publicity generated so much business that I dropped out of grad school again and quit my other job, which was spraying annoyed women with perfume in Neiman Marcus sixty times an hour.

School. I was twenty-six years old and still didn't have the master's degree I'd started four years earlier. I had only one more year to get back into my program or I could forget the credits I already had.

"What do you need a degree for?" my mother said time and again. *"You're the famous Dating Diva of L.A.! You should be out gallivanting, not burying that gorgeous face in textbooks."*

Education wasn't a priority with my mother. Good-looking, wealthy men were.

Scratch that. One good-looking, wealthy man in particular was her priority: my father.

"If I looked like you, I'd be out catching myself a wealthy husband and a hot gorgeous boyfriend," my mother had said more than once. *"Hey, maybe you'll meet a winner while you're evaluating a date and you can steal the guy!"* she'd commented when I showed her the *L.A. Magazine* article.

"I have a boyfriend, Mom," I'd reminded her.

And she would flutter her eyes and change the subject. Charlie was both good-looking and wealthy, but she didn't like him.

"He's not the one, angel," she said over and over.

I loved my mother dearly, but she wasn't exactly someone I'd take relationship advice from.

Maybe Charlie was the one.

Then again, maybe not.

When the *L.A. Magazine* reporter heard that I wasn't married or in a long-term relationship (I'd just started dating Charlie then), he was surprised that I had only a useless bachelor's degree in psychology, a job as a perfume sprayer and a lackluster track record in the love department. I'd explained that I'd fallen into the date guru business through a friend, who'd asked if I'd critique a first date with a guy she really liked. She was turning off men, she'd said, and she didn't want to keep blowing it.

I laughed when Cara kept asking me to spy on her dates—what made me an expert on men and dating?

"You might not always have a boyfriend, Zoe—because you don't want one, I might add—but every time we go out, guys swarm all over you, and every date you have calls you the next day and sends you flowers. And that's because you know how to act. Or not act. You're totally yourself. I watch you sometimes and wish I could come across like you—completely natural, confident but not intimidating, warm, funny, smart. Everything guys want! I want to learn why I'm not coming across like that on dates."

Buttering me up helped. And so, despite feeling funny about spying on her date and judging her, critiquing her—or anyone, for that matter—I arrived ten minutes before she did at the bar where she was meeting Mr. Potential, a stockbroker named Mike. We'd prearranged for me to sit at the end of the bar while Cara would sit at one of the little round tables just to the side of it so that I could see and hear them clearly.

"Just don't let a guy pick you up during my date!" she said, and I laughed. "I'm not kidding!" she added. "Some guy sees you sitting alone at the bar and you'll miss my whole date! Bring a textbook, so it'll look like you're studying. A med student's textbook, so that you'll be too intimidating for anyone to approach."

I shook my head and laughed, but borrowed an oversize textbook on Contract Law from my next-door neighbor (I still lived in the same off-campus housing—a cute apartment I used to share with a roommate but now had to myself—that I'd moved in to as a nineteen-year-old sophomore), which I figured would be intimidating enough.

It was. I sat at the bar with my hair covered by a baseball cap, wearing baggy jeans and prescription-free glasses

I'd picked up at the drugstore for five bucks, and buried my nose in the textbook while taking many furtive glances at Cara's table. My notebook and pen were at the ready for "notes," and no one bothered me.

And very unexpectedly, from the moment Cara's date arrived and she talked nonstop about herself, from what kind of juice she liked to drink in the morning to the movie she'd seen the previous night to one too many stories, albeit amusing, about this and that, that and this—I'd found myself writing up five pages on what could potentially turn off her date. I was afraid I'd hurt Cara's feelings, but she'd so appreciated my analysis that she'd taken me to dinner afterward and told me I should hang a shingle. And a week later she reported that my critique had been such a success for her that a new Mr. Potential had asked her out for date number two right in the middle of the first date.

So instead of talking nonstop on her dates, Cara now spoke nonstop about her "amazing friend Zoe Solomon," the date analyzer who could pinpoint exactly what you were doing wrong so you could correct it and find love. And my little business was born. Friends of Cara from graduate school and her group therapy sessions called to test me out. And they told two friends and so on and so on and so on.

That was four years ago. When the article came out last year, I began to work all the time, morning, noon and night. I'd eat my scrambled eggs at the table next to a client on a breakfast date. I'd play tennis (and once badminton) on the court next to a client on sporty dates. I'd gone on Ferris wheels (tricky), long walks on the beach, jogs in the park, for ice cream, countless dinners and lots of club sodas. And the dates were none the wiser that one Zoe Solomon, ex-perfume sprayer and unmarried—in fact, barely boyfriended herself—was spying on the sweet awkwardness of a first date.

It was at one of those countless dinners that I met my boyfriend. I was critiquing a date in a very popular gourmet pizzeria. I sat at the bar, eating my own personal pizza for one, pretending to be studying for a real estate exam, my notebook open.

"Eavesdropper," accused a male voice.

I redirected my attention from my client's blind date, which was about as bad as a first date could get (the problem wasn't her, but the guy, who was a real schmuck) to my textbook. "Excuse me?" I said in my most leave-me-alone voice.

"You're eavesdropping on my cousin's date."

That got my attention. I glanced up to find a very cute guy in a UCLA sweatshirt and faded jeans trying to wedge himself into the slightly open spot beside me at the crowded bar. "Your cousin?" I asked. "The woman or the man?"

"The man," he said and then ordered a Bass from the bartender. "Don't you see the family resemblance?" With a grin, he turned to show me his profile and pointed to his dimple. I almost laughed, but then I collected myself. I was working!

But the more I listened to his cousin wax on to my client about how long he could hold his breath under water (he was a surfer) while he checked out every woman in the restaurant, the more I tried to remember that schmuckiness didn't necessarily run in families. Still, I couldn't exactly talk up the cutie in front of me and earn my fee at the same time. Turned out it wasn't a problem, since Cutie's own date arrived a moment later. She eyed me up and down, then suggested that they grab a table on the other side of the restaurant.

Cutie gave me something of an *Oh-what-might-have-been* expression, and then his date gave me one of those *I'll claw your eyes out if you flip your hair or cross your legs his way* looks, and off they went.

The very good-looking distraction gone, I wrote on and on in my notebook about how my client had been polite and accommodating above and beyond the call of first-date duty, that she had said and done just about everything humanly possible to include herself in the date and that if he didn't call, she should consider herself very lucky, and if he did, she should change her telephone number.

Fifteen minutes later, I noticed Cutie heading my way, but he walked past me with a devilish smile and disappeared into the men's room. A few minutes later, as he passed me again, he slipped his business card under the bowl of peanuts in front of me. On the back it said, *I'm on a first date from hell, like my cousin seems to be. Though I have no doubt that my high-maintenance cousin is the date from hell in his case. Tacky as this might seem under the circumstances, I really wish* you *were my date. If you're interested, call me and I'll redeem myself, I promise.*

I covered my mouth to hide my smile and happy laugh and slipped his card into my bag, then forced myself to concentrate on my client's date. I didn't have to work too hard, since a minute later she stormed out, then returned a moment after that for her purse. Cutie's cousin was already chatting up the two women at the next table. "You can have him," she yelled at them, and stormed back out.

I called her that night and told her to keep her money—to pay for a critique of that Technicolor nightmare would add the clichéd insult to injury. We shared a good laugh over bad dates that you couldn't do a danged thing about, and then I called Charlie.

That was fourteen months and five or ten or twenty marriage proposals ago. Charlie had proposed on our fifth date, and I'd been telling him I wasn't ready ever since.

Why? Didn't I love him? Wasn't he what I wanted?

If he was, then why did I always come down with a cold whenever I thought I should just say yes already? Every time I decided I was nuts for not accepting his proposal, my body seemed to tell me I wasn't. I came down with heartburn, the flu, hives, migraines.

I didn't want to marry Charlie, and I didn't know why. I didn't know if it was just a not-yet kind of thing or a not-ever kind of thing.

It was driving me crazy. And driving him away.

He'd proposed again two weeks ago, with his mother's heirloom two-carat marquise diamond ring in a diamond-studded platinum setting and a hansom-cab ride. When I'd told him I still wasn't ready, he'd jumped out of the carriage, slammed shut the ring box and told me he was getting really tired of waiting. That if I loved him, I'd commit.

Was that how it worked?

I was supposed to be pro-commitment, he'd said, since I was the only person he knew whose parents had been married for twenty-five years.

Hello? My parents divorced *after* twenty-five years.

My father had been having an affair with a twenty-four-year-old student. A little over a year ago, he'd broken the news to my mother that he was leaving her for another woman. My mother had called me in a hysterical panic, and I'd called my father to find out what the hell was going on.

"She's everything I've ever wanted," my father told me when I'd driven to his house that night to see him. *"Don't*

hate me, Zoe. This is what it's all about. Love. Incredible love. This is all I can ever want for you, too."

He hadn't mentioned that night that the woman who was everything he'd ever wanted was my friend Giselle. My friend who I'd introduced to him without a second thought when we ran into him in a popular brunch spot in Santa Monica.

"Dad, this is my friend Giselle Archweller," I'd said.

"Giselle Archweller. What a lovely name," he'd said.

And apparently, he'd remembered it. There weren't too many Giselle Archwellers in the L.A. area, and he'd looked her up and called her, and that, as they said, was that.

That was also the end of my parents' marriage.

Giselle and I hadn't been best friends or particularly close friends, but we probably would have been had fate not intervened in the form of my father. (Was that fate? I was still unsure a year later.) But we'd been budding friends and I'd liked her. She was the kind of friend I hadn't had since high school. And since my three high school friends had scattered across the world—Lauren was in France with the chef she'd met in a two-month-long French cooking class in Paris; Deb was in Switzerland, doing something involving banking and skiing; and the other Debbie was in an African country, deeply involved with the Peace Corp—I was sorely in need of a gal pal.

Giselle and I had met at Neiman Marcus, right before I quit to become the Dating Diva full time. We were both well-paid floor model slash perfume sprayers with psychology degrees from UCLA and no idea what we really wanted to do. Co-worker quips led to coffee breaks and then lunch breaks and then shopping trips. Giselle had a one-year-old baby whom she adored (the happy result of an unhappy relationship with a wanna-be rock star who'd told her it couldn't be his kid), and the three of us had just begun to spend time together on Saturday afternoons, at the beach or park, when Giselle suddenly stopped being so available a couple of months into our friendship.

At first I was sure I'd done something to offend her, but finally she told me she was seeing someone new and was crazy in love, but didn't want to jinx it by talking about it.

My father and Giselle were very careful. I didn't have a clue that they were involved. Until the day my mother called me, sobbing hysterically on the phone.

"We meant to tell you ourselves," my father had said later. *"We felt that I should tell your mother first, but we hadn't realized that she'd tell you right away. We thought we could then come over to your place, sit down and explain what happened. That we fell in love. Didn't mean to hurt anyone. That love is love."*

They'd been dating for two months. Two months. And that was love? Apparently it was love enough to destroy a twenty-five-year-long marriage.

And a daughter's faith.

"Honey, we're deeply in love...it just happened. So sorry you got hurt. I feel terrible that your mother is beside herself. Age is just a number.... Would I break up my family if this weren't the real thing? A woman half my age with a one-year-old baby, for God's sake?"

I hadn't talked to my father for two months after that. And I'd refused all calls and visits from Giselle, who tried for months to explain that she simply couldn't help falling in love with my father, a man twice her age, a man who was married to my mother.

My mother thought it was just another affair (I hadn't known there *were* affairs, let alone that my mother knew about them) and ran to get Botox injections, booked an emergency appointment with her colorist and hired a personal trainer to come to the house four times a week. She went for counseling, group therapy, and even tried to hire me to analyze her as a human being. She bought push-up bras and black stockings with seams down the back, high heels and leather. She shopped in stores like Bebe and started wearing Seven jeans.

And my father complimented her on how great she looked, adding that she'd surely catch a young stud in no time.

My father had always been clueless.

And my mother had gone nuts.

First, it was *"I'll never grant that son of a bitch a divorce!"*

Then it was *"Whyyyyyyyyyyyyyyyyyyyyyyyy?"*

And finally, *"That son of a bitch won't live a peaceful moment while I'm alive!"*

She meant it too. Which was why I'd booked myself on the first flight to New York City that wouldn't cost me a thousand bucks, tomorrow night's red-eye. My mother was somewhere on the loose in Manhattan.

"Zoe, honey, it's Mommy," she'd said in her usual voice on my answering machine an hour ago, which I checked before every date to make sure the date was still on. *"Don't worry about me, dear, but I'm on my way to New York to shove your father's engagement announcement up his ass. Do you believe he had the goddamn nerve to send me one? 'See, Judith, it was the real thing,' he wrote on the inner envelope. Well, he and his child bride aren't going to have a wedding, because I'm going to ruin their goddamned lives!"*

And then she'd slammed the phone down and called me back a moment later. *"Zoe, sweetie, my anger wasn't directed at you, you know that, right, doll? Bye now!"*

My mother was crazy. My father was crazy. Giselle *had*

to be crazy to want to be with my father, so good riddance.

Deep sigh.

My father and Giselle had been together for a year now. They'd gotten engaged on their anniversary, which was two months ago, bought a penthouse apartment on Park Avenue and insta-decorated it, and then, two weeks ago, they'd begun sending out the engagement announcements.

If my father had planned to tell me about his engagement himself, the announcement had beat him to it.

"Zoe, it's time to forgive and forget," my father said over the two lunches we'd had in L.A. since my parents' breakup, his ubiquitous sunglasses shielding his sincerity or lack thereof. *"Giselle is just beside herself that you won't speak to her. Not only did she lose her friend, but she feels like she destroyed your relationship with me, as well."*

No, you *both* take that honor, Dad.

"Zoe, I tell her nothing could destroy our relationship, but she thinks that you keep your distance because you're upset with us."

Ding! And he's won one million dollars!

When you were in a good mood, without a care in the world, there was no one better to be around than Bartholomew Solomon. The man was always up, always ready to take on the world. If you were down, he'd tell you to snap out of it, that the world was too full of novelty and surprises to waste one second being depressed.

A divorce? A broken family? No big whoop!

"You could use some therapy, young lady!" my mother had once snapped at Ally on the telephone. I was ten or eleven, so Ally must have been eighteen or nineteen. Silence, and then; *"Well, I'm not surprised to hear that you are seeing a college psychologist, because you really need to deal with your issues, Allison. You're an adult now. And it's time to grow up and stop expecting your father to be your daddy."*

It was a pivotal moment when you realized that you didn't agree with your mother about fundamental things, when you realized that your values were completely different. It was no surprise to me that my parents' marriage worked and for so long. They were peas in a pod. They both swept everything under the rug. My father wore sunglasses indoors. And my mother got a lot of plastic surgery.

What the hell did Giselle see in my father? That was the one thing I couldn't figure out. She wasn't an airhead or an under-the-rug-sweeper or a wanna-be film star (my father was a movie producer).

And besides her looks and her brains and the fact that she was once a very nice person, what did my father see in a woman half his age?

"She's the love of my life," my father said for the hundredth time.

"She's younger than I am," I countered.

"Age is just a number, Zoe."

He said that a lot.

Age is just a number, Zoe, had also become my mother's line when I asked her why she was having so much plastic surgery. She'd seen a television show about a woman who'd had over twenty-five surgeries to look like a human Barbie doll. *"Why shouldn't I turn back the clock, be the beauty I used to be?"* my mother said. *"To look at me, who would think I was ever a contender for Miss Orange County?"*

One year. My father and Giselle had been together for one year, and now they were getting married. I'd been with Charlie for a few months longer, and I was no closer to getting married than I was when I met him.

Now, as I watched Amber scooch closer to her date, I wondered if it was really worth all she was putting into it. Paying me two hundred and twenty-five bucks to tell her what? That she shouldn't be herself? That she was doing something wrong? My mother had spent twenty-five years doing everything she possibly could to keep my father interested, and he'd dumped her for a woman half her age. I had a boyfriend I couldn't commit to. What the hell did I know?

Amber and her date left the bar together, hand in hand.

Sarah

As Griffen and I collected our doggie bags (containing one chocolate cupcake each), put on our jackets in what felt like slow motion, and made our way to the door of Julien's restaurant, Griffen was hit in the ankle by the smallest baby stroller I'd ever seen. I watched him peer inside at the sleeping infant, and I was quite sure he was about to throw up on the baby.

He managed a "sorry" to the mother, eyed the two wild-eyed children who refused to put on their coats and shot a glance at the father, who was struggling to get the little girl's arm through her denim jacket when she was busy trying to stuff a bread stick down her brother's pants. The father grabbed the bread stick, startling the girl, and she started bawling. The couple sitting to the left of them apparently had had enough, took final sips of their wine, threw a pile of bills on the table and left, dirty looks all around.

In the five minutes it took to get out of the restaurant, Griffen didn't say a word. Not a sarcastic "And you want to have one of *those?*" Not an offensive "Are you one hundred percent sure it's mine?" He just clutched his doggie bag in his white-knuckled fist, held open the door for me and out we went into the oddly warm October air.

As we passed the entrance to the Seventy-seventh Street 6 train, he didn't run down the steps. He didn't hail the taxi that was stopped at a red light. He didn't flee west around the corner to make his escape home through Central Park.

He didn't do or say anything. He just walked, staring down at the sidewalk.

A few blocks later, at Eighty-fourth Street, he stopped. "Are you absolutely sure?" he asked me, glancing at the traffic for a moment, then at me, then at the sidewalk, then back at me. "I mean, did you see your doctor?"

I nodded.

"We can wait a few hours for the blood test results to be one hundred percent conclusive," Dr. Scharf had said four days ago, *"but you're definitely pregnant. Your uterus is enlarged. Congratulations!"*

It was interesting that the only two people who'd offered me congratulations were the doctor I saw every two years for birth control (lawsuit!), and a stranger in a restaurant.

When I'd walked out of Dr. Scharf's office, Lisa at my side, the words *Your uterus is enlarged* had echoed over and over in my mind. Lisa had taken my arm and led my dazed and confused self to Barnes & Noble, sat me down in a big green leather club chair near the magazines, disappeared for two minutes and returned with three books: *What To Expect When You're Expecting, The Girlfriends' Guide To Pregnancy* and *But I Don't Know How To Be Pregnant!*

And then we went to my favorite coffee bar, the very one where I'd met Griffen in the first place. She bought me a large decaf cappuccino and a Linzer torte ("Gotta watch the caffeine—in chocolate too," she said), pointed at an overstuffed sofa and handed me *But I Don't Know How To Be Pregnant!* while she started reading *What To Expect.* And so I drank and ate and read. We sat there for two hours, reading, flipping pages. Staring at truly frightening pictures of fetal development. I learned about the placenta. Sonograms. Arm buds. That I wouldn't *have* to drink milk, after all, but that I would have to avoid aspirin and cough medicine and soft cheeses and any fish containing too much mercury. Caffeine, to be safe. Alcoholic beverages. Hot dogs, bacon, and anything with nitrites.

Oh, and I could expect my brain to go on hiatus.

"Ready?" Griffen asked, startling me out of my thoughts.

"As I'll—"

Ever be, I'd been about to say. But I realized Griffen wasn't talking about the pregnancy. He was talking about resuming walking.

We turned the corner of Eighty-fourth Street and walked down to First Avenue, something of a hike from Lexington Avenue when you weren't saying a word.

Again Griffen was almost hit by a baby stroller.

There were a lot of baby strollers in my neighborhood. I'd never really noticed them before, except to want them out of my way. Now I wanted to peer in every single carriage and ask the mother questions.

Griffen stopped in front of my apartment building. The last time he *stopped* in front of my building was our first date.

"Do you know what you want to do?" he asked.

I wondered what he was thinking. *Get rid of it. Say you want to get rid of it!* I imagined him silently chanting.

Was he foaming at the mouth to tell me he'd pay all expenses?

"My doctor said I'm due on May fifteenth."

He looked positively ill. Really. Like he was about to throw up on the street.

"That'll make the baby a Taurus," I rambled on. "My mom was a Taurus, and it's definitely not true that Taureans—or is Tauri?—are stubborn, so..."

I trailed off as he stared down at the street. Now he looked as if he wanted to cry. "Are you really going to do this?" he asked, desperation in his voice. "I can't believe you're going to do this." He covered his face with his hands, then shoved them in his pockets, then dropped down rather dramatically on the bottom step of the brownstone next door to my building. "Are you really going to do this?" he asked again.

I nodded.

He sucked in a breath. A deep, ragged breath. "So you're going to do this. You're really going to do this."

Just remember the daze you were in when you found out you were pregnant, I reminded myself. *That's how he feels now. Be very kind.*

"I am going to have this baby, Griffen," I said. I laid a hand on his shoulder. He flinched, and I pulled it away. "I know it's an incredible shock. I don't know what else to say myself, other than that I'm pregnant and I'm having the baby."

He let out a whoosh of breath and dropped his head between his knees. "I need some time to digest this. Okay?"

"Okay."

"I'll call you," he added, and then he shot up and walked away. Fast.

I imagined him stopping just around the corner on Second Avenue, hyperventilating into his doggie bag.

★ ★ ★

I'll call you. I'll call you. I'll call you.

A month ago, I'd gotten Astrid's gold star raised eyebrow and a "Write it up" when I suggested "What He Really Means When He Says He'll Call" as an article. I'd boldly stopped twenty-five guys on the street, from hot to very not, from early twenties to early forties, stuck a microphone in front of their mouths and asked the age-old question.

According to my own survey, the odds that a guy would call when he said he would were slightly less than fifty percent.

I considered those odds promising for my current situation.

Then again, I hadn't exactly given the men hypothetical situations to mull over, such as: *"Uh, a chick you've been seeing for a couple months tells you she's pregnant, and you say you need some time to digest it and that you'll call. Will you?"*

Tape recorder in hand, I'd asked: "At the end of the evening, you tell your date you'll call. Will you?"

Mark, 30: "If I like her, yeah. If not, no."

Me: "Then why say you'll call?"

Mark: "Sometimes I say it just to get away from the girl, you know?"

Me: "From the *woman,* you mean."

Mark (rolls eyes): "I wouldn't call you if you said something like that on a date."

Me: "Good."

Jim, 34: "You just say it. It doesn't mean anything. It's like when someone says, 'How are you?' It's like a rhetorical question. They don't really expect an answer."

Me: "But isn't the woman expecting a call?"

Jim: Blank stare.

John, 29: "If I say I'll call, then I'll call. Guys who don't give nice guys like me a bad rap."

George, 21: "I'd definitely call *you*. I like older women. Seeing anyone?"

Me: Big smile and a proud "Yes, I am."

Paul, 37: "I call exactly three days later. You don't want her to think you're too into her. Women like a man with an edge."

Robert, 28: "I don't even realize I'm saying it." (In other words, what Jim said.)

Griffen (yes, *that* Griffen), 32: "I mean I'll call."

Me (smiling): "But *when* will you call? Tomorrow? In three days? Two weeks? When you're bored? If you want sex?"

Griffen (smiles back and taps my nose with his finger): "When did I call you after our first date?"

Me: "The next day at work. You said you had a great time and asked me out again for the weekend."

Him: "I'm a stand-up guy, huh? You're pretty lucky."

Me (kissing his neck): "Oh, yes. Yes, yes, yes."

And then we had sex. Great sex.

That flirtatious little conversation over chocolate fondue and strawberries, a few glasses of white wine and a lot of sexual innuendos was one month ago. I was pregnant then.

I'd been pregnant for just about our entire relationship.

But it wasn't the fondue or the wine or the sexual innuendos.

I was pregnant because of a large iced mocha.

And because my air conditioner had conked out yet again.

And, indirectly, because of my Don't-You-Dare-Do-It sister, Ally.

Two months ago, on a hot, humid late August morning, the kind that wakes you up with its stickiness, I'd decided to spend the sunlight hours at the very air-conditioned DT★UT, a coffee lounge around the corner from my apartment. I took a cold shower, threw on a tank top, jeans and my flip-flops that annoyed even me with their clickety-clackety on the sidewalk, twirled my hair up into a messy bun, grabbed a bunch of competitive women's magazines and a pad of paper and headed out. I planned to write a "What the Competition Is Doing and What *Wow Woman* Should Be Doing" memo to Astrid, since it was my month to report on the competition. After the stifling heat of my apartment and the sauna outside, the cool air in the coffee lounge was almost too cold, and I ran back home for a meshy cardigan.

I was standing at the condiments counter with a large iced mocha into which I was stirring an extra packet of Sweet'N Low, when someone backed into me.

The cutest guy I'd seen in a long, long time.

"I am so sorry," he said, grabbing a wad of tissues and handing them to me, his expression full of apology. He grabbed another wad of tissues. "I hope your sweater isn't ruined. It's nice."

I beamed. Was there a stain on my sweater? Was I standing in a coffee bar? I had no clue. I felt as though I'd been transported to dreamland. That was how instant the chemistry felt. To me, anyway.

I looked down at myself. My new pale pink Banana Republic cardigan, the one Ally had bought me because she'd been offended by the ratty black one I'd shown up in for lunch a couple of weeks ago, was soaked with a combination of espresso, milk, chocolate syrup and whipped cream.

From the breasts down.

He was looking at the stain. At my chest?

"Here," he said, reaching into his back pocket. He pulled out his wallet and handed me a card. "Call me when you get the bill for the dry cleaning. I'll pay for it. That sweater looks expensive."

"It's really no problem," I said. "Easily could have been the other way around."

He smiled. And a tingle shot up both my legs.

Thick, silky blond hair. Real blond. Baby blond. But brown eyes. Pale brown. And long, boy eyelashes. One dimple, in his left cheek. He was tall and lanky, with delicious shoulders, and dressed guy Gap-y in army green cargo pants and a white T-shirt and sneakers.

I realized I was staring and hoped I wasn't salivating. "You could—"

"I'm really sorry again," he interrupted, "but I'm so late. I have to go." He pointed to the card he'd given me. "Call me when you get the bill and I'll send you the money. I'm good for it."

And before I could say another word, he was out the door with his take-out cup of iced coffee.

I looked at his card. Griffen Maxwell. Producer at Fox News.

I whipped out my cell phone and woke up Lisa.

"Don't wait for the dry cleaning!" she shouted. "Call him tonight! He sounds gorgeous!"

"But—"

"No buts," Sabrina insisted when I called for her opinion. "You like the guy, call him. Why do you think he gave you his card in the first place? He was in a rush, didn't have time to get your number, so he whipped out his card."

For once, Lisa and Sabrina were in agreement.

"Talk about cute meet," Lisa said. "You can write it up for a *Wow* How-We-Met sidebar!"

"Don't you dare call him!" Ally advised later that day

when she called to ask if I'd gotten our father's engagement announcement with the Wedding Fest event time card. (Yes, I had. I'd shaken my head and flung it across my room with a *Yeah, right.*)

"Sar, if he was interested, he wouldn't have run out of the coffee shop like that," Ally said. "He would have asked you your name and gotten your number. When a man is sexually attracted to a woman, nothing keeps him from sniffing out a date. Men are always throwing around their cards, especially if they're proud of their jobs. Don't call a guy who isn't interested."

Can you spell KILLJOY?

"Do what you want," Ally said when I complained that she was always raining on my parade. "But trust me—he'll say okay to getting together because he figures it's easy sex, and suddenly you're nuts about a guy who never liked you to begin with."

How did you respond to that? Did you simply hang up in your sister's ear or did you tell her off first?

I opted for a "Whatever, Ally," the response that always tended to annoy her the most, then I did the opposite of what she'd suggested. A little habit of mine.

That night, I picked up the telephone and put it back down five times. Finally, I picked it up and forced it against my ear and dialed. "Hi, Griffen, this is Sarah. We met at DT★UT this morning?"

"Sarah?" he repeated.

I waited a second for my face and stained breasts to register.

Silence.

Panicking and thinking that perhaps I should have listened to Ally was another habit of mine.

How many women had he met at DT★UT that morning?

"You spilled my coffee on me?" I reminded him.

Moment of silence. "Ah, that's right," he said. "Of course. The woman in the pretty sweater. So what do I owe you?"

Not the pretty *woman* in the pretty sweater. Just the pretty sweater.

Shut up and talk, Sarah!

"Um, well, my sweater's still at the cleaners," I said. "They'll definitely be able to get the stain out."

"Great," he said.

Silence.

Shit.

"It'll be ready tomorrow, though," I rushed on, "so I thought maybe we could meet at DT★UT, and you could buy me a cup of coffee to make it up to me." Flirt, flirt. Coy, coy.

Silence.

Shit.

"Or whatever," I said, disappointment and Ally's words of unfair wisdom filling my stomach.

"Tomorrow's no good for me," he said. "Thursday's okay, though, for a quick cup of coffee. Around seven?"

Smile. Big smile.

Ha! Ally had been wrong, wrong, wrong. If he wasn't interested, he wouldn't have made the date. He would have told me to call him when I'd paid the bill. Okay, granted—a "quick cup of coffee" wasn't exactly dinner. It wasn't even really meeting for coffee. But it was a start.

And so on Thursday night, I spent an hour dressing for a quick cup of coffee (sexy-casual, which was much more difficult than my standard business-casual or casual-casual).

He didn't even recognize me. Hadn't remembered me at all. But then we'd sat and started talking about our work—both our jobs were entertainment-focused—and then movies, and it turned out we were both huge Woody Allen fans and huge Chris Rock fans and huge Yankees fans and huge fans of Indian food, and twenty minutes later we were having Indian food in a narrow red restaurant with thousands of Christmas lights way down in the East Village, sharing Taj Mahal beer and chicken tikka and salmon tandoori. And two hours later, as we walked uptown, on the lookout for a taxi, we'd passed by Veniero's, the famous bakery, and I'd commented on the cupcakes.

And then he'd called the next day and asked me out for Saturday night.

It was one heck of a date. We had chicken enchiladas, margaritas, saw a Jennifer Lopez movie, and then went back to my apartment and made a baby.

"I'll call you?" Sabrina said, slamming her palm on our little round table at Starbucks. "That's what he said to the news that you're pregnant—and then he just *walked away?*"

Hurried away was more like it.

While Sabrina muttered the word *dick* and Lisa shook her head, I stared out the window, counting baby strollers. In the two minutes we'd been sitting down with our coffees, my already dog-eared *But I Don't Know How To Be Pregnant!* next to my Linzer torte, which I'd craved a second ago and now couldn't imagine eating, I'd counted eight. Wait a minute—I spoke too soon. Make that nine.

Yesterday, before I'd gone to meet Griffen for the big tell-him-the-news birthday dinner, Lisa and Sabrina and I had arranged to meet this morning at the Starbucks around the corner from my apartment. The plan was for me to sleep on Griffen's reaction so that regardless of whether he got down on one knee or went screaming out of the restaurant, I could come to my own conclusions before anyone else's opinions got thrown into the mix.

Here were my conclusions: I'd expected Griffen to call last night even before he got home. I envisioned him in Central Park, shivering in his denim jacket by the Boat House, staring at the water and pondering deeply. I thought he'd call me on his cell, suggest we meet for a drink to talk things through. But he didn't. And he didn't call an hour later, or two hours later. Or three hours later. At four in the morning, I finally fell asleep with the telephone on my pillow.

And then the process began all over again this morning. I stared at the phone, expecting it to ring. It didn't.

As Sabrina flipped through pages of *But I Don't Know How To Be Pregnant!* and asked questions like "What the hell is an umbilical cord stump?" and Lisa filled her in, sharing a nausea-inducing story about her older sister's cat making off with her nephew's fallen off umbilical cord stump, I wondered what Griffen was doing now. Staring at the ceiling and saying *Why, God, why,* over and over again?

Lisa covered my hand with hers. "Sarah? Are you okay?"

My nod must have been very pathetic because Sabrina slung her arm around me, and Lisa patted my hand.

"He'll call," Lisa assured me. She took a sip of her chai tea. "He'll definitely call, Sarah. He just needs time to digest it, like he said. You had four days to think about it. He had five minutes. He'll call."

He'll call, I assured myself. Griffen was indeed a caller.

"But what if he doesn't?" Sabrina asked. "Or what if

he does and says, 'I can't deal. I don't want anything to do with you or the baby'? Are you prepared for that, Sarah?"

"Jesus, Sabrina, you're scaring her to death," Lisa chastised. "She has enough to think about without what Griffen's going to say and do."

"But what Griffen's going to say and do has a lot to do with what Sarah's going to be able to do," Sabrina countered. "I just want you to be prepared, Sarah. If it's just you, honey, you're facing a lot."

Just me. It had been *just me* for so long that it didn't sound frightening. But that was idiotic. Taking care of myself, my share of the rent, half of a few utilities bills and making sure I had enough money for a Metro Card every week wasn't exactly neuro science. I had no idea how to be pregnant, how to have a baby, what that really meant.

What did it mean?

"Here's what it means," Sabrina said. "It means getting *huge.* Big as a house. It means not drinking coffee, drink-drinks or taking cold medicine when you have a nasty bug. It means being exhausted all the time, losing your mind, barfing your brains out, waking up five times in the middle of the night to feed a crying infant. It means bloody nipples. It means a *lifetime.* You can't ever go back to the way things were."

"Jesus, Sabrina!" Lisa snapped. "Leave her alone."

"I just want her to know what she's getting into," Sabrina said. "It's not about a cute little baby. It's about reality."

I felt like I was going to hyperventilate. I stood up and ran to the bathroom, but you needed a key to get in. I burst into tears and slid down on my butt against the bathroom door.

Lisa and Sabrina were beside me in seconds. "Sarah," Sabrina said, cupping my face in her hands. "I'm sorry.

I'm really, really sorry. I didn't mean to be a bitch. I'm just scared for you."

Me too.

After Lisa and Sabrina had helped me calm down, I'd had a sudden and desperate urge to know everything there was to know about what was going on inside my body and what I could expect. And so I'd grabbed *But I Don't Know How To Be Pregnant!* and *What To Expect When You're Expecting* and headed for the playground in Carl Shurz Park, where I could watch mothers and nannies and babies and children and be among this sudden new kind of mine.

Two hours later, I closed *What To Expect* (I read up through the fourth month) and opened to my bookmark in *But I Don't Know How To Be Pregnant!* It was the chapter on what a baby cost for the first year.

Infant Car Seat: $70. Good, I thought. We're off to an inexpensive start, since I don't have a car and therefore don't need a car seat. And then I read the parentheses, which stated that you couldn't even leave the hospital after giving birth without an infant car seat.

Diapers: $13 for a package of 48. *Expect to change baby's diaper six to ten times per day.* Six to ten times per day?

Bottles: $10. Reasonably self-explanatory, except apparently there were around twenty-five different kinds—and nipples—to choose from.

Breast Pump: $180. Breast pump? What the hell was a breast pump, and how did you use it, exactly? The paragraph went on to discuss hospital-style pumps, mini-electric pumps and manual pumps. Oh God. Oh God. Oh God. Skip.

Crib: $200-$500. Ah, now this was something I understood. A crib. *Some parents like to use a bassinet or a cra-*

dle because the small-size bed makes a newborn feel more secure. So did I need *both* a bassinet and a crib? And where exactly was I going to put the crib?

Thermometer (rectal), nasal aspirator, baby nail clippers, gas drops: $25. Okay. I knew what a thermometer was. And I had dim memories of a rectal thermometer from early childhood, but hadn't there been thermometer advancement since then? I mean, couldn't you just stick a thermometer in the baby's *mouth?* I had no idea what a nasal aspirator was.

Receiving Blankets: $50. I wasn't sure why they were called receiving blankets. Apparently, they were just thin baby blankets that you used to wrap or swaddle (another new word) the baby in.

Bathtub and Bathing Paraphernalia: $40. *For the first couple of weeks, until the baby's umbilical cord falls off, baby will be sponge-bathed.* Oh God. Oh God. Oh God.

Stroller: $200–$300. Now there was another something I thought I understood. But according to page 200, there were countless makes and models, with varying degrees of bells and whistles, to choose from. There was something called an umbrella stroller, but it didn't seem to mean that it came equipped with an umbrella.

Layette: $100–200. Layette was French for baby's wardrobe. It included everything from receiving blankets to onesies (there was a little drawing of a onesie, which looked like a T-shirt slash bodysuit), sleepers, which were footed pajamas, and various little shirts and pants.

Monitor: $20. Hear baby's every peep or *lack thereof.* Oh God. Oh God. Oh God.

Rocking Chair: $100. Sounded nice enough.

Bouncy Seat: $30. *Buy one of these baby chairs with a vibrating feature and soothe a fussy baby.*

Changing Table: $100, plus pad: $20. Apparently, you could turn a dresser top into a changing area if you laid a curved, waterproof pad on top of it to change baby on.

Nursing Pillow: $25. Looked a bit like a life-preserver cut in half around your waist.

BabyBjörn: $89. The premier baby carrier. *Wear baby against your chest and he'll feel safe and secure and your arms will be free!*

Diaper Genie: $20. *Just drop the soiled diaper in the top, turn the little lever, and voilà, no odor!*

Crib Bedding: $100-$300. Expensive sheets, I understood all too well.

Burp Cloths: $20. *Buy at least twelve of these for baby spit-up alone.*

Pacifiers: $5-$10. *All babies like to suck,* the writer said, *but some people worry that using one at all means baby will demand his binky until second grade.* Apparently, there were many "controversial" issues involved in the raising of infants. *Be prepared for relatives, friends, even total strangers, to offer their opinions on this and many, many other aspects of baby rearing.*

About to throw up (from fear and not from morning sickness, which had yet to plague me), I opened my pregnancy journal, a gift from Sabrina, and jotted down some sorry facts:

My income: $31,500 per anum.

My monthly expenses:

Rent: $812.

Gas & electric: $30 (in summer, $60).

Phone: $30.

Cable: $35.

Subway: $45.

Coffee and lunch: $200.

Groceries: $50.

Laundry: $30.

Visa: $50 to $60.

Student Loan: $115.

Grand Total: Frightening.

And I lived with a roommate. Once I got my own place, I'd have to double rent and utilities.

My Net Worth: $0.

Which meant my choices were:

A) Win the lottery.

B) Rob a bank.

C) Ask my father for help.

D) Get promoted to senior editor, which came with a $10,000 raise in salary (because senior editors were considered management, despite having no one to manage except an occasional editorial intern).

E) Pray that Griffen didn't mysteriously disappear.

Choice *A* was impossible, since I couldn't afford lottery tickets and had never been a particularly lucky person, anyway. I couldn't do *B,* since the experience of my mother finding out I swiped a Bazooka bubble gum from the bodega on our corner and making me return it and apologize and sweep the floor for four Saturday afternoons turned me away from a life of crime forever. Forget *C.* You might think that as the daughter of a major movie producer who made sick money, there might be a generous wad of cash in my birthday card every year, but there never *was* a birthday card. *"I'm not good at birthdays or holidays, pumpkin, you know that. Here, here's a fifty. Go buy yourself something nice."* Which was accompanied by a pat on the head and a run-along-now look.

Every year for the past eleven years, since my mother's death from a sudden and senseless brain aneurysm, Ally had bought me something for my birthday that she thought my mother would have given me that year had she been alive. The card always said, *I think Mom would have liked to see you in this,* and it would be something I desperately needed but would never think to buy myself, like a raincoat. Despite how bossy and pushy and overbearing Ally was, she was all I had. Which was basically the reason why I wouldn't ask her for financial help. She'd give it to me, because she had it to give and because I was her sister. I was pretty sure that Ally would do just about anything for me.

D, the promotion, was the answer. *E* was a toss-up that I couldn't depend on, so it was up to me. I couldn't imagine Griffen ducking out on his financial responsibility to the baby, but he wasn't exactly making a fortune himself, either. So even if Griffen did magically propose marriage, we'd still come up short if the list of what it cost to raise a baby was accurate. And if it was accurate in anywhere, U.S.A., it was even more expensive in New York City.

D was my only option. Since I hadn't suffered from morning sickness once, perhaps my luck had turned after all. No one at work would have to know I was pregnant until it was obvious. I could work my butt off for the promotion. And according to *But I Don't Know How To Be Pregnant!,* I had a good four to five months before my belly swelled to showing proportions.

A woman wheeled a baby carriage past my bench and I put down *But I Don't Know How To Be Pregnant!* for a peek at the results of pregnancy. The baby was sleeping inside what looked like a tot-sized sleeping bag. The sleeping bag was navy blue, so I assumed the baby was a boy. He looked very peaceful. He wasn't crying at the top of his tiny lungs or passing gas or pulling his mother's hair. The woman sat down at the far end of my bench, smiled at me and pulled a paperback book out of the diaper bag hanging on the push handle. It wasn't a book on babies or how to stretch your salary. It was a novel. She gently rocked the carriage with one hand and turned pages with the other.

A peace came over me, a cuddly, warm peace, and I touched my belly.

And then, from the other side of the playground, a baby screeched so loudly that it woke up the baby near me. The woman put down her book and picked up the infant and hugged it to her, shushing and cooing. The baby wouldn't stop crying.

"Are you hungry?" the woman singsonged to the baby. "Still tired? Too hot? What? Tell your mama what's wrong."

The baby wailed. The woman tried a bottle. The baby turned red. She burped the baby. The baby wailed louder. "Well, if you're hot, Nicholas, we have to go home. It's too cool out to take off your fleece bundler."

And so she put the wailing Nicholas back into the stroller. The moment she moved the stroller, the baby stopped crying. "You just wanted to keep moving, huh, Nicky-wicky?" the mother singsonged, blowing kisses.

She forgot her novel on the bench. I picked it up and ran after her. She turned around and looked at me as though I were handing her a paper towel or a leaf. "Like I'll ever have time to read half a page," she said with a laugh, thanked me, and then continued wheeling Nicky-wicky around the playground.

Deep breath. Deep breath. Deep breath.

I lunged for my cell phone and called Lisa and told her that my baby's first year would take one third of my salary.

"That's what baby showers are for," Lisa said. "My sister had a shower and got two car seats and two playpens.

She won't have to buy baby clothes for a year. You've got nothing to worry about."

Somewhat relieved, I went back to *But I Don't Know How To Be Pregnant!* and read for another half hour. I skipped the section on breastfeeding out of pure fear, then realized that breastfeeding was free and started reading.

The things you found in your husband's pockets and drawers when you knew he was cheating on you made you wonder if you'd been blind, an idiot or simply in total denial. Evidence of Andrew's indiscretions were all over our bedroom, his office, even the downstairs bathroom's little wicker trash can, which contained one well-buried used condom.

The last time Andrew and I used a rubber during sex was thirteen years ago.

Bastard! Bastard! Bastard!

And I was a fool, fool, fool.

How could I not have noticed a used condom? A pair of panties that weren't mine? Lipstick stains on his shirts from colors I didn't use?

In the dry-cleaning hamper (in four of his pants pockets), I found:

Six women's phone numbers, including a Ginger who dotted her *i* with a smiley face.

Three hotel room receipts, two in the city and one here in Great Neck.

Two Victoria's Secret receipts. (I hadn't received a lace teddy from Andrew for years.)

Six florist receipts—red roses.

Under our bed, next to a few dust bunnies, last month's issue of *Wow Woman* and the current *Vanity Fair:* one pair of black thong panties, size small (I was a medium).

In his office, on his desk: countless bar tab and restaurant receipts in the high hundreds.

His shirts smelled of perfume I never wore. The Armani sweater I bought him "just because" had a fuschsia lipstick stain on the *hem.*

For a second I considered grabbing everything Andrew owned (or at least what I could lift), stuffing it into his precious Jaguar (which was in the garage because it was raining), and burning it all up the way Angela Bassett had in *Waiting to Exhale.*

And then I remembered a case my law firm had won a few years ago, *Arnock v. Arnock,* in which Mrs. Arnock had done exactly that to the belongings of Mr. Arnock. The replacement value came out of her settlement. Maybe I wasn't a fool, after all.

Shit. Shit. Shit. Shit! I was the biggest fool of them all. *Trust me, Kris, if Andrew were even thinking of cheating on me, I'd know it. We've been married for eleven years, and we dated for two years before then. I* know *the man.*

I shook my head and dropped down onto my bed. My husband had been making a fool out of me for years. And no one had told me.

"Who would tell you?" Marnie had asked when I'd gone to her house this morning to confront her.

Oh, you bet I had.

Not right away, though. Turned out that when you caught your husband of eleven years cheating on you in front of your eyes, in your own house, in the hammock he bought for you for Mother's Day the first year you were married because "One day you'll lie with our children in the hammock, reading them Dr. Seuss," something other than anger could take over, like pain.

Last night, after I slapped Andrew and ran out the door with Mary Jane, I drove to a hotel near LaGuardia Airport, checked in under the name Polly Smith, paid a clerk to run out and get me a few cans of Alpo and then flung a lamp across my generic, ugly room. In five seconds I received a phone call from the front desk asking if everything was all right, to which I'd replied that it most certainly was not, that my husband was a fucking cheating bastard, before I slammed the phone down.

And then I'd stared at the phone and picked up the receiver, needing to call someone, and I put it back down and slid to my butt on the side of the bed and cried.

Who was I going to call?

My mother was gone. My father would probably take Andrew's side, since he was a serial adulterer himself. My sister Sarah had her own problems, and besides, I wasn't about to tell Sarah that my life was falling apart.

I wasn't about to tell anyone that my life was falling apart. Especially not my girlfriends, who were really just women I knew from the country club, women whose husbands Andrew played golf with. And I couldn't tell Kristina. We were work friends and reasonably close, but I couldn't handle the thought of being a "told you so," lumped into the categories of cheating she'd been talking about this afternoon.

And so I sat on the floor of the hotel, against the bed,

clutching Mary Jane to my chest, and stared into space for a few minutes. And then the tears came.

After an hour or so, I picked myself up off the floor and lay down on the bed and finally slept. I slept until six this morning, then ordered two pots of coffee and looked out the window for a few hours at planes taking off and landing. And then I decided to drive home and confront the bastard.

But instead of making a left off the exit, I made a right, toward Marnie's condo complex, where I'd gone many times for private Pilates and yoga lessons. I didn't think, didn't form questions. I just drove. I had a feeling that Marnie could provide me with more answers than Andrew could. Truthful answers, at least.

I left Mary Jane in the car with the window cracked and her favorite car bone, rang Marnie's doorbell and seconds later saw her peek out the bay window and then dart back inside at the sight of me. Scaredy-cat. It started to drizzle. A minute passed. Again I saw her part the curtain. Another minute passed. Two. Five. I sat down on the single step and waited, the raindrops fattening. Again I saw her part the curtain.

Finally she opened the door. She wore her usual tiny sports bra over her supersized chest and yoga pants over her minuscule hips and butt. The familiar thick blond hair was in a knot atop her head, two sticks in the bun.

"I can take you, Ally," she said, one hand on the door, the other on her hip. "And you know I can. So if you've come here to try to beat me up, don't bother."

When you slept with women's husbands, women who were your own well-trained, hard-bodied Pilates clients, you clearly expected, like a seventh-grader, to get your ass kicked.

I rolled my eyes at her. "I've only come for the truth,"

I said. "Woman to woman, Marnie, tell me the truth. Are you having an affair with my husband? Was it a onetime thing? What?"

Woman to woman was Marnie's own favorite little thing to say. *Woman to woman, Ally, you should think about liposuction for your tummy. It's reasonably flat, but you're in too good shape for that little jiggle. Woman to woman, Ally, you shouldn't wear so much beige. Yes, I know it's classic and elegant, but it washes you out.*

She stared at me for a second, taking measure of me just the way Andrew had last night, then gestured for the sofa.

I'd sat on that blue-and-white-checkered sofa countless times for Marnie's special just-squeezed vegetable juices, which began all her sessions. Now I wondered how many times Andrew had sat on that sofa, Marnie straddling him.

"Do you really want the truth, Ally?" she asked. "Because if you do, I'll tell you. But be sure you want it. Most people don't. They can't handle it. Ignorance is bliss and all that."

She was suddenly a fount of wisdom?

"I'm a lawyer, Marnie. I understand the consequences of the truth."

"Okay," she said with a shrug, and again gestured for the couch.

I sat. I listened. I turned down a glass of wine because a) I was driving, b) I didn't want to lose my anger or my grip on reality and c) what was she, my *friend?*

Given what Marnie told me, you'd think I didn't graduate summa cum laude from Cornell or make law review at Stanford. I made $230,000 a year because of how perceptive I was, and yet for years Andrew had been screwing his way through HotBods Health Club's hot-bodied staff and I'd had no clue.

According to Marnie, Andrew was successful at enticing the young lovelies into bed or backroom blow jobs because he was good-looking and hot-bodied himself, married, offered incentives in the form of gift certificates from Victoria's Secret and diamond stud earrings (which, mind you, he got practically free since his brother was a dealer in the diamond district) and because he was discreet.

"Why would anyone get off on sleeping with a married man?" I asked.

She said something stupid about it involving danger and excitement. Oooh, falling naked off a hammock into a pile of dogshit—how exciting and dangerous!

I thanked her for her honesty, then told her I thought she was a skank, to which she shrugged and said, "Save your hostility for your husband. Oh, and I'm sure you won't try to hurt my business, because I'm sure you won't want everyone to know your husband is cheating on you."

I was a bitch?

She slammed the door shut behind me and I threw a "Fuck you" over my shoulder (now who was the seventh-grader?). Then I drove home, ready to confront my husband.

But he wasn't home when I arrived. My first thought was that he was out looking for me, but then I realized he was very likely spewing a poor-me routine to some diner waitress and hoping for a quickie in the bathroom. For fifteen minutes, I sat on the sofa in the living room in a daze, unable to comprehend that this house that I'd lived in for eleven years had changed in a moment. Before the hammock moment, it had been my sanctuary, my beloved home. This morning, it was like a stranger's house.

Mary Jane's bark had startled me out of my catatonic state, and I was suddenly obsessed with the idea of searching for evidence of Andrew's infidelities just in case he tried to give me the *Marnie is just trying to break us up* crap. I could just hear Andrew in his supposedly sincere voice, the one I'd heard him use so many times in white lies to business associates and neighbors. *She's just a jealous cunt, Ally. She came on to me, got me a little drunk, and I didn't know what I was doing. You're not going to listen to her over your own husband, are you? Ally, I love you.*

In a matter of minutes—really and truly just ten or fifteen minutes—I'd found the hotel and bar and Victoria's Secret receipts in his pants pockets. I'd found the lipstick-stained sweater. After finding a bra that wasn't mine wedged behind the little trash can in the downstairs bathroom, I'd been compelled to examine the contents of the trash can.

With Andrew's tweezers, I dug out the used rubber and carried it upstairs at arm's length, then set it down on his pillow, next to the lacy thong.

And after I nixed the idea of burning up everything he owned in his precious little Jaguar, inspiration hit. If a friend were in a similar situation, I would advise her to immediately pilfer pertinent financial files, just in case the bastard tried to pull any funny business if things got ugly.

On the desk in his office was our wedding photo. I picked it up and looked at it, but I couldn't even recognize the smiling young couple. Had I been that young? That full of hope? That innocent?

We had once loved each other. Really loved each other.

Andrew and I hadn't had one of those thirty-thousand-dollar weddings with rubber chicken and goofy bands that sang a lot of Kool & the Gang. We'd gotten married on the beach, on the whitest sand I'd ever seen in front of a turquoise ocean. And that night, our wedding night, we'd made love in the sand, and I'd felt loved. Cherished. We were going to be married forever, unlike both our parents. We were going to be happy.

What the hell had happened?

I set the picture frame facedown on his desk and yanked on the long drawer, but it was locked. I jimmied it open with scissors and threw the photo inside with a "Fucking bastard!" at the top of my lungs.

The photo landed on a box of Trojan condoms. "Ribbed for her pleasure."

Bastard! I'd been on the pill for years before Andrew and I had stopped using birth control in order to start a family. I grabbed the condoms—there were three left in a box of sixteen—and flung them across the room, then searched through the file folders and papers underneath.

Amid a bunch of ordinary papers was an insurance-claim form, dated five years earlier, for a vasectomy.

I was packing when Andrew came home.

"Oh, come on, Al," he said, tossing his jacket on the bed. Hands on hips, he watched me fold my clothes and place them in my suitcase, which lay open on our bed.

Our bed. Ha! It was his bed now.

I turned around and stared at him, sure he'd look different now that I knew the whole truth, the extent of his lies and manipulations. But he didn't look different. He looked exactly the same as he always had, just slightly older than the very good-looking guy I'd married eleven years ago.

"Al-ly." He drew it out, trying for sexy and cute. "C'mon, baby. Let's sit down and talk."

I ignored him and continued packing.

"Ally, don't you think you're being a little overly dramatic? Taking this a bit too far? C'mon, let's talk this through. That's what *adults* are supposed to do."

"You're not an adult, Andrew. You're an adult*erer.* And the adulterer in this room doesn't deserve to be heard."

"Oh, so you're just jumping to conclusions," he said. "Is that what they taught you in law school? To jump to conclusions?"

"Andrew, I think you're confusing me with the brainless women you fuck. Don't waste my time playing games. They won't work."

"So you're just going to believe what Marnie told you?" he said, throwing up his hands. "Great, you go talk to that little bitch and she fills your head with lies about me because she's jealous, and you believe her over your husband. She told me everything—including that she wants me to leave you and marry her. She's just trying to break us up, Al."

Was there really any reason to respond to that?

"Great, Ally," he said. "So you're just going to believe her over me. That really makes me feel good."

"Oh, Andrew, you're right! You poor thing! I am so sorry!"

His eyes lit up, and I realized he didn't even know me well enough to know that I was being sarcastic. "Wait a minute," he said. "Are you—"

"Yes, asshole, I am being sarcastic. And, in case you forgot, catching you screwing another woman with my own eyes helped me 'jump to conclusions.'"

"Ally, you don't know what you think you saw," he said.

Was that English?

"What you think you saw and what really happened could be two very different things," he added.

"Really. So you weren't having sex with another woman on the hammock?"

"No. I wasn't," he said.

Amazing. "Andrew, maybe you're forgetting that what I learned in law school was that people lie through their capped teeth with the most innocent expressions and without the slightest wrinkle on their foreheads. Liars come in all forms, even husbands you trusted five minutes before they destroyed your marriage."

"Ally, sweetie, you *can* trust me. You can. I've been worried sick since you left last night." He put on his worried expression and came around the bed. "I left at least ten messages on your cell phone."

Andrew was wearing good black pants and a charcoal gray shirt, his "going out to dinner" standard outfit. Which meant he'd just come home from wherever he'd gone after I'd left last night. He was worried sick? What, while he was screwing some other woman?

"Ally, c'mon," he said, touching my arm, which I wrenched away. "Let's sit down and talk about this."

"Andrew, just shut up." I handed him the vasectomy claim form.

It's interesting to watch people when they're confronted with the inalienable truth of their deception. Momentary shock replaced by the wheels spinning to think up a new angle.

He sat down on the loveseat in front of the window and sighed. "Ally, look—"

I threw down the two suits I was folding into my suitcase. "No, you look, you lying son of a bitch!"

He leaned back the way he did when he was tired of our conversation. "You were so hellbent on having a kid, Ally. From the minute we got married. I wasn't ready then, and I'm still not really ready."

"But you said okay to trying to have a baby," I pointed out. "We had sex how many times without protection?

What did you think *I* thought we were trying to do? Not get pregnant?"

"I said okay because I couldn't take it anymore, Ally. Having a baby was all you talked about. And you wouldn't listen when I told you it wasn't time. You never listen, Ally. So I made sure it wouldn't happen. When I'm ready, I can reverse it. We can have a baby, Ally—when we're *both* ready."

I laughed in his face. "Are you thinking for a second that I might continue in this shitty, sham marriage? You've been lying to me for five years about the most important thing in the world to me."

"There you go, Ally. Having a baby is the most important thing to you. Not me."

I stared at him for a second. "That's not true. Wasn't true, anyway. But it doesn't matter now, Andrew. *We* don't matter now."

"Ally, don't get all melodramatic. I hate when you do that."

"Well, I hate *you,* Andrew."

"Ally, I know you don't mean that."

"Oh, but I do."

And I did. I knew exactly how I felt about Andrew Sharp.

For the past few years, Andrew and I had started to become known in Great Neck as The Couple Trying To Have a Baby. *"I hear you're trying for a baby,"* acquaintances would say as conversation openers, and with a deadly combination of embarrassment and the human desire to discuss what was fervent in my heart, I'd launch into a monologue about our rate of intercourse and my basal temperature. *"And when are you two going to start a family?"* strangers would ask at parties or at the health club or at work dinners.

Just as soon as rude people like you are obliterated from the earth, I always wanted to yell back. What if I couldn't have a child? Huh? How would a question like that make me feel, then?

I knew exactly how it would make me feel. Like how I felt when my father tried to explain to six-year-old me that he was leaving, even though my mother had just brought my brand-new baby sister home from the hospital. Like how I'd felt when that baby sister told me, eighteen years later, that our mother had died suddenly from a brain aneurysm while painting a watercolor in the living room of our house. Like there was a hole inside me, so deep inside I couldn't feel it, couldn't touch it, certainly couldn't fill it with too much chocolate, alcohol, sleeping pills, exercise or bitchiness.

And now I could add like how I felt when I saw Andrew having sex with another woman in the hammock in our backyard and like how I felt when I found the claim form for the vasectomy.

Andrew stood up and stepped toward me, but my expression halted him. "All right, Ally, I'll stop. I promise. I stand here right now before you and promise you that I will never even *look* at another woman. Doesn't that tell you how much I love you?"

"Andrew, you're free to look at all the women you want," I said, throwing my cosmetics bag on top of my clothes and snapping shut the suitcase. "All packed. Goodbye, Andrew. Have a nice life."

He shot up and grabbed the suitcase out of my hand. "Ally, I don't have one friend who doesn't have a little cake on the side. It never means anything. There are no emotions involved. It's just sex, some release, like watching porn. Are you really going to throw away eleven years of marriage—thirteen years together—over nothing?"

There was definitely something wrong with him.

"Andrew, you're the one who threw away our marriage."

I grabbed the suitcase back from him and headed downstairs.

"Ally. Ally, c'mon. I can have the vasectomy reversed. Next year, when I'm ready to start a family—"

"Just shut up already!" I screamed, and ran for the door.

He stood at the top of the stairs, hands on his hips. "Ally, if you leave now, you're telling me you're not willing to work things out. *You're* the one who's bailing, not me. Despite our problems, I love you. My vows were for *life.* Maybe you just forgot the 'for better and for worse' part."

Ah, so it wasn't that I was a fool or blind or even in denial. Andrew was simply that good at manipulation. Gold star. A-plus. Top of the class.

I was a chump, was what I was.

When Andrew and I got engaged, my father asked me if I was planning to take my husband's last name or keep Solomon. When I told my dad that Andrew and I had agreed that I would hyphenate, Sarah said, "I wouldn't if I were you. You'll be Ally Solomon-Sharp—which means your new initials will be A.S.S."

I had definitely earned that monogram.

6

Zoe

My flight to New York was leaving in a little over three hours, and my client's date was late.

C'mon. C'mon. C'mon. Show up already!

I was sitting at the long mica bar of an out-of-the-way bar/restaurant, my notebook open, my pen tapping and my prop copy of Contracts Law in front of me. What I really needed was a prop volume called *Places To Look For Your Mother in Manhattan When She Goes Crazy.*

I'd called my mother's cell phone five times since she left her I'm On My Way To New York To Destroy Your Dad and His Child Bride message yesterday afternoon. Apparently, it was turned off or not working across the country. She'd left another message for me on my home machine, at a time when she knew I wouldn't be home, letting me know that she'd landed just fine at LaGuardia early this morning, had a lovely vegetarian entrée on the plane and gave a gypsy cabdriver the what's what when he tried to charge her seventy bucks for a thirty-dollar ride into Manhattan. She didn't say where she was staying, how long she was staying or what she was planning to do in terms of ruining my father's life. She only said she was fine, that the city sure was busy on Saturdays and I shouldn't worry, and that she'd call in a few days to say toodles.

I imagined my mother stalking Giselle and following her home from work one night, waiting for the right moment to throw her in front of oncoming traffic.

No. My mother was crazy, but *good* crazy. She wasn't psycho crazy.

This morning, I'd called my dad to let him know that I was flying out tonight and would arrive very early Sunday morning on the red-eye—and why.

"Honey, don't worry about your mother," my father said. "I'm not worried about her in the least."

I held my tongue, which was something I'd learned in my four years as the Dating Diva. My father had never been worried about my mother. He wasn't a worrier by nature.

"It's not the L.A. way," he always said. *"It's the New York way, which is why I wanted to move to the land of sunshine."*

Perhaps now that he was a New Yorker again, he'd start worrying. Perhaps today or tomorrow or the next day, when he was taking a shower and found my mother parting the curtain with a pair of hedge clippers and aiming for the family jewels, he'd start worrying.

Mom, where are you? She had no relatives in New York. And she'd lived there so briefly as a student (when she'd met my father) so long ago that she'd lost touch with anyone she might have known then. There were countless hotels in New York. I wouldn't even know where to begin.

I glanced at my watch. It was seven-fifteen. My client's date was set for seven, and I wanted to be on my way to the airport by eight.

C'mon, Date Boy, show up already!

My client, Tammy, was gnawing her lip and glancing at her watch at her table a few feet from my spot at the bar.

Twenty-one-year-old Tammy thought she was boring her dates to death, which was hard to believe when you first saw her. A perky blonde with saucer-blue eyes, an ample chest accentuated by a tight V-neck cashmere sweater and long legs encased in knee-high black leather boots, she was a hot package. But unlike Amber, her problem wasn't coming on too strong and making sexual innuendos.

"The last guy I dated told me to stop talking so much," Tammy had explained over coffee a few days ago. "Once, during a movie, I think it was the third *Harry Potter.* Oh, wait a minute. Maybe it was the third *Lord of the Rings.* Did you read the books? Weren't they great? Omigod, I loved them. I know to look at me, you'd think I only read *Cosmopolitan,* but I love to read. I swear I keep Amazon in business. My mother is uncomfortable making online purchases—she thinks there are little thieves in the computer, stealing her credit card numbers. I've already starting ordering Christmas presents online. It's so convenient, and—"

"Tammy," I interrupted, "I think I'll be able to help you."

"Whew! Fabu! Oh hey, that rhymes!" She cackled for a moment. "Did I mention I wrote poetry? Of course, the last asshole I dated told me I wasn't exactly Wordsmith. Wait a minute—that's not right. Words*worth*. Yes, Wordsworth. Do you like poetry, Zoe? The guy I'm meeting tonight was buying a book of poetry for his mom 'just-because' when I met him. Isn't that sweet? It was a book on the Romantics. No, wait, the Victorians..."

I loved poetry. Especially the Victorians. But the idea of discussing anything with Tammy seemed truly painful. Despite how attractive and sexy she was, I was beginning to wonder how she managed to get dates at all.

My game plan for Tammy, which I'd explained to her in detail to keep her from talking, was to closely watch her date's face and body language for clues that he was getting antsy. If his eyes started to glaze over and he began looking at his watch, I was to signal her, and we'd meet in the ladies' room where I'd quickly explain why she was losing him and how to rectify the situation. I had a feeling all Tammy had to do to score a second date with anyone was to barely speak on the first date and let the guy do most of the talking. In my years as the Dating Diva, I'd noticed that men on dates with exceptionally sexy women like Tammy tended to want to talk themselves up and impress their way into a make-out session later. If she let the guy talk, she'd have him.

Hey, my job was only to get her to date number two. Not marriage.

The guy she was meeting tonight, who was now twenty minutes late, had made such an impression on her that she was willing to "put a muzzle on it," which was what that ex-boyfriend had said to her during the third *Lord of the Rings.* (She had finally gotten back to that tangent.)

Mr. Poetry was edging toward twenty-five minutes late. Tammy glanced at me and bit her lip; she looked like she was about to cry. First dates on a Saturday night had that extra zing of pressure and anticipation, and getting stood up on a weekend was a lot worse than getting stood up on a Tuesday, when you could go home and watch *Will & Grace* and comfort yourself with the fact that you had to get up early for work anyway.

There was nothing I wanted more than to hop in a taxi and get to the airport, but I gave Tammy the "Give him a few more minutes" sign and she nodded and settled back down. As the clock ticked toward thirty minutes late, Tammy's lower lip quivered and she stood up.

Jerk! Why did he ask her out if he was just going to stand her up? Sometimes I didn't understand men at all. Not that I claimed to understand them, but when it came to dating, I just wished that men (and women too, of course) would think first and ask out later. I closed my notebook and grabbed Contracts Law, then signaled the bartender to close my club soda tab.

"Omigod! You're finally here!" I heard Tammy say. "I was about to leave, but then I remembered a scene from this movie where the guy—"

I was about to signal Tammy to meet me in the bathroom for an emergency shut-up now session, but when I glanced over to see her date, I was struck speechless.

Her date, Mr. Poetry, Mr. Tall, Dark and Hot, Mr. Made Such An Impression on her, Mr. Thirty Minutes Late, was…Charlie.

My Charlie.

My boyfriend of over a year.

He was dressed for a date. Black pants. Charcoal-gray button-down shirt. He looked very Banana Republic.

"I'm sorry I was so late," he said to Tammy. "I—"

"Charlie?" I blurted out.

He spotted me at the bar and paled. "What are you doing—" He glanced at Tammy, then bit his lip. "Oh, shit, did she hire—"

"You two know each other?" Tammy asked. "Omigod, it is *such* a small world. Once, I was on a date, and who came in and sat down right next to us, but my high school English teacher, who I'd had a mad crush on. So

I tell my date this piece of information, and he didn't appreciate it one bit. Not with the guy sitting next to us. But everyone has crushes on their teachers. I mean…"

"Tammy, this would be a good time to stop talking," I said. "Do you see my expression? Your *date's* expression? That should signal you to *stop talking.*"

Clearly confused, she looked at me, then at Charlie. At least she shut up.

"Zo—I—" Charlie began, and then he stopped talking too. He leaned his head back and let out a whoosh of a breath. "I can't believe this."

He couldn't believe this?

Was I on *Candid Camera?* Was this some new kind of reality television show? Get the relationship guru?

Charlie was a straight shooter. Pranks weren't his style.

"Hel-lo," Tammy said. "Does one of you want to tell me what's going on?"

"I'll tell you what's going on, Tammy," I said, staring at Charlie. "My boyfriend here is cheating on me."

Tammy's eyes widened, and she covered her mouth with her hand. "Omigod! You're two-timing the Dating Diva? With me?"

Now, that was one for the tabloids.

"Zoe, can we please talk—in private?" Charlie asked.

"Don't you think you owe *me* a talk, too, Charlie?" Tammy asked, crossing her arms over her chest. "You asked *me* out. You're supposed to be on a date with *me.* I think you owe *me* an explanation."

Suddenly Tammy was quite concise.

"Look, Tammy, I'm really sorry. But I need to talk to Zoe right now."

"Asshole!" she snapped. "I hope she dumps your sorry two-timing ass." She grabbed her purse and stormed off.

Again, she was quite to the point.

"Zoe, hear me out, okay?" Charlie said. "Please?"

It made no sense. I knew Charlie. Or at least I thought I did. There were guys you knew were capable of lying to you, of cheating on you. Charlie wasn't one of them.

Yes, and that's why he's here, Zoe, meeting another woman for a date.

"Zoe, I've been asking you to marry me for eight months. But you've been putting me off, and putting me off and two weeks ago—" He shook his head and sat down at the bar.

I sat down next to him. "Charlie, if you want to marry me so badly, what are you doing on a date with another woman?"

He took my hand and I grabbed it back. "I asked her out because she's not the least bit my type. When I met her, she rambled on about astrology for ten minutes. I asked her out because she was safe."

"What the hell are you talking about?"

"Zoe, if you're not going to commit, I'm going to date other women. Period. I used to think you were really commitment phobic, that I could work on you, but I've started to think that it's not you—it's me. Maybe I'm just not the one for you."

Was he? *I love you, I love you not. I love you. I love you not.*

"Do you love me or not, Zoe?" he asked.

I don't know. I don't know!

What the hell was wrong with me?

"Charlie, I don't know what it is. I just know I'm not ready. I'm only twenty-six years old. Maybe that's it."

"No, Zoe. Maybe it's that I'm just not it for you. And you didn't answer my question, either."

"It's not you," I told him. "It's ambivalence."

"Well, I don't want the woman I love to be ambivalent about me. I want her to want me as much as I want her. Look, Zoe, I've really had it. It's either yes or no."

"Well, I can't give you an answer right now. I have to be on a plane to New York in two hours. I have to get to the airport."

He shook his head. "Wait a minute. You're going to New York? Tonight? And you didn't even bother to tell me?"

Shit.

"Charlie, it all happened really fast, and I didn't have time today to call you, and—"

"You know what, Zoe? I've had it. You couldn't see me last night because you were working. You couldn't see me tonight because you were working. And now you're flying off to New York for who knows how long, and you didn't even think to mention it. Whatever. I'm sick of it. You know how many women come on to me a day? Between work and the gym and hanging out with my friends?"

"Goodie for you, Charlie," I said.

"Yeah, goodie for me, because now that I'm a free agent, I can make up for lost time. A waste of time."

"You can start right now," I countered. "There's a bar full of single women right here."

"Maybe I will," he said.

"Fine," I said.

"Don't make me out to be the bad guy here, Zoe. This conversation could have gone a lot differently, but you led us here."

"You're the one on a date with another woman, Charlie."

But he was right and I knew it.

"Whatever, Zoe."

And then he turned and walked out.

★ ★ ★

In a city of eight million people, how was it possible that the first person I saw when I landed at LaGuardia Airport bright and early Sunday morning was Danny Marx, who'd asked me out at least a hundred times between junior high and high school?

I'd never said yes.

"Maybe that's why my standards are high," Danny said, grabbing my suitcase from the carousel the moment I reached for it. "No one I meet lives up to you. Not even my new girlfriend. And she's spec-tac-ular."

"How'd you know I needed an ego boost?" I asked, trying to suppress a yawn. The red-eye from L.A. to New York was a killer itself without adding a few hours of crying to the mix.

Six hours later I still wasn't sure why I was crying: because Charlie and I had broken up, or because I was beginning to really wonder if something was wrong with me? I'd had a good guy. A great guy. Why would I just let him go?

Because there's something wrong with you, that's why.

"Geez, what do you have in here?" Danny mock-complained, hefting my suitcase as we walked toward the exit. "Dating Diva reference manuals?" He laughed. "And c'mon. Who are you kidding—Zoe Solomon needs an ego boost? Impossible."

That was pretty much the reason I'd never said yes to Danny Marx. He'd put me on a pedestal in the eighth grade and I didn't want to get knocked off.

Which meant I could never be myself around him.

Which was the real reason I'd never said yes.

"The Dating Diva in the flesh," Danny said, wiggling his eyebrows like Groucho Marx. "I read the article about you in *L.A Magazine* last year. I wanted to call you, but I also read about your boyfriend. You see how skinny I am—I figured he'd kick my ass if I asked you out."

He might have, until eight hours ago.

Besides, Danny wasn't all that skinny. He'd filled out. And he was tall. He was sort of cute, with his puppy-dog brown eyes and light brown mop of hair. But he'd always be Anthony Michael Hall in *Sixteen Candles* to me. Sweet and goofy and immature, yet just slightly wise enough to make him tolerable.

"Well, Danny, you don't have to worry about getting beat up. The boyfriend and I are history."

I said it aloud to test out how it felt to say it, for it to be a true statement. It felt funny, sounded funny. A year was a long time for your life to suddenly change in an instant.

"One minute you're married and your life is great or even just fine and status quo," my mother had said a few months ago, *"and the next, your husband is running around with a woman who was in diapers when he had his first child. Some people say that's just the way life is. But I say screw that! Life is what you make it. Not what it is!"*

My mother always made sense up until a certain point. And then you wouldn't know what the hell she was talking about. Life wasn't what it was? What?

"Let me put it this way, Zoe," she'd said. *"Someone drops a bomb on your life, what are you going to do? Live in a ruin? Or are you going to fight back?"*

"What if there's nothing to fight?" I'd asked. *"What if you're simply defeated?"*

"That's what seeking vengeance is all about, dear."

And that was what my mother was up to this minute. I knew it. There was nothing and no one to fight, because my father couldn't be less interested in having a casual or serious conversation with his ex-wife. That left my mother one option: retribution. What *kind* of retribution was beyond me, though. Phony phone calls in the middle of the night? Phony calls to Giselle claiming to be his gal on the side?

Daniel dropped my suitcase and froze in mock shock. "Zoe Solomon is a free agent? Figures that I'm taken now. Because I know if I weren't, you'd be panting to date me."

I laughed. Danny Marx had elicited my first smile in eight hours.

"And it's *Daniel* now," he said. "I stopped being Danny when I turned the tassle on my high school cap."

"Ah, yes," I said in my best Queen's English. "Daniel it is."

"Daniel is an architect now," he said. "What do you think of that? Class clown Danny Marx ended up doing pretty well, eh? My firm opened a New York City office a few months ago, and I volunteered to transfer and *voilà*."

"Very impressive," I agreed. "I remember you used to draw buildings all the time. Tall, New York buildings."

His eyes lit up. "Zoe Solomon remembers anything about me? Unbelievable. Next you'll tell me you always had a secret crush on me in high school."

"No such luck," I said, grinning. "I remember the drawings because I always dreamed of moving to New York one day, and you used to draw New York."

"Well, fancy that," he said as we followed a throng of people toward the exit. "And here you are."

"Well, I'm not really here. I'm chasing after my mother. Ah, it's a long story."

He glanced at his watch. "Well, my friend's flight is delayed a half hour, so I've got time for a long story."

"My parents got divorced last year," I said. "Another woman."

Daniel nodded. "That's what got my parents. A long time ago, though."

"Well, now my father's marrying that other woman, and my mother flipped when she saw the engagement announcement. My father actually *sent* her one. He was married to the woman for twenty-five years and didn't know her well enough not to do that?"

"Sounds like he just got caught up in his own excitement," Daniel said. "It was pretty insensitive, though."

"My mother thought so too. And she flew out yesterday to destroy his life. Or so she said."

Daniel laughed. "I always liked your mother. Very theatrical."

"How do you know my mom?" I asked.

"Are you forgetting that I was an esteemed member of the Desmond Hills High School's thespian group?"

Ah. My mother had been a little too involved in my school. She was assistant director and head set designer for the drama club, which I had never joined for that reason. Couldn't act, sing, dance or memorize lines, for that matter. I'd graduated from Desmond Hills eight years ago, yet she still donated her time to the school.

"Do you know where she's staying?" he asked. "I'm sure you'll be able to talk some sense into her. I remember Mrs. Solomon as being very dramatic but ultimately reasonable. One year we did *Romeo and Juliet,* and your mother spent an hour trying to convince the head director to let them live at the end. She's just a romantic, Zoe. Maybe once she sees that your dad is happy, she'll back off."

"I don't know about that," I said. "My father's happiness isn't number one with her. And I don't know where she's staying. I don't even know where to look."

"I'd look in your father's closets," Daniel said.

I laughed. "That's probably exactly where she is."

"Hey, can I hire you while you're in town?" he asked.

"Hire me? I thought you said you were taken."

"Well, I am, sort of," he said. "She's on the way to *becoming* my girlfriend, but she's not there yet."

"And what's stopping her?"

"A lack of serious interest in me," Daniel said.

I laughed again. "Well, that would stop her, yes."

"We've gone out a few times and I really like her," he said, "but you know when someone's being halfhearted and ambivalent. Even a dolt like me knows."

"Your ambivalence isn't exactly confidence-building, Zoe," Charlie had said a few times. *"You're halfhearted about us."*

"I'm not," I would tell him. *"This is just how I am. I'm not Miss Burst of Enthusiasm."*

"I've seen you enthusiastic, Zoe. I've seen you bursting with enthusiasm."

Oh.

"I don't know what I'm doing wrong," Daniel continued. "Once or twice—okay, more than once or twice, I've seen her eyes glaze over. You could accuse me of a lot, but being a killer bore isn't one of them."

I bit back my smile. I could imagine Daniel on a date, trying to impress a woman, going a bit overboard with his shtick.

"How long have you been seeing her?" I asked.

"We've gone out five or six times. I think she's at the point where she's gonna dump me or commit—to sleeping with me, at least."

I glanced at him. Sex and Danny Marx didn't seem to belong in the same sentence. I couldn't imagine even kissing him on the lips.

He shifted my suitcase to his other hand as we headed outside to the taxi line. "And once we're, shall we say, intimate, I can work on her from there. It's easier to make a woman fall in love with you once she's slept with you."

My eyebrow shot up. "Where'd you read that crap?"

"It's a known fact," he said with a grin. "You see why I need your help?"

"Oh, I see, all right." I grinned back at him and punched him on the arm as I untied my sweater from around my hips and slipped it on. "You need a lot of help, Mr. Marx. So what exactly do you want—a critique of your relationship?"

"Not the relationship, just my skills at relating. I want the Dating Diva's gentle brutality."

I laughed, which I'd been doing a lot of since running into him. "Sounds like you relate just fine, Daniel."

"I would have gotten her into bed by now if that were the case."

He got another punch on the arm. "Maybe she's just the wrong woman for you. Did you ever think of that?"

"Nah, no chance," he said. "I really like this woman. A lot. She's special, you know?"

I stopped and looked at him. "You really like her, huh."

He nodded.

"I'll tell you what, then, Daniel. I'm not too sure what my schedule will be over the next few days or how long I'll be staying in New York, but if I find some spare hours, you've got a critique on me, for old times' sake."

He grimaced. "Ack, don't say that. Old times' sake. I was every girl's best friend. 'You're so nice, Danny. I wouldn't want to ruin our *friendship.* I just like you as a *friend,* Danny. You're such a *sweetie.*' Well, screw that horseshit. I'm trying to perfect my inner jerk."

"For that, you get the Dating Diva's private cell phone number." I handed him my card. "Really, though, Daniel,

I'm not sure if I'll even have time. I'm not too sure of anything right now."

He looked at me. "Are you all right? I didn't want to pry before, but I figure your parents divorcing when you're twenty-six ain't too much fun, and I don't know what happened to the boyfriend, but I'm sure you'll be snatched up in about five minutes."

"Well, thanks," I said. "But I think I'm going to concentrate on stopping my mother from maiming my father." I was next in line for a taxi. "Thanks for waiting with me, Daniel. And if I don't talk to you, good luck with the girlfriend-to-be. I really hope it works out."

A moment later I was in a yellow taxicab. Danny leaned down and made a funny face against the window, then waved as the cab sped away. I turned around to look back, and Daniel was standing there, watching.

My father had one of those amazing New York apartments you only saw in old Woody Allen movies like *Hannah and Her Sisters.* It was a penthouse apartment on Park Avenue in the low nineties. There was even a maid's room, where Zalla, housekeeper and Zone chef, did indeed live.

Zalla took my suitcase and disappeared down the hall. A moment later, my father appeared, looking a lot like Ralph Lauren.

My father always looked as if he just returned from vacationing on a Caribbean island. He was tall, tanned, had silver-brown thick hair and was a very good-looking man. As he came toward me, big smile, I half expected my mother to jump out from a corner with an electric razor and buzz his hair off. *"He's all hair and tanned skin and flash,"* my mother had taken to saying recently. *"You cut the hair, lose the tan and the Rolex, and he's just an old man. A dirty old man."*

My mother's therapist managed to do some very good work, but it lasted only a day or so. Then my mother would be back to, *"He's the only man I'll ever love. He just needs to see that she's a teenager and he belongs with a woman. We have history! A child together! A child older than the baby he's marrying!"*

My father pulled me into a hug. "You look great for someone who's been on a plane all night."

Actually, I looked like shit. I was surprised Daniel had even recognized me. My crying jag had obliterated my makeup, I had dark circles under my eyes and my hair was in a ponytail under a baseball cap. I wasn't sure if my father always thought I looked beautiful because he was my father or if he just never really saw me.

"Giselle was thrilled when I told her you were coming," he said, putting on his suit jacket. "She already left for school, but she can't wait to see you tonight."

I could wait to see her.

He grabbed his briefcase from a gorgeous secretary desk in the hallway. "I wish I didn't have to head out, Zo, but it's 8:00 a.m., which means I've got to hit the office. Dinner's at seven." He kissed the top of my head, then slipped on his sunglasses, despite how overcast it was. "We'll catch up then. Oh—there's a surprise for you in the guest room."

The surprise turned out to be my sister Ally and a second bed, a cot. Ally was sitting on the edge of the full-size bed, next to an open suitcase, twisting her wedding ring around her finger. She was crying.

I stood in the doorway, unsure if I should go in or not. "Ally?"

Her hands dashed to her eyes and she shot up, busying herself in her suitcase. She started unfolding and folding a red sweater. "Dad mentioned you were coming."

Was that why she was crying? I knew she wasn't crazy about me, but I wouldn't think my presence could reduce her to tears.

I stepped into the room, unsure where to stand. I sat down on my bed. "Are you okay?"

"Yeah, fine," she said, unfolding the same sweater and then folding it again.

"Are you staying for a while?" I asked.

"Look, Zoe, I don't mean to be rude, but I'm really not in the mood for Twenty Questions, okay?"

O-kay. I wanted nothing more than to conk out for a couple of hours, but I could see that Ally needed some privacy. "I'm going for a walk around the neighborhood. Can I bring you back anything?"

"That's another question," she said, and unfolded a pair of black pants, then refolded them.

"Righto," I said, and left the room.

Ally tried to come across like an intimidating bitch, but it was a facade. She was a marshmallow, like most cranky, bitchy people. I found that out on Thanksgiving, ten years ago, when she'd blown my head off for saying something about her mom, who'd died earlier that year of a brain aneurysm. I was trying to say something nice, about us being a family, but she told me to "mind your own fucking business."

"You're such a bitch!" Sarah had snapped at Ally from across the table, and both Ally and I had stared at Sarah, surprised.

And then I noticed the tears well up in Ally's eyes for just a second, before she blinked them back and asked my aunt Ramona to pass the cranberry sauce. Then Ally slipped her hand inside her husband's and he squeezed it, and I realized that she was hurt.

Ally had always scared me to death. But from that

minute on, I saw her as vulnerable. I'd tried to develop a relationship with her and with Sarah, who was closer to my age, but neither of them would bite. Not for invitations to hang out at the house for the summer, or for a week at the holidays or for skiing trips. Nothing.

"Why do my sisters hate me?" I'd ask my father, and he'd say they didn't hate me but that they were victims of divorce.

"But then aren't you to blame?" I'd ask.

In answer he'd pat me on the head, hand me his credit card and send me off to the mall with Zalla.

"Why do my sisters hate me?" I'd ask my mother, and she'd say it was because they were jealous of me. Because I had their father, whom they wanted.

"But shouldn't they have him too?" I'd ask.

"They need to grow up," my mother would say. *"They're immature and spiteful. They don't even have a civil word for me when they visit."*

Maybe because you're mean to them, I always thought. *And you broke up their family.*

I'd grown up being aware that another woman could swoop off with my father, take him two thousand miles away to another family, a new daughter, a new stepmother who wouldn't like me. But it never happened.

And then I met Charlie, the king of commitment, and I started to think marriage could mean something. That it wasn't just two people bound by a legal piece of paper and pretty vows to love, honor and cherish.

But then my own parents contributed to the fifty percent divorce rate.

"Stop making excuses about divorce rates, Zoe," Charlie would say. *"Marriage is about commitment. Love. Respect. And a willingness to grow with another person. It's the want*

to do it with a certain person. It's not about other people and their marriages."

And now it wasn't even about Charlie.

Hear ye, hear ye, the famed Dating Diva of L.A. is a failure at relationships, including with her own family.

I waited a few minutes to see if Ally would come after me, to apologize or say she'd go out with me, but she didn't.

Sarah

I used to be able to climb the stairs of my fifth-floor walk-up apartment building in about three minutes. Now, at only seven weeks pregnant, I was taking about a minute per step. How was I supposed to make this hike when I was seven *months* pregnant? And with a baby stroller? Mothers couldn't even manage to get a stroller through a door. I was going to lug it up four flights of stairs?

And given that tomorrow marked one week since Griffen had said, "I'll call you," I could pretty much count on carrying that stroller all by myself.

"You are so out of shape, Sarah!" announced my roommate, Jennifer, when I opened the door. She was sitting on the couch in one of her teeny-tiny stretch tank tops and yoga pants; her boyfriend and constant guest was sprawled out, his head in her lap. He was staring at the TV—vintage *Star Trek*. "You're totally out of breath!" She tsk-tsked.

I wasn't about to tell her why, not yet anyway.

I'd been living with Jennifer Futterman for six months, ever since Lisa, my former roommate, moved in with her boyfriend. I'd heard about Jennifer and her need for a roommate through an acquaintance at *Wow;* she had a real two-bedroom (the apartment I'd shared with Lisa was a one-bedroom convertible, which meant two fake walls and zero sound privacy), and I managed to afford my share of the higher rent and utilities by cutting back on food and walking to work more often. Jennifer and I had never become friends. Maybe because she left her dirty underwear on the bathroom floor, her dirty cereal bowls on the coffee table, and her dirty boyfriend all over the couch.

"Did you stay over at Griffen's last night?" she asked. "I ran into your bedroom to see you first thing this morning, and you weren't there."

"Uh, yeah," I lied. I'd been unable to sleep and had gone out at the crack of dawn to stare at the East River for a couple of hours before heading to work.

"I can't believe you've been standing there for, like, five minutes, and you still haven't noticed my rock!" she said, wiggling her left hand.

My gaze immediately went to her hand, and there on her ring finger was indeed a rock. It sparkled in the dimly lit living room.

She held up her hand and waved her fingers. "That's what I wanted to show you this morning. We got engaged last night!"

As she related the tale of her engagement, complete with hansom cab ride in Central Park and a one-point-five-carat marquise-shaped diamond, I almost burst into tears.

"Oh, and Sar? I'm really sorry, but, um, now that we're engaged, I finally said okay to living with Jason, so, um, he's going to move in at the end of the month. Officially, I mean. He's basically going to live here starting today."

She started stroking his stomach and kissing his neck. "Isn't that right, Pooh bear?"

I wondered if my sudden queasy stomach was the result of morning sickness, impending homelessness or *Pooh bear.* "But—" *There really isn't room for him. There's barely room for the two of us as it is.*

"Jesus, I'm trying to watch this," Jason complained and pushed Jennifer's hand away.

She played with his hair instead. "I'm really sorry, Sarah, but it *is* my apartment, and I'm sure you'll find another place fast. You have two whole weeks. Omigod, I have to call my friend Julia. I can't believe I forgot to tell her that I'm an engaged woman!" She grabbed the phone from the coffee table.

"Hey, quit moving around and keep it down!" Jason snapped. "This is the classic 'Trouble with Tribbles' episode."

Enjoy your prince, I thought, and went into my bedroom.

I flung myself on my bed. Don't freak out, I told myself. Don't burst into tears. Everything will be okay.

I thought about my options. Sabrina had two cats, to which I was allergic. Lisa lived with her boyfriend. Ally was both insufferable and a major commute away and had the smarmy husband besides. Griffen was digesting. And besides, we weren't at that stage in our relationship.

How pathetic was that?

I was not spending another night under this roof with that idiot Jason. I'd suffered through enough embarrassing episodes of waking up in the middle of the night to use the bathroom only to find him masturbating in the living room to the *Robyn Byrd Show.* If he was living here, I wasn't, two weeks to go or not.

Where could I go? Where would I find another roommate?

Oh, hi, I'm looking for an apartment to share for me and my baby. Yeah, he or she will wake up wailing at 2:00 a.m. every day for months and will spit up on all the furniture and rugs, but you can add the cost of earplugs and cleaning supplies to my portion of the rent.

Which I might not be able to pay, anyway, if I don't get that promotion.

Which I might not get if I sleep through my alarm again. (Actually, I'd only done that once during the past two weeks, and Lisa was sure it was psychosomatic exhaustion due to reading about the symptoms of pregnancy.

Did I mention how grateful I was that Lisa was a coddler?)

I couldn't have a roommate. I would already have a built-in roommate in seven months. It was time to find my own place.

But the cheapest studio apartment in the dinkiest section of the Upper East Side, which was both the most inexpensive and the most expensive neighborhood (cheap if you lived way east on a side street and a million miles from the subway), was twelve hundred bucks. I couldn't afford that on my current salary.

Anyway, could I live in a studio with a baby? And how was I supposed to pay a rent like that and raise a baby, even if I did get most of the starter stuff I'd need at my baby shower? Was someone going to give me diapers for life as a gift?

Like it or not (not) I had two choices. Ally or my father.

Given that Ally came with a commute on the Long Island railroad and the smarmster of a husband, she immediately had two strikes against her. She also knew I was pregnant and would nominate and declare herself captain of the pregnancy police. *Don't eat that! Did you take your prenatal vitamin? You already had one cup of coffee this month! What would Mom say if she saw you doing that?* Living with Ally was out of the question. From birth to when Ally left for college when I was twelve, I had shared a bedroom with her in a small two-bedroom apartment on the Lower East Side, which had been an inexpensive neighborhood in those days (apparently my father had offered to pay for a bigger, more luxurious apartment, but my mother wanted to be self-supporting). Sharing a bedroom with a teenaged Ally, as snappish as she was now, had turned me off the idea of overnight visits to her house forever, despite the swimming pool and hot tub. So there was no way I could stay with her indefinitely or until I found a new place, whichever came sooner.

That left my father, who did conveniently live in a penthouse with a few extra bedrooms. One had been converted into a bedroom for Madeline, his fiancée's toddler, but there were two other guest bedrooms. I tried to imagine myself waking up every morning in my father's house.

Good morning, Dad.

Morning, honey.

Silence.

Bye, Dad.

Bye, honey.

I wasn't exaggerating. Here was most of the last conversation I'd had with my father, a month ago, when I'd called to congratulate him on his engagement, which of course I'd heard about via the mailed announcement:

Me: "It's a women's magazine, Dad. I've been working there for four years."

Dad: "Ah, that's right. For some reason, I thought you were working for a publishing house, on books."

Me: "No, it's a magazine."

Dad: "Well that's great, Sarah. Just great. Have you been working there long?"

Silence.

Me: "Uh, four years, Dad."

Dad: "That's great, Sarah. Just great."

Silence.

Me: "Well, congrats again on your engagement."

Dad: "Thanks, honey. And come for dinner any time, Sarah. Giselle and I would love to have you."

That was another plus for Dad. He was free and easy with the invites *and* he lived in his own private Idaho, a place that didn't include noticing subtleties, like other people's problems. Which meant a rent-free, hassle-free, pry-free, very nice place to live until Griffen either called and proposed marriage and carried me over the threshold of that two-bedroom high-rise on the Upper West Side, or I figured out how to manage my new life-to-be on my own.

For reasons I couldn't fathom, my two sisters were A) in my father's apartment, B) sitting next to each other on one of the four butterscotch leather loveseats in the living room, and C) staring at six identical photographs pushpinned into a bulletin board on an easel.

As I trailed after Zalla, who insisted on taking my suitcase (was my secret out or was I just not used to a housekeeper greeting me at a front door?), I peered around her down the long, narrow hallway to get a glimpse of the photographs that held everyone rapt.

"Take your time, girls," my father was saying. He stood to the side of the easel and examined the photographs with the fascination one might devote to Mona Lisa in the Louvre. "Really look at each one and let me know which you think rocks."

My father's vocabulary needed work.

"Dad, they're *cummerbunds,*" Ally said, examining her nails. "It's not that big a deal."

"Oh, but it is, Ally," my father said, pinching her cheek. "I want every detail of this wedding to be perfecto. What do you think, Zoe? Really look at them. Do you see the ruched effect of the second one on the top? I think it adds a really hip touch."

Bartholomew Solomon was obsessed with hip.

"I like them all, Dad. Really," Zoe said.

Zalla came to a stop under the archway of the living room. "Mr. Bart," she said, "Miss Sarah is here."

My father and sisters turned around, each one looking more surprised than the next.

"Sar!" My father pulled me into a hug. "All my girls in the same room. Fabulous!" He eyed the suitcase. "Zalla, add another cot in the guest room, please." He glanced at his watch. "I've got a major phone call coming in. We just might land Leonardo DiCaprio for the coal miner film. A year we've been in negotiations to make this film, and we still don't have even a working title. You gals like Leo? Of course you do. What woman doesn't? Okay—" he clapped his hands "—dinner's at seven, so why don't we all meet here for cocktails at six-thirty. Giselle should be home about then." He picked up the easel. "We'll take another look at the cummerbunds after dinner. You can really make a look with just the right one." He leaned the easel against a wall. "All rightie! I'll see you girls in a little while."

Gee, Sarah, what brings you here? And with a suitcase, no less. Is something wrong? Tell Dad all about it and if I can fix it, I will.

I'd stopped expecting anything from my father a long, long time ago. Then again, at least I didn't feel the need to call first to let him know a small detail like the fact that I was moving in for who knew how long. Whether I said I was staying overnight or for a few years, it would be *just great, sweetheart!* And, no, that wasn't fatherly *mi casa es su casa* stuff. He simply didn't listen, didn't hear. A few weeks from now, he'd notice me having a bowl of cereal in the kitchen or brushing my teeth in the bathroom, and he'd say, *Nice of you to spend a few days, Sarah. Wonderful to have you.* Pat on the shoulder. Exit scene stage left.

Like I said, my father wasn't one to notice that you were a nervous wreck. He didn't really see you, so when you didn't want him to know something major about you, like that you were pregnant, homeless and that the father of your baby was *digesting,* you didn't have to add his awareness of you to your list of worries.

"Sarah, you look terrific," he said, cupping my chin in his palm for an instant. "Just terrific." He smiled, blew a kiss in each of our directions, and then disappeared into his study.

"You don't look terrific," Ally contradicted, raking me up and down with those never-miss-a-thing blue eyes. "You look exhausted. Are you getting enough rest?"

"Yes, yes, yes," I said. "I'm fine. Hi, Zoe. When did you fly in?"

"Almost a week ago," Zoe said. "I arrived the day after Ally, and we've been bunking together ever since."

If anyone looked exhausted, it was Zoe, and now I understood why. Sharing a room with Ally could be very taxing. I'd never seen Zoe look anything but perfect. She was one of those natural beauties you saw in soap commercials, women who looked amazing while splashing water on their face in slow motion. She had longish light brown hair, silky and slightly wavy, and a long, lanky body. She even had a beauty mark next to her lip, like

Cindy Crawford. But she did look really wiped. Dark circles under her eyes, no makeup and the expression of someone who'd been worrying.

I knew a lot about that expression. I'd seen it every time I looked in the mirror these past two weeks.

"So what brings both of you here?" I asked. "For a week already."

"Where's the third cot going to go?" Ally asked no one in particular, completely ignoring my question. She pulled a compact out of her purse and began arranging pieces of her hair, which she'd cut short and *tres chic* in a Meg Ryan style meets Debra Messing color. I eyed Zoe, but she started braiding and unbraiding her own Pantene commercial hair. O-kaaaaaay. "There's barely room for the two beds in there already," Ally added.

"So why are you two staying here?" I asked again. "And why in the same room?"

"I'm just here for another few days," Zoe said. "Maybe another week."

"Me too," Ally said.

"Why?" I asked, looking from one to the other.

Zoe began braiding her hair again. "I thought I'd help out with the wedding plans."

That was crap. According to Ally, who heard a brief version of the story from Dad a few months ago, Zoe wasn't exactly hunky-dory with her new stepmother-to-be.

"And you?" I asked Ally.

Ally looked away. "Same reason."

Yeah, right. Something was definitely up with both of them. I'd spoken to Ally during the past week; she'd asked how things went with Griffen during the big birthday conversation, she'd asked if I was taking my prenatal vitamins, she asked if I was getting enough vitamin C. But she never once said, *Oh, and by the way, I'm staying at Dad's and sharing a room with Zoe.*

"What brings you here, Sarah?" Zoe asked me.

"Same reason," I said.

The three of us eyed each other with very unsisterly skepticism.

I wasn't about to let Ally know I was homeless—I'd get lectured for an hour, and then she'd insist on taking me apartment hunting on the spot. And I wasn't sure I wanted Zoe or my father to know I was pregnant until I myself had answers to the obvious questions they'd ask.

"Well, I'm going for a walk," I said. "See you for *cocktails* in the main drawing room," I added in an English accent.

"Yeah, and I have to meet a friend," said Ally.

"I'm going for a jog," said Zoe.

And we all, quite uncomfortably, headed out the door in different directions.

The dining-room table was set for seven. Six, really, if you didn't count the high chair.

"Sit wherever you want, girls," my father said, taking the head of the table on the left.

Ally grabbed the seat farthest from him, Zoe the seat closest. I parked myself in between them.

"Sorry I missed cocktails," Giselle said as she walked into the dining room, her two-year-old on her hip. "A certain little girl named Madeline wouldn't put on her pants, would she?" She tickled Madeline's stomach, and the baby started laughing. "Okay, Madeline, time to go in your high chair." The second Madeline was seated, she grabbed the spoon from the tray and started banging. "She'll stop when she realizes there's a new face to study," Giselle added, and, indeed, Madeline glanced around the table with wide eyes, examining faces, looking away, and then staring.

Her big hazel eyes landed on me, and she wouldn't look away.

"It's so nice that you're all here," Giselle said, smiling around the table. She looked at Zoe, who had ended up directly across from her, but Zoe stared at her fork, and Giselle turned to me. "It's great to see you again, Sarah."

I'd met Giselle once, about four months ago, when she and my father had come to New York supposedly for business but really to penthouse hunt. The happy couple and Ally and I had met for dinner at an expensive, dull restaurant. My father had dominated the conversation with movie talk and how great New York was, how happy he was to be "home," and I hadn't gotten to know Giselle at all. She seemed nice enough.

"The baby's going to get overstimulated with all these people!" announced a gravelly-voiced, reed-thin woman. She stood in the doorway with a partitioned plate full of teeny-tiny pieces of food.

"Madeline's fine, Mom," Giselle said. "Her preschool class has more people than this. And there's only one more person here tonight."

"In my day, you didn't overwhelm a baby," Giselle's mother muttered, and sat down next to Madeline's high chair.

"Sarah, this is my mother, June Archweller," Giselle said. "Mom, this is Bart's middle daughter, Sarah."

The mother eyed me, then began feeding Madeline. "Nice to meet you," she said, handing the baby what looked like diced chicken.

"Well, folks, let's dig in," my father said. "Zalla's quite a cook."

It turned out that my father was on the Zone diet,

which covered a good twenty minutes of conversation, and about which Giselle's mother had quite a bit to say. Nutrition was her thing. The next twenty minutes were taken up by wedding chitchat and an overview of Wedding Fest events. My father discussed cummerbunds for another ten minutes.

Madeline began flinging peas and chicken pieces at Giselle's mother, who was surprisingly patient with the toddler. Given her snappish conversational style, I'd pegged her as the ungrandmotherly type, but the woman was truly remarkable with Madeline. She was able to be firm and sweet at the same time; Madeline listened to her.

I had a million questions for Giselle about Madeline, from what it felt like to be much more pregnant than I was at the moment, to what the hell Lamaze class was all about, to giving birth, to changing a diaper, which I had never done in my life. I especially wanted to ask her what it was like being pregnant alone. Being a single mother. According to Ally, who heard the story from my father last year, Madeline's father was a wanna-be rock star who'd denied the baby was his.

At least Griffen hadn't done that.

"Giselle, how did you and Dad—" *Meet,* I swallowed as all eyes swung to me. "Decide which caterers and bridal boutiques, et cetera, to try," I added fast. Idiot. I almost forgot that they'd met through Zoe at some chance meeting in a coffee bar. I glanced at Zoe; she was slicing her filet mignon into shreds.

Zoe and Giselle had been friends, and then Giselle had stolen Zoe's father away from her mother. It was hard to remember that when you looked at Giselle. She had one of those absolutely open faces, like she'd give you the shirt off her back if you needed it. She was super pretty like Zoe, but in a different way. Zoe was almost classically beautiful because her features and her hair and body were so annoyingly perfect, but Giselle was beautiful in an exotic way. She had wildly curly light blond hair, to her shoulders, very light brown eyes, like Griffen's, and a dusting of freckles. There was a lot of her too, but she was incredibly sexy, and she showed off her ample bod. She was wearing tight brown leather pants and a to-the-waist ruffly sheer shirt with a camisole underneath. She wasn't a skinny-minny like my mother and Zoe's. My father's first two wives were so alike physically that everyone said he simply married a younger version of the same woman. Giselle was as opposite from the tall, dark, thin, regal type as you could get. She was more Anna Nicole Smith but with an Audrey Hepburn demeanor.

Every time I saw Giselle, I wanted to blurt out: *What the hell are you doing with my father?* She was twenty-five years old, gorgeous, smart (she was starting a master's program in clinical psychology at Columbia in the spring), and she had a doting, if overbearing mother to baby-sit Madeline. What could she possibly have in common with Mr. Materialist himself, the king of the schmoozers, a completely superficial filmmaker partial to tanning in the winter and thick gold bracelets? My father got pedicures, for God's sake, and Giselle didn't even seem to wear makeup.

"So how long are all of you staying?" Giselle's mother asked us, her shrewd eyes glancing from Solomon daughter to Solomon daughter. She turned to Ally. "You and Zoe have been here, what, a week now?"

"How long are *you* staying?" Ally snapped, and the woman blushed and turned her attention to Madeline.

"Everyone in this room is welcome to stay for as long as you like," my father announced. "A toast—to my six girls!"

"I'm hardly a girl," Giselle's mother muttered, but she lifted her glass. I wondered what she thought of her daughter marrying a man her own age.

Ally, Zoe and I lifted our glasses as though they were weighted with bricks.

"Zal, honey, get a picture, will you," my father said, and the housekeeper disappeared and reappeared with a camera. "First get Sarah, Ally and Zoe together, and then get a group shot."

"Say cheesebiggers," Zalla said.

"Cheese*burgers,* Zalla," Giselle's mother corrected. *"Burgers."*

"Burgers," Zalla repeated, and clicked. Smiling on "burgers" didn't exactly elicit grins.

Photos snapped, my father clapped his hands for attention, a bad habit of his.

"Sarah, I've got Ally and Zoe already thinking about this, and now I'd like you to join the think tank. Plaza, W, St. Regis, the Paramount? We're thinking of a hotel wedding, but then something at the seaport might be nice too. Thoughts?"

Bartholomew Solomon carried on all conversations as though he were at an L.A. meeting.

"Dad, you've had *two* weddings already," Ally pointed out, "so surely you know what you want and don't want."

If my father caught her sarcasm, he didn't bite. "But that's just it, Al," he said. "I really don't. I just want it to be spectacular. Spectacular like my Giselle."

Giselle blushed and smiled. "I'd be fine with a small family wedding, but your dad really wants to go all-out. Ally, I heard your wedding was incredible. It was at the seaport, right?"

You had to hand it to Giselle for trying.

Ally sucked down some wine."Yup. And what a waste of forty grand that turned out to be."

All eyes swung to Ally.

"I mean, all that expense," Ally continued, "all that planning, and for what? *One* day. Not even a day—five or six hours. The next day it's business as usual."

I was about to say something sarcastic, like *Oh, that's romantic,* but there was a reason Ally was here, and it wasn't to help my father pick out a cummerbund.

"As I recall, Ally," my father said, pointing at her with his fork for emphasis, "the *next day,* you and Andrew arrived in Greece for a two-week honeymoon. Ah, Greece. What a beautiful country."

Ally speared a piece of asparagus with a little too much force.

"Um, Dad," I said, "where are you and Giselle planning to go for *your* honeymoon?"

"We're thinking an African safari," he replied. "We're going to ride elephants through the jungle." He then told a five-minute story about a trained elephant in an upcoming romantic comedy he was producing. "You'd love the film, Zoe." He looked at her, then around the table. "Zoe's a romantic comedy freak."

Zoe's only response was a tight smile. She then went back to slicing her steak to bits and playing with her vegetables.

"Speaking of comedies," my father continued, "I was thinking about a movie theme for the wedding. Maybe the wedding party putting on minifilms at various points during the reception. Doesn't that sound hip?"

We all stared him, including his future wife. He continued on about how the bridesmaids and ushers would get to be stars for the day too.

"Since the three of you are all here together," Giselle

said when her fiancé took a breath, "this seems like a great time to ask if you'd all be bridesmaids. It would mean the world to us." She eyed Zoe, who stared at her plate, then looked at Ally and me.

"Do you even have a wedding date?" Zoe asked. It was the first thing she'd said in forty minutes.

"We're thinking of June," Giselle replied. "I'd love to add Central Park or the Brooklyn Botanical Gardens to the list of venues, but your dad isn't too keen on an outdoor wedding, in case it rains."

"Gissy baby," my father said, "if your heart is set on it, let's add the park and the garden to our list."

Giselle smiled. "Thanks, honey. So can I count on you three as bridesmaids?"

If I can fit into my dress, I thought. "Sure," I said.

Ally nodded.

All eyes swung to Zoe.

"June?" Zoe repeated. "I might be out of the country. I'm not sure yet. Can I let you know?" she added, looking at the platter of asparagus instead of Giselle.

"Sure," Giselle said. "I just hope that you can, Zoe."

Can you spell TENSION?

I wondered if the Zoe-Giselle ex-friendship was all that was bothering Zoe. If it were, she probably wouldn't be here, wouldn't have survived a day, let alone a week.

And there was definitely a reason Ally was here. I had never seen her so distracted. She usually loved to try to embarrass my father with how self-absorbed he was, and I fully expected her to say something like, *Don't you love the boots I got Sarah for her birthday?* And then my dad would look at me quizzically and say, *Oh, gosh, that's right! I had it marked on my calendar, but then yesterday was such a wild day.* And then Ally would say, *Her birthday was a week ago, Dad.* And without missing a beat, he'd smile and say, *Everyone, raise a glass to Sarah!*

But Ally wasn't doing anything to antagonize our father. Like Zoe, she too was pushing her food around on her plate, staring at her watch, staring at her food. Perhaps the reason had something to do with Smarmdrew, her husband. During cocktails earlier, which had turned into another cummerbund session, I'd asked her privately why she was staying here, and, clutching her little dog for dear life against her chest, she'd said something about Andrew being in Tokyo on business and the kitchen being renovated. But maybe she was lying.

"How's Andy's business these days, Al?" my father asked, filling his wineglass. "The market's tough right now."

Ally stiffened. It was for just a moment, but she stiffened.

"Business is great," Ally responded. "He's in Switzerland right now, hammering out a new deal."

An hour ago it was Japan. Now it was Switzerland.

"Well, I'd better turn in," Ally said. "I have to walk Mary Jane, and then I've got to prepare for a killer meeting first thing in the morning." She stood up. "Good night, everyone."

We said our good-nights, and Ally practically fled.

"You know, I think I'd better hit the sheets myself," Zoe said.

No way was I being stuck at the table alone. My sisters and I might not have spoken five words to each other, but there was still solidarity in sisterhood.

"Me too," I chimed in. "Dinner was just great," I said to Giselle before I realized she had nothing to do with it. "Well, good night."

"Amazing," my father said. "A two-year-old can stay

up longer than my daughters!" He laughed and rushed over to Madeline, lifting her out of her high chair. "And what do you think of that, Maddy-Waddy? Huh? What?" He tickled her, and the toddler started a giggle-fest.

I watched him from the doorway. I remembered him being like that with Zoe when she was very little, when Ally and I would fly out to California to stay with him for a couple of weeks during the summer. If he was like that with me or Ally, I didn't remember it. Maybe we were too old by then. Then again, I'd never lived in the same house with my father.

"Let the baby digest," Giselle's mother complained. "It's me she's going to spit up all over later, not you."

"You won't spit up all over Grandy, will you, pumpkin pie?" my father singsonged to Madeline. "You're way too sweet for that!" And he continued the tickle and giggle-fest, then began swooping her high in the air, much to Grandy's frown and Giselle's delight.

"Oh, Sarah?" Giselle called just as I turned to go.

I turned back.

"Will you let Ally and Zoe know that I'll be tacking wedding gown photographs to the bulletin board later and that I'd love their opinions any time before our bridal boutique appointments next month?"

"I'll tell them," I said.

She smiled and joined her fiancé and daughter in the fun.

Weird. I thought I was long over feeling funny about watching my father interact with a new family. But apparently, that funny feeling never went away.

The moment your marriage ended, you had a tendency to notice the world was full of couples, baby strollers and love songs. The young couple in front of me in line at Au Bon Pain were making out. Kissing with tongue at eight in the morning on a Monday, when most people were half-awake and in a bad mood and on their way to work.

"What are you getting, snookums?" the guy kisser asked, his tongue darting in the woman's ear. The slacker probably didn't have a job. The eyebrow ring was a dead giveaway.

"Whatever you're getting," she breathed back at him. "I want to experience what you're experiencing."

Could I throw up all over them?

They began making out again, their hands in each other's hair.

"Hel-lo," I snapped. "Could you get your tongues out of each other's mouths long enough to move forward? You're holding up the entire line."

They whipped around and stared at me. Someone behind me giggled.

"Next," called the clerk behind the counter, and the slackers finally moved.

The woman kisser turned around and shot me a nasty smile. "We're always cranky about what we don't have, aren't we, *ma'am?*"

I held up my left hand and waved my wedding ring at her. "Nice try, sweetie."

"Like married people get any," she countered, and she and her boyfriend laughed.

"Just forget it," the male kisser said, playing with her hair. "Unhappy people hate it when other people are happy."

"I happen to be very happy," I announced.

"Whatever, lady," the male kisser said.

"Could this line move any slower?" I snapped around him at the clerk.

I hated being called "lady." It reminded me that I wasn't twenty-two anymore and that I looked like a *ma'am* to twentysomethings. It reminded me that I *wasn't* "getting any" because I *was* married.

Ha. That was a joke. I glanced at the wedding ring I'd just waved around. Talk about an empty gesture.

I *was* unhappy. Plenty unhappy.

I'd walked out of my house with a suitcase one week and two days ago, and Andrew hadn't called once. Not that I'd talk to him.

And I was living in hell. Between the pregnancy books Sarah had under her pillow, and the wedding bulletin board in the living room, I was surrounded by babies and marriage.

I'd surprised myself by ending up at my father's apartment. A week ago last Saturday, I'd left my house with a suitcase in one hand and Mary Jane in the other and had no idea where to go. I'd thought about staying in a hotel, but the two-hundred-dollar bill I'd received for breaking that cheap, ugly lamp, plus the loneliness of waking up in a hotel room when you weren't away on business, was too much to bear. At least at my father's, there were people I knew walking around, but the plus was that my father tended to mind his own business because he didn't care about anyone but himself. What I hadn't counted on was having Zoe as a roommate. Or Sarah.

I had to do something. Something to distract myself from myself. From images of Andrew in the hammock with that skank. From my father's and Giselle's beaming faces at six in the morning. From my sisters' curiosity. Last night, I felt eyes on me, only to find Sarah staring at me when I thought she was absorbed in *But I Don't Know How To Be Pregnant!* (Which she read facing me and not Zoe, since she didn't want Zoe or my father or Giselle to know she was pregnant.) And twice I found Zoe watching me when I thought she was busy doing her usual thing of staring at the ceiling or contorting her body into yoga positions in a very small space in front of her bed. Granted, I watched them too, since Sarah's favorite answer was *I don't want to talk about it,* and I wasn't exactly comfortable asking Zoe anything personal. So I watched them and they watched me. We watched each other.

If I was going to stay at my father's for a while—until I figured out exactly what I was going to do with myself, if I was going to rent an apartment in the city or buy a house of my own in Westchester, or visit a sperm bank and knock myself up—I needed to do something. Something proactive. Something to make me feel good about myself.

Like I needed another facial, massage, shopping trip or an island vacation.

What, then? What, what, what?

Make appointment with good divorce lawyer was first on my list, but I wasn't one hundred percent ready to deal with that yet.

Corn muffin and coffee in hand, I sat down at a little table as far away from the kissing couple as I could get. I bit into my muffin and stared out the window.

"I met him on a FindAMate.com," a late-thirties woman at the next table whispered to her female companion. "He's *amazing.* Forty. Divorced and over it. Loaded. And as good-looking as his picture." She leaned close to her friend and flipped her long, curly red hair behind her shoulder. "I came for the first time in three years without the help of a vibrator."

Her friend's mouth dropped open, and both women looked around to make sure no one was listening to them. (Lawyers learn in law school how to make potential confessors feel like the lawyer isn't even in the room.) "You had sex with a man you met *online?*" the friend asked. "A *stranger? Are you insane?*"

"He wasn't a stranger when I slept with him," the redhead responded. She wrapped her hands around her cup of coffee and breathed in the aroma, her expression satisfied. "I e-mailed him a note, he e-mailed back, and we went back and forth for a couple of weeks. Then we spoke on the phone a few times, long conversations, and when I felt comfortable, I arranged a date."

"I don't know," the friend said, biting into her bagel. "Still."

"Still what?" the redhead asked. "I'd *still* be single if I hadn't given it a try. Single at Thanksgiving and Christmas and New Year's? No, thanks. I met a great guy. No one needs to know I met him online. Not that I'm embarrassed about it."

"I always thought personal ads and online matchmaking services were for losers," the friend said, taking out a compact and powdering her nose. "Sorry, but a lot of people feel that way."

"I'm doing it," the woman countered. "Am I a loser?"

Her friend colored. "I didn't mean *that.*"

"There are people on it just like me." The redhead grabbed the compact and checked her lipstick. "Just like you. Just like anyone. Where are we supposed to meet a man otherwise? In a bar? At work? On a blind date? Please. Online dating is totally mainstream now. You read through profiles, see who looks good to you, you write to each other, and when you're comfortable, you make a date in a private place. You don't like the guy, you leave in two seconds, no hurt feelings. You like each other, suddenly you're on a date with a promising guy and there's no busybody fixer-upper asking you questions."

"I guess that sounds pretty good," the friend said. "So you really like this man, huh?"

The redhead beamed. "I'm planning on taking him home for Thanksgiving, if we're still dating in a month. For the first time in three years, I won't have to listen to my relatives say, 'Your time will come too, sweetie, but it might come quicker if you lost a few pounds and got a good haircut.'"

"I hear that crap too," the friend said. "I am so sick of it! Okay, I'm sold. Maybe I'll check out the site tonight."

The redhead had me sold too. I needed a distraction? I needed something to make me forget my husband? I needed to retaliate? I'd found it.

I pulled out my Palm and wrote: FindAMate.com. And underlined it.

★ ★ ★

The room I was sharing with my sisters was slightly smaller than my bedroom at home, the one I used to share with Andrew. He and I were rarely in that bedroom at the same time, yet now, I was sharing the same-sized room with two other people. And two people who took up a lot of room. Not physically, of course. Sarah was only two months pregnant and thin as usual, and Zoe was a rail. But they both had mega presences.

At the moment, the three of us were on our beds, which were lined up, hotel fashion, next to each other. Beside each one was a round table upon which sat a tiny Tiffany lamp that I assumed was fake—but at my dad's you never knew for sure, since he could afford the real thing—a travel alarm clock and a tiny crystal bowl of lemon balls, which I happened to love. Sarah was in the middle, making notes for an article for *Wow* and sucking on lemon ball after lemon ball (which I attributed to cravings). Zoe was lying on her stomach, her arm outstretched in front of her and staring at a wallet-sized photograph of a guy. Boyfriend, I assumed. And I was typing FindAMate.com into my Web browser, this morning's eavesdropped conversation swirling in my head.

Sarah flopped onto her stomach and hung over the side of her bed, trying to pull her suitcase up and over onto the bed.

I lunged off my bed and grabbed it out of her hands. "You're not supposed to lift anything! Jesus, Sarah."

"This suitcase weighs about half a pound, Ally. The ba—" She glanced at Zoe, who was now eyeing us with curiosity.

"Do you want some privacy?" Zoe asked. "I can go examine wedding gown photographs on the bulletin board or something."

Sarah laughed. "I wouldn't wish that on my worst enemy. And besides, Ally was about to go back to minding her own business. Weren't you, Ally?"

I sat back down on my bed and dragged my computer onto my lap. "Do what you're supposed to do, Sarah. If you would, I wouldn't *have* to mind your business."

"How's Andrew?" Sarah snapped. "I haven't heard you mention him once since I got here three days ago."

"How's Griffen?" I snapped back.

"I'm going to give you guys some privacy," Zoe said, and she slipped out the door.

"I don't care if she knows," Sarah told me. "I'm getting tired of lying on my right side to read my pregnancy books so she won't see. According to *But I Don't Know How To Be Pregnant!*, I'm supposed to lie on my left side."

"That's right," I said. "I remember reading that. How are you feeling, anyway?"

"Okay," she said. "A little tired."

"So you still haven't heard from Griffen?" I asked.

She shook her head.

I tossed her a sourball. "Under the circumstances, Sarah, I guess he's got a little leeway to spend some time thinking things through. Taking over a week seems a little excessive, but I'm sure he'll call in the next few days. I don't know what he'll say, but I'm sure he'll call."

Sarah didn't say anything. She popped the sourball into her mouth, flopped onto her back, clasped her hands over her stomach and stared at the ceiling.

"What do you want him to say?" I asked her.

"I don't want to talk about it, okay?" she said without looking at me.

"Fine," I told her. "Check your e-mail tomorrow. I'm going to send you some links to some good pregnancy Web sites."

"Ally, I've been reading. I know the basics."

I doubted that. And not only was I sure she didn't know the first thing about expecting a baby, she didn't have the means or wherewithal to take care of a baby. Until she found out she was pregnant, she didn't even *want* a baby. She wanted her sort-of boyfriend to fall in love with her. She wanted to go to Puerto Rico with her friends to celebrate her birthday (guess who planned to buy her the ticket as a surprise). She wanted a black leather jacket, which I'd gotten for her from our mother (I'd bought Sarah a birthday present from our mother every year since her death). Sarah wanted a bigger bedroom and bigger breasts (which she'd now get). She wanted a pair of knee-high black leather boots from Steve Madden. She wanted to see the new Drew Barrymore (her favorite actress) movie. She wanted to be able to afford a venti-sized latte at Starbucks. She didn't even seem to want a real life.

And yet she was pregnant. My dream in life.

"If you knew the basics, Sarah," I told her, "you wouldn't have been about to lug that suitcase. You're not supposed to lift anything heavier than a hardcover book. You can have caffeine once a week. No alcohol, ever. Have you been taking your prenatal vitamins?"

"Ally—"

"Humor me, Sarah."

"I always do, Ally."

There was a soft knock at the door. "It's me again," came Zoe's voice.

"You don't have to knock, Zoe," Sarah called out. "This is your room too."

Zoe came in and shut the door. She sat down on her bed. "Dad and Giselle are in the living room, staring at photographs of tuxedo shirts. I couldn't take it. Sorry."

Sarah laughed. "At least cummerbund weekend is over."

"Cummerbund weekend?" Zoe repeated. "Try cummerbund *week*. It's all we've talked about since last weekend. And Ally arrived a day before me. She had to suffer it out all alone."

"That's right," I said, tossing Sarah another sourball. "So I deserve a little peace."

"Peace? You wanna *piece* of me," Sarah said in her best Brooklyn Robert DeNiro accent, putting up her dukes, and the three of us laughed. "You wanna piece a me?"

Zoe sat on the edge of her bed, facing Sarah and me. She sobered up. "You want to know why I'm staying here?" We stared at her, dying of curiosity. "Because my mother's on the warpath about Dad getting engaged. He sent her an announcement with an idiotic personalized note, and she went ballistic and flew out here vowing to ruin his life."

"I don't blame her," I said. "He's marrying a woman younger than her own daughter. It's vile."

Sarah and Zoe stared at me as though they couldn't believe I actually said it aloud.

"I'm really worried about my mom," Zoe continued. "She came here over a week ago, and I have no idea where she is. She's left me a couple of messages on my home phone to say she's fine and not to worry."

"So maybe she is fine and maybe you shouldn't worry," Sarah said. "She was probably just being funny when she said she's going to ruin Dad's life."

"Funny?" I repeated. "That I doubt. I remember Zoe's mother."

Sarah shot me a look. If I'd offended Zoe, it didn't show in her expression.

"Well, why are you so worried about her?" Sarah asked. "Do you really think she's going to do something crazy?"

"I don't know," Zoe replied on a sigh. "She's gone nuts as it is with plastic surgery to try to look younger to win him back. She dresses like a trendy teenager. She's a size four. She got her boobs done—bigger and lifted. She grew her hair even longer and made it even blonder. And when all the extremes didn't work—I just don't know what she's capable of doing."

"What *is* she capable of doing?" Sarah asked. "We're not talking Lorena Bobbitt, are we?"

"I don't think so," Zoe said. "But honestly, I don't know. I don't know what she thinks she *can* do. She wants Dad back so badly she'll do anything. That's what I'm scared of."

I shook my head. "You know what, Zoe? I don't really think it's your father she wants back."

"What do you mean?" Zoe asked me.

"I don't claim to know your mother that well," I said, "but I'd bet anything it's her dignity she wants back. Not your father."

"Her dignity?" Zoe repeated.

I nodded. "Getting plastic surgery, dressing like Britney Spears—she's trying to look like she's twenty-five because she associates youth with dignity. She was treated like a queen when she was young and beautiful, and now she feels she's being treated like shit. So she associates youth with dignity, instead of associating it with herself, with self-esteem."

"Very impressive, Ally," Sarah said. "Does that sound right to you, Zoe? You know your mom best."

Zoe nodded. "It sounds exactly right. But I don't get why my mom flew out here, then. If she's after her dignity, why not just go meet a new man who'll appreciate how well preserved she is? Why come after Dad? Why work so hard to get him back?"

Because she's a beast like Dad, that's why. They were made for each other.

I understood Judith Gold Solomon and Bartholomew Solomon as a couple. What I'd never understood was my mother and Bartholomew Solomon. I got why he wanted her—she was beautiful and the kindest person there ever was. But I'd never understood why she'd fallen for him, why she'd married such a superficial person.

"Why would you marry someone who'd just up and leave you one day for someone else?" six-year-old me had screamed at her when she told me my father was leaving, that he fell in love with someone else. She'd picked me up in her arms and sat with me on the rocking chair by the window in our midtown apartment, and I'd screamed and cried and shaken my fists at her as though it were her fault. She'd held me against her, tight, trying to hold my beating fists, and soothed me with shushes and strokes of my hair and told me that my father was a good man, but that sometimes people changed, and if they did, you had to let go, had to let them be who they were. *"You didn't even fight for him?"* I'd asked, crying and kicking again.

"Oh, Ally," she'd said over and over. *"Everything will be okay, you'll see, baby girl."*

And everything had been okay, basically, because my mother, with an angry six-year-old and a newborn, was a strong person. We'd moved to a smaller and dinkier apartment on the Lower East Side, near my mother's grandmother, and once a year Sarah and I flew out to California to stay with my dad, Judith and Zoe for two weeks.

Why would you marry someone who'd up and leave you one day for someone else...? Oh God, Mom, I thought now. I am so sorry. I am so, so sorry.

"Zoe, your mom didn't work so hard to get *him* back," I said, "she worked so hard to get herself back. You said your mother was here in New York to ruin Dad's life, not to get him back. When you want someone back, you don't go about it from a 'destroy their happiness' angle. Unless you're insane."

"Your mom's not insane, is she?" Sarah asked Zoe with a smile.

Zoe laughed. "She's just normal crazy."

"Like all of us," Sarah said.

"Trust me, she doesn't want Dad," I said. "She's after something else."

Zoe lay down on her bed, on her stomach, and folded her hands under her chin. "I guess you're right, Ally. I didn't really look at it that way."

"You know," I added, "I never got the feeling that Dad and your mother really even liked each other. I mean, *really* liked each other, the way you really like a friend."

"They were married for twenty-five years, Ally," Zoe pointed out.

"Yeah, because they probably didn't really care," I said. "So they never actually fought and got along fine."

"They cared about each other," Zoe snapped. "I was there."

"Yeah, you were," I snapped back.

Sarah looked between us nervously. "So what are you saying, Ally? That a marriage based on something other than love will work just fine, but that a marriage based on love is doomed?"

"You're generalizing," I told her. "I was applying that strictly to Dad and Zoe's mother."

"You really hate her guts," Zoe said. "Don't you?"

"I'd have to *care* to hate her, Zoe," I pointed out. "And I don't. I'm sorry, but I don't."

Zoe's mother had been vicious and vile to me and Sarah from the get-go, preferring to think that her husband didn't have two other daughters back in New York. Once, during our annual two-week summer visit, when I was nine and Sarah just three, I'd come inside from the pool to use the bathroom, careful not to drip all over the rug (she'd had a major cow over that one year), and as Sarah splashed happily in the pool, the ever-present nanny watching with one eye while the other was on newborn Zoe, I'd overheard the witch trying to convince my father that a two-week visit was too long, that one week was surely plenty, since he flew to New York to see us twice a year for a day or two. The next summer, when we were invited back for two weeks as usual, I stopped hating my father, and my chronic headaches at age ten went away. I didn't like him, but at least I didn't hate him. In his own way and very indirectly, he'd chosen us over his new wife. That had meant something to me.

"Whatever," Zoe said. And then she stood up, took off her clothes (except for her underwear), put on a T-shirt and low-rise yoga pants, slipped into bed and faced the wall. "Good night," she added after a moment.

"Good night, Zoe," Sarah said, shooting me a look.

I shrugged and turned back to my laptop but my hands were trembling and I couldn't use the keyboard.

I had no idea how the three of us were supposed to share a room without strangling each other. Sarah and I kicked and screamed, but we were able to have a relationship. I'd never been able to get along with Zoe. She was perfectly nice, but her very being bothered me. Her very being had bothered me from the moment she was born when I was nine.

Amazing. When Zoe was born, Giselle, our stepmother-to-be, hadn't even been a twinkle.

* * *

According to FindAMate's matching system, 226 men met my criteria. While Zoe tossed and turned, and Sarah snored (she'd fallen asleep with her cheek mashed into page 178 of *But I Don't Know How To Be Pregnant!*), I chose men to potentially meet. Talk about distracting. FindAMate.com was almost too much fun. In a matter of minutes, I'd forgotten all about angry little girls and terrible summers and marriages gone wrong and sisters who most likely wanted to wring my neck. I'd spent a half hour familiarizing myself with the site, then began clicking on everything I wanted in a man, from hair color to salary range to how often he visited a house of worship, and seconds later, 226 thumbnail photos and lengthy profiles appeared before my eyes. You didn't like the looks of someone, you simply scrolled past him. You liked someone's face, you clicked on his picture and it became bigger. And then you read his profile, his questionnaire, his likes and dislikes and his personal essay—what he was looking for in a woman, in a relationship.

I whittled down the two-hundred-plus men to fifty, based on who I was attracted to, physically and mentally—at least as mentally as their personal statements and little essays allowed me to get a glimpse of who they were. And then I scrolled through those. At least twenty-five men interested me, some ruggedly blond, others the always delicious tall, dark and handsome, and some David Caruso red. There were lawyers, doctors, journalists, investment bankers and real estate developers.

The only problem was that most of the men I was interested in were interested in women aged twenty-one to thirty-four. Out of the twenty-five whose profiles and pictures reeled me in, twenty-two of those men wanted women younger than me, despite the fact that they were my age or older.

Twenty-one years old? What would a thirty-seven-year-old man want with a twenty-one-year-old kid? Honestly. I didn't get it. Yeah, yeah, they were young and inexperienced and lithe and beautiful. Whoo-hoo. You could have great sex with a lithe and beautiful and experienced thirty-five-year-old, a woman your own age, a woman who got your references, who grew up when you grew up, who knew what you were talking about, why you found something funny or nostaglic. Why date a woman you had nothing in common with? Why date a woman who was playing spin the bottle when you were climbing the corporate ladder? What would you really talk about? Perhaps I should nip down the hall and ask my father.

So now what? Did I forget about those men I was interested in and look for ones whose age range I met? They were jerks anyway, weren't they?

Or were they? I myself had scrolled past every man with a receding hairline, anyone who clicked on *husky* to describe his body type, anyone without an advanced degree and anyone who misspelled a single word or used numbers to represent words, like *Looking 4 U.* Taste in the opposite sex, types, was very individual. If Sarah were picking *her* FindAMate preferences, she'd ignore the Andrew Sharp types, the financial geniuses who made fortunes on Wall Street and owned sailboats and houses in the Hamptons, and she'd go straight for the writers and painters who were really waiters—the more silly facial hair, the better.

So what to do? My taste was the twenty-five men I'd carefully selected. Their taste was a woman younger than myself.

I decided to come back to that dilemma and create my own profile so that whoever I did e-mail could check me out, decide if he liked the look and sound of me.

Click here to create your profile and you could have a hot date tonight! I clicked. *Name (no last names please.):* Ally. *Age:* 34—I deleted the thirty-four and typed in thirty-five, since I would be thirty-five next month, on Thanksgiving Day.

Thirty-four looked better than thirty-five.

Twenty-nine sounded better than thirty-four.

I tapped the *2* key with my nail. What to put, what to put?

I deleted the thirty-five and typed thirty-four. Then I deleted the thirty-four and typed twenty-nine.

I stared at the number. It looked ridiculous. I'd been twenty-nine a long time ago, and it had been a fine year. My baby sister was twenty-nine, for heaven's sake.

Yet all the men you selected want a woman under thirty-four, Ally. Perhaps once they see you, see that you could pass for twenty-nine (barely, perhaps), they won't mind when they find out you're really six years older than that.

After all, surely there were little white lies involved in the online dating biz.

I deleted the twenty-nine and typed thirty-four, which was technically true for an entire month. I was still in the youth demographic, dammit!

I stared at the blinking cursor and deleted the thirty-four. *Age:* 29.

I moved on before I could change it back. At the foot of my bed, Mary Jane cocked her head at me. *Tsk-tsk,* she seemed to be saying. I patted her head with my foot, and she closed her eyes and dropped her little head on her paws.

Marital Status... Now that was another toughie. There was a box to click on for *Separated,* but whose business was that? Then again, I couldn't click on *Married,* since that would suggest that I was married and looking for an affair. I couldn't click on *Divorced,* since I wasn't. Then again, I wasn't twenty-nine, either. Oh Lord.

But I wasn't divorced. And I wasn't ready to apply that word to myself.

I clicked on *Single.* I considered myself single, and that was what mattered.

For *Job* and *Salary Range,* I was tempted to click on *Clerical* and *$25-$50,000,* since some men were intimidated by high-powered women. But did I want to meet one of those men? No. I clicked on *Professional* and *Over 200K.*

Use the space below to describe the kind of man you're looking for in forty words or less:

My fingers typed before my brain even had a chance: *I'm looking for a man to make me feel like a woman.*

Huh? Was that what I was looking for? What was I looking for? I didn't even know. I wasn't looking for a relationship. I wasn't looking for a friend. I wasn't looking for sex.

So what the hell was I doing?

I set the laptop on my bed and lay back and stared up at the ceiling. What *was* I doing?

You're looking to distract yourself, Ally, I told myself, running my toes along Mary Jane's silky fur. You're looking for someone to make you feel special again. You're looking to sit at a table for two with an attractive man who's flirting with you, interested in you. And if you should be inclined to have sex, then so be it. Your marriage is over.

I sat back up and pulled the computer back onto my lap.

Upload a recent photo of yourself. I scrolled through the photos I had online and chose my very favorite, which was taken five years ago. I'd been sunbathing in Central Park with Mary Jane when Sarah happened to settle down on the Great Lawn with a blanket and a girlfriend. She'd recognized Mary Jane and sneaked over with a camera, catching me unaware. She told me she'd never seen me look so relaxed, so at peace, as I did lying there on my side, reading a book.

The book, which you couldn't see in the photo, was *Get Pregnant Now.* The night before, Andrew had said yes to having a baby. *You can finally stop asking me if I'm ready, Ally-cakes,* he'd said, *because the answer is yes. Baby, let's have a baby!*

And so I'd thrown out my birth control pills and bought a basal thermometer. I'd bought the bikini I was wearing in the photo. Andrew couldn't get enough of me then. We had sex morning and night. No protection. I'd thought we were making a baby. But month after month, I got my period.

A man had made a fool out of me for the past five years. It would never, ever happen again. From now on, I would be in control.

Five minutes later, all clicked and uploaded and my twenty-five-dollar monthly fee taken care of, I was a member of FindAMate.com.

Zoe

My cell phone rang, and I snatched it off my bedside table. "Mom?"

"No, it's Daniel. But I saw your mom a few minutes ago."

Daniel? Ah, Danny Marx. "You did? Are you sure?"

"I'm sure," he said. "It was only for a few seconds, and when I ran over, she was gone. Bloomingdale's is pretty crowded for a Wednesday morning. I looked for her for a while, but I couldn't find her."

My mom was alive and well and in Bloomingdale's. I let out a deep breath and lay down on my bed, but then a wet-haired Sarah wearing a robe and slippers came into the bedroom. I figured she wanted some privacy to dress for work, so I took the phone into the living room.

"Bloomingdale's," I repeated, dropping down on the loveseat by the window. I should have figured I'd find her in an upscale department store.

"She was in the cosmetics department," he said. "Bobbi Brown, to be exact."

"What were *you* doing in the cosmetics department?" I asked.

"Well, now that you're in town, I thought I should spruce up a little."

Was he serious?

"Kidding, Zoe."

"Sorry," I said, parting the filmy drape and peering out the window. "My sense of humor is definitely off."

"The woman I'm dating works there," Daniel explained. "Joy. That's her name. She works behind the Estée Lauder counter."

"Ah," I said, distracted by the wedding bulletin board in front of the fireplace. Seven eight-by-ten glossies of wedding gowns.

"I use Estée Lauder," I said absently.

"I could get her to give you a discount."

"That's all right, Danny."

"Daniel," he reminded me. "And not that you need any makeup."

"Well, thanks for letting me know about my mom, Daniel. At least I know she's in the range of normal for her if she's getting makeovers at Bloomie's. It's one of her favorite things to do."

"She looked good, too, by the way," Daniel said. "You'd never know she was fifty. Like Morgan Fairchild."

"Well, thanks a lot for letting me know," I said again, itching to get off the telephone and run to Bloomingdale's to look for Mom. "I definitely owe you one."

"Glad to hear you say that, because if you can swing it, I have a date tomorrow night with Joy, and I could really use your expertise, Zoe. I've seen her a couple of times since I ran into you at the airport, and it's been eye-glaze both times. I'm worried this might be my last chance before she gives me the big brush-off."

"Sounds like a job for the Dating Diva," I said. "Okay, Daniel. It's a deal."

"Oh, and Zoe—be brutal."

I had a feeling that Danny Marx on a date would indeed require brutality.

Someone was hogging the bathroom. I was about to knock when I heard the distinct sounds of retching. Someone was throwing up.

I knocked. "Are you okay in there?"

Sarah opened the door. She looked positively ill. She didn't say anything.

"I guess I'm not supposed to know, Sarah, but I didn't miss the allusion Ally made the other night, and I did see *What To Expect When You're Expecting* peeking out from under your pillow. Morning sickness?"

She nodded and ran back in and leaned over the bowl. I collected her hair and held it up for her.

"I'm okay now," she said, moving to the sink. She brushed her teeth and splashed cold water on her face. "Thanks," she added, then headed back to the bedroom.

I followed her. "Are you sure, Sarah? Can I get you a cracker or something?"

"I'm okay." She dropped down on her bed and took a deep breath. "That was the first time I've gotten sick. I have a feeling it was the half pound of fudge I ate in the middle of the night, though, and not morning sickness. God, I crave fudge."

Our father was a fudgeaholic and always kept a pound of the best fudge in the world in the kitchen.

"Well, you'll never go without here," I said. "Can I get you anything? A glass of water or tea?"

"No, really, I'm okay." She glanced at the little alarm clock on Ally's bedside table. "Oh shit, I am so late for work, and there's a staff meeting this afternoon that I haven't even prepared for. I'd better go."

"Can I call in for you? Let them know you'll be late?"

Relief lit Sarah's face. "Oh God, would you? I'd be so grateful. Don't say I've been hurling though. Just that there was a family emergency, okay?"

"No problem. And, Sarah, if you need anything or I could help in any way, you'll ask, right?"

She smiled. "Thanks, Zoe. I appreciate that. Oh, and Zoe? I hope Ally didn't get to you too much the other night, about your mom."

I shook my head. "There's a lot of history there. She has a right to her feelings."

She nodded and smiled, and I waited to see if she wanted to talk more, say something else the way people did when they wanted to talk but felt inhibited, but she just took some clothes out of her suitcase and began pulling on a pair of black tights.

"Do they even make maternity tights?" she asked.

"I'm sure they do," I said. She glanced at her skirt and sweater next to her on the bed and I realized she wanted some privacy. "Well, I'll see you tonight, then, Sarah."

"Thanks for before," she said. "Hey, speaking of your mom, have you heard from her?"

"No, but I just got a report of a spotting. Someone saw her in Bloomingdale's getting a makeover."

"That's a good sign, right?" she said.

"I think so. I'm going to head over there now and see if I can find her."

We wished each other luck, and I slipped out of the bedroom.

I was at the front door when Giselle called my name. Damn. Damn. Damn. I was so close to escaping. For the week and a half I'd been staying in her home, I'd managed to avoid her, except for an occasional family dinner and a pass-by in the hallway on my way or her way out. She usually left early in the morning for school, and I made myself scarce at night.

I turned around, and she was coming toward me, carrying Madeline on a hip. "I wanted to know if you were free for lunch today," she said.

She'd asked me that every day since I'd arrived.

"Um, sorry, but I just made lunch plans. Maybe some other time," I said.

I smiled at Madeline, grateful that I had somewhere to look other than at Giselle.

She shifted Madeline on her hip. "I'd really love the chance to sit down and talk, Zoe. If you don't want to talk about us, about the past, I understand. But maybe we can just put that behind us then and start anew." All of a sudden, Madeline started screaming at the top of her lungs, complain-screaming. Giselle tried to calm her down, but Madeline screamed more and grabbed a fistful of her mother's hair. "Saved by the baby, I guess," Giselle added with a smile.

I involuntarily smiled back, and she disappeared down the hall into Madeline's room.

Daniel's almost-girlfriend was pretty.

I sat at the bar, two feet from their little round table by the window, my notebook open, my pen at the ready.

And, boy, was there a lot to write.

Daniel talked too much, too fast, laughed at his own jokes (most of which were, indeed, funny, though the girlfriend didn't always get them), gulped his drink in the middle of a story, and twice stopped dead in the middle of one of those stories to say, "You are so beautiful," with absolute sincerity and awe in his voice.

I understood why Daniel so strongly felt her ambivalence. She seemed to like him and find him annoying at the same time. One of those was going to win over the other, and my job was to get him to get her to choose *like.*

At the moment he was telling her how much he loved the movie *The Mighty,* and how he walked out fighting tears, mortified that he was actually crying. I smiled. The object of Daniel's affections, however, Joy Ross, flinched for a half second.

A few months ago, Charlie and I had gone to see a tear-jerker, and he'd burst into tears on the street, two blocks from the theater. Delayed reaction. I'd found the movie a little too manufactured, and Charlie's reaction irritated me, as in how could you be taken in by manipulation? He'd gotten mad at me for not agreeing that the movie was heartbreaking, and we'd gotten into a fight and hadn't gone home together that night. We'd made up the next day, but the difference between us had bothered us both. I felt it in Charlie's voice, his slight distance, but a few days later it was gone. We'd joked about how ridiculous it was to let something so silly cause tension between us.

But it had been there and there had been lots of those "differences." Things that perhaps shouldn't matter, little stupid things. But they did seem to matter.

"Never go to bed angry," my elderly neighbor, Mrs. Gutleman, had said a few times. She lived next door to the house I'd grown up in, and she'd baby-sat me for years. *"I know, I know, you've heard it before. But don't. Abe and I never went to bed angry. In sixty-one years. You love someone, you don't go to bed angry. You never want to be against the one person in the world who you truly love."*

I'd gone to bed angry at Charlie countless times.

I tried to imagine being angry with Daniel; I couldn't,

really. With that cartoon smile, those ridiculous jokes and story for every occasion, it would be like getting angry at Snoopy.

Snoopy. *When you love someone, really love someone,* Mrs. Guttleman said three or four times, *his voice, his presence, just the thought of him, will make you want to do the Snoopy dance.*

And I'd see Snoopy, spinning around in utter joy over mean Lucy, his ears flopping, his black nose in the air, little hearts fluttering out of his chest. And I'd laugh and Mrs. Guttleman would hug me and cut me a piece of checkerboard cake.

The Snoopy dance.

Daniel was sitting across from a woman, doing the Snoopy dance. His eyes were sparkling, he was leaning forward, he hung on her every word and had something either funny or insightful to say in response to everything that came out of her mouth.

As a "relationship guru," I rarely if ever critiqued a date as though I were the one sitting across from the client. It wasn't about whether or not the date appealed to me or offended me or bored me; it was about how the client came across universally. Whether the date was uptown, downtown, buttoned-up or goofy, the important point was for the client to learn about his or her own behavior. Did goofy types turn a particular client into a chastising jerk? Did smart types intimidate a particular client into not saying a word lest she appear less than brilliant? Maybe.

As I watched Daniel, though, I heard and saw him through the eyes of a woman sitting across from him, and I liked him. Yes, he did that and this, this and that, but for some reason, it worked.

Except for Joy.

So which was it? Was Daniel supposed to change the way he acted on his dates with Joy to appeal to her? Or was he supposed to be himself, and if she didn't appreciate it, screw her?

Not literally.

Suddenly Joy glanced at her watch and hopped up, and Daniel also stood.

"Well, I have an early day tomorrow, so…" She kissed him on the cheek. "No, no—stay and finish your nachos. There are a ton of cabs." And then she dashed out the door, hailed a cab and jumped in before Daniel could even say good-night.

He shoved his arms into his chest as though she'd stuck a dagger in his heart and kneeled down to the floor and fell over.

"Sir! Sir!" a waiter yelled. "Are you okay?"

Daniel popped up, an apologetic look on his face. "Kidding, sorry. No food poisoning. No lawsuit."

The waiter grimaced and hurried away.

I couldn't help it. I burst out laughing.

"C'mon, kid," he said. "You can give me the awful report outside."

He put out his arm and I took it.

I looked like Cousin It. The wind had whipped my hair around to practically cover my face, so Daniel suggested we get out of the windstorm and into a café for dessert and coffee.

"That way, when you explain in detail what a loser I am on a date," he said, "everyone in the café will hear. I love having my flaws and foibles put out there."

I laughed and pushed him into Netta's, a fifties-style coffee bar. With coffees and a crumb cake to split, we sat down on two overstuffed chairs.

"Okay, sister, let's have it, Ms. Solomon."

"Honestly, Daniel, you're fine."

He raised an eyebrow. "That's what people pay you two hundred bucks an hour to hear?"

"This is on the house."

He ripped open three packets of sugar and shook them into his coffee. "I really like this woman, Zoe. C'mon, let me have it. All of a sudden she had to get up early tomorrow morning?"

"Did you ever stop to think that the two of you just might not be compatible, or that she doesn't 'get' you, or that if she doesn't like your jokes, then maybe she's not the right person for you?"

He shook his head. "Absolutely not. Well, it's possible, but—no. I know I can come on a little strong, be a little too loud, tell a little too goofy a story. If it's going to interfere with a relationship I want to work, then I want to work on how I come across. And that's where you come in."

"I thought you were fine, Daniel. More than fine. Really. But I can tell you where I noticed she seemed to zone out a little."

"More than fine?" he said, popping a crumb into his mouth. "That's not bad, coming from you."

"I'm—" No big deal, I'd been about to say. Daniel looked at me, really looked at me, and I realized why I didn't love Charlie. Why I'd been unable to commit to him.

He wouldn't have looked at me. Wouldn't have wondered what I was about to say. Wouldn't have been curious. Daniel suddenly reminded me of the Richard Dreyfuss character in *Once Around,* a movie that Charlie and I had caught on cable. Charlie had thought Richard Dreyfuss's over-the-top love for Holly Hunter had been suffocating. And maybe it was. But I'd liked it. To be loved so totally, to feel so safe inside it.

"What are you thinking about?" Daniel asked, and I wanted to jump up and hug him.

"I'm thinking that you were great on your date with Joy. You're a great guy, Daniel. Why would you want to change to appeal to anyone?"

"Zoe, I have self-esteem, okay? I want to win over this woman. Gimme the skinny."

I shook my head. "All right. I'll tell you what I saw from an *objective* standpoint."

Daniel leaned forward and licked his lips. His mop of thick, silky light brown hair fell over his face, and he pushed it back.

"When Joy came in, you immediately stood up and announced that she looked amazing—twice. And then, a second or two later, you interrupted yourself to tell her she looked *really* amazing."

He beamed. "She does look amazing, though, doesn't she? God, she's pretty."

I laughed. "Well, maybe you could just tone it down a little. You can tell her she looks amazing, but not with such force and drama. Maybe you don't have to *stand* to say it."

"So it's not a good thing to tell a woman she looks amazing with force and drama?" he asked.

"Hey, I'm the one who said you shouldn't change a hair on your head, Daniel. But maybe with this particular woman, it's not a good thing. You said yourself, it's not about you, it's about her."

Suddenly I wondered if the reason Daniel's high opinion of me had made me so uncomfortable in high school wasn't because I knew I'd eventually fall off the pedestal he put me on, but because *I* didn't think I belonged up there in the first place. À la Groucho Marx, if you didn't want to join any club that would have someone like you as a member, was it because of you or the club?

"So what is it about Joy, anyway?" I asked. "Maybe we should start there. What's special about this woman to you?"

"She's smart, has her act together, knows what she wants, has confidence. I like a strong woman. She's putting herself through college, she really cares about her major, which is teaching. She talks about everything with passion."

Passion. That seemed to be what was missing from me and my life. I'd once been passionate about graduate school and studying to become a psychologist or a therapist, but now that had become a vague dream, a "one day" kind of thing. Critiquing dates paid too well and was too easy.

When had I become so lazy?

"The other thing I like about her is that she really listens when I talk about something important," Daniel said. "Yeah, she tunes out my silly side, but when I'm talking about limestone or the boring glass canopy I'm working on for a hospital entrance, she listens and asks questions. The last woman I dated blew smoke in my face and started freshening her lipstick when I talked about architecture. At least I've stopped droning on and on about my work the way I used to. I give Joy the brief version—maybe that's why she listens."

"But that's so wrong, isn't it?" I asked. "I mean, one woman isn't interested in hearing about your work, so you figure it's a boring subject and avoid it on dates, when actually that particular woman just wasn't a good match."

"I guess so," he said. "But isn't that the way anyone

learns to do anything? You get burned, you're twice shy. Did I get that cliché right?"

I laughed. "Yeah. It's my new motto."

"Why?"

See, he'd gotten me again. A line like that with Charlie wouldn't have elicited a *why*. He would have just gone on talking.

"Are you telling me that the boyfriend burned you, and not the other way around?" Daniel asked.

"Burned me bad," I admitted. "Guess who showed up as a client's date right before my flight out here?"

His mouth dropped open. "Oh, Zoe. I'm really sorry."

I burst into tears. I had no idea why or where they came from, but the tears came and my hands flew up to cover my eyes. Daniel shot out of his chair and kneeled down next to me. He pulled my hands away from my face.

"Zoe, he's a jerk. You're better off without him. Any guy who wouldn't consider himself the luckiest man on earth to be your boyfriend deserves to be in a mental hospital."

I shook my head. "He's not a jerk. I pushed him to it."

He cupped my chin. "Oh, you pushed him to go on another date? To cheat on you? Do I need to send you on the Dr. Phil show?"

"He asked me to marry him a bunch of times, and I kept telling him I wasn't ready. The date was his way of testing the waters for himself, I think. Doing something proactive."

"Zoe, I don't give a shit how open-minded you are. It's not proactive to date other women when you're proposing to your girlfriend. It's passive-aggressive, if you ask me."

"I didn't ask you," I said.

"Well, you told me."

I let out a deep breath. "I'm sorry, Daniel. Charlie really shocked me, and I'm worried about my mother, and I'm staying at my dad's and so are my sisters, and there's a lot of tension there and then there's Giselle."

"Giselle?"

"My dad's fiancée," I explained. "We used to be friends. I'm the one who introduced them."

"That's what broke up your parents' marriage?" he asked.

I nodded.

"Ah. So that's why your mom's on the warpath. Not about her, but about you."

"What?" I asked.

"*You* got betrayed too, Zoe."

God, this felt good. To feel validated. To feel like someone was taking a soothing balm and rubbing it all over my body. It felt as good as a hug. Charlie's response to my bringing up my father and Giselle was to tell me it was just an excuse to keep him at arm's distance, that I should get over it.

Daniel squeezed my hand. "I think you've got a lot on your mind, Zoe Solomon. Good thing I left you the last bite of crumb cake." He forked it and twirled it in the air to my mouth as though trying to feed a stubborn child. "Open up. Yum-yum."

I laughed and opened up.

"So you haven't heard from your mom?"

I shook my head. "I went to Bloomingdale's yesterday after we spoke and looked in every department that I might find her in, but no luck. I've called her cell constantly, but it's not turned on. I don't even know what's got me so worried—her state of mind or what she's going to do to my father— Ack. Enough of my melodrama. Do you—"

"Don't minimize what's going on in your life, Zoe," he said. "It's not melodrama."

I smiled at him and squeezed his hand. "Thanks, Daniel. I mean that."

He smiled back.

"Do you have plans to see Joy again?" I asked.

"She invited me to a party at her school for the graduate students. I always figure that's a good sign, since it lets the entire male population at the party know she's taken."

"See, Daniel. Maybe she likes you just fine. Just as you are."

"Who are you, Mark Darcy?"

"*You* saw *Bridget Jones's Diary?*" I asked.

"A date dragged me."

"Well, it's a good line, Daniel. That's what we're all really looking for, right? Someone to love us just as we are."

"Except us neurotics with issues."

I laughed my head off.

10

Sarah

It took Griffen two weeks to call. Two weeks.

He phoned me at work this morning and suggested—with a lot of "ums" and pauses for a fifteen-second conversation—that we meet tonight at DT*UT "to discuss the situation."

What was he going to say? What did I want him to say?

Marry me, Sarah. We'll work it out as we go. We're having a baby. We're in love. Let's make a commitment and go from there.

Was that how it worked? I had no idea. I certainly didn't have a background in marital commitment to look to. Many times over the past six days I'd wanted to ask Ally's opinion of "the situation," but she was still very distracted, grumpy and either not around or asleep. I had no doubt that something was wrong in her marriage, but she clearly didn't want to talk about it, and though she was queen of the priers, she would send a killer glare if you dared ask *her* a personal question. Day after day, though, she sent e-mail links to every imaginable pregnancy Web site with every imaginable article: "What To Eat During Your First Trimester;" "Why Prenatal Vitamins Are A Must;" "Don't Fight the Fatigue;" "What's Happening in Your Body, Week Eight;" "Maternity Clothes With Style!" That last one had stopped my breath. Maternity clothes? I hadn't figured buying a new wardrobe into the mix of my expenses. According to *But I Don't Know How To Be Pregnant!,* my bible, I wouldn't need maternity clothes until I was five months along. So I had three months before I had to worry about where that extra money was coming from.

I thought about confiding in Giselle and asking her some of my burning questions, but she wasn't home very often either, and when she was, she was busy with Madeline. There was also something so unreal about Giselle that I almost didn't feel entitled to have a personal conversation with her. You saw a lot of Giselles in New York City, especially if your office was on Fifth Avenue near Union Square, like mine, but you didn't personally know them, the megawomen who looked like actresses or models or like they skied in Aspen all winter.

I certainly couldn't talk to Zoe, despite how nice she'd been to me a couple of days ago. She was crankier than I'd ever seen her. I rarely did see Zoe over the years, maybe a few times at holidays, but she was always trying to talk to me and I was always trying to keep her at a distance. Now she was as distant as I usually was. She slept with her cell phone on her pillow. She was either waiting to hear from her mother or waiting to hear from a guy. It was hard to imagine Zoe waiting for a guy.

And then there was Danielle Ann, who I usually tried to avoid at work, but who I now couldn't get enough of. If I spotted her in the kitchen, making a pot of decaf, I stared at her belly until she stared back at me. I watched her in meetings, noting just how many minutes it took for her eyes to start drooping. And I jotted down how many times she ran to the bathroom. *"Can I* help *you with something?"* she'd snapped at me when I was standing in the doorway of her cubicle, staring at her bare feet. Her socks and ugly black shoes were next to her chair. *"They swell, okay?"*

And I'd skulk back to my cubicle, wondering when my feet would start to hurt. I spent so much time listening for Danielle's movements that twice Lisa had to touch my arm to get my attention.

After work I'd stopped off at my father's apartment and stuffed some of my favorite outfits into a bag, then headed to my old apartment, where I still officially lived for two more days. I was milking those days for storage time. I didn't have much—a bed and a dresser and a ton of books and my tiny clothing collection, but penthouse or not, I doubted any of it (except the clothes and a couple of boxes of books) would fit at my dad's. Some of my clothes had started to get a little tight, and I wanted to try a few things I'd left at the old place to find just the right outfit.

I stood in front of the full-length mirror attached to my closet door, a small pile of clothes at my feet, which I kicked away in frustration. I tried on my always-perfect black stretch bootleg pants—too tight in the hips. I tried on my always-perfect just-past-the-knee black matte jersey skirt—too tight in the butt. My slightly tight, slightly cropped cashmere-esque black sweater with the tiny black rose on the left chest—too tight in the bust. How was it possible that nothing fit already? Oh God. *Was* it time for maternity clothes? I was only eight weeks pregnant!

I settled on a black wool miniskirt that Ally had bought

me in a size too large. She gave it to me last year, and it still had the tags on it. Now the skirt fit perfectly. The "boyfriend" sweater, which was naturally a little loose and my new black leather knee-high boots, and at least I didn't look pregnant.

"Ooooh, someone's got a date. Where are you going?" Jennifer asked from my doorway.

"Out somewhere," I said. *Go away. Go away.*

"You're wearing that?" she asked.

I looked at my reflection in the mirror. "What's wrong with this?"

She braced her hand on the door and her diamond ring sparkled. "Sar, don't take this the wrong way, okay, but it sort of makes you look pregnant. You just need to lay off the scones and the M&M's. Like, last year, I wanted to lose five pounds for Jason's company Christmas party, so I gave up frappucinos because they're made with *two* percent milk and not skim. You'd be surprised how that adds up, Sarah. Ooh—phone's ringing! Have fun, Sar!"

"I don't even really know you," was what Griffen said when we sat down with our coffees, mine a decaf, and the chocolate cupcake he insisted on buying for me. If Jennifer had walked by, I was sure she'd snatch it away with a wag of her finger. "You're going to be the mother of my child," Griffen continued, "and I don't even really know you."

"Griffen, we've been seeing each other for two months." The past two weeks not included, of course. "You know me."

"You know what I mean, Sarah."

"No, I really don't," I said. "I understand that we haven't known each other for very long in the scheme of things, but we've spent a lot of time together, talked a lot, shared a lot of personal stories about ourselves. I feel like I know *you.*"

He gave me one of those *uh-huh* looks. "What did you expect me to say, then, about the pregnancy?"

He had me there.

"You don't know me, Sarah. You can't possibly."

"So what are you saying? Why don't you just say what you're saying?"

He glanced down, then up at me. He looked me directly in the eye. "I'm saying that I'm not ready to be a father. Sarah, I am really sorry that it took me two weeks to call you, but I've spent these past fourteen days walking around like a zombie because I don't sleep at night. All I've been thinking about is the pregnancy. What it means. How I feel. What's fair. What's right. What's wrong. And when I couldn't *not* face the truth anymore, I called you."

"And the truth is that you're not ready to be a father?" I asked. "I'm not ready to be a mother, Griffen. But I'm going to be."

"The truth, Sarah, is that I don't *want* to be a father. Not yet, anyway, not by a long shot."

But you are a father, idiot. You are going to be a father whether you like it or not, whether you're ready or not.

Did I *want* to be a mother? Yet? Absolutely not—and to quote Griffen, not by a long shot. Did I want the baby? Absolutely yes. I already loved the baby inside me.

Griffen took a sip of his coffee. "I'll help you financially. I definitely will. I want you to know that you won't have to worry about money. I don't make a fortune at the station, but I do okay…."

"Are you saying you don't want anything to do with the baby?" I asked, my cupcake sludging around in my stomach.

He looked away, then nodded, then looked back at me.

"At least right now, anyway." He covered his face with his hands and shook his head wildly. "Sarah, I can't even deal with the fact that you're pregnant, that you're really going to have a baby. My baby. I can't wrap my mind around the fact that I'm going to be someone's father. I'm not ready, Sarah. I can't handle it. Not even the idea of it."

"Me either," I said.

A look of surprise lit his face. "So why do it?" he asked almost excitedly, as though he realized he might have a spark of hope talking me out of it. "I mean, you're not ready. I'm not ready. You don't really want a baby right now, so why do it?"

Because I'm pregnant, I thought. *You don't know how you're going to feel until you know you're actually pregnant. Until you see the pink line or the doctor says Congratulations, and you touch your stomach.*

"I can't explain it rationally, Griffen. I only know that when I found out I was pregnant, I felt joy first. Absolute joy. Then I felt fear. But I never felt 'I don't want this baby.'"

"But, Sarah—"

"You want to know what I feel? I feel extraordinarily happy and extraordinarily scared that in seven months, I'm going to have a baby. I used to think about seven months in terms of saving up to go on a trip, or losing fifteen pounds, or working my ass off for a promotion. And now, in seven months, I'm going to be a mother. I don't know what to do with this baby or how to have a baby and I'm not even ready to think about how my life is going to change, whether the father is there or not. But I still have never once thought about not having the baby."

"Well, I have thought about how my life is going to

change," he said, "and I don't want to be a father now. It's not really fair for you to make me be one."

What was I supposed to say? It wasn't really fair. But I was pregnant. If I weren't pregnant, he wouldn't have to be a father now.

"I won't be just a guy anymore," Griffen went on. "I'll be someone's father. Financially, my life completely changes. I have to think of someone else first—so mentally my life changes. Spiritually, emotionally. Every way. I like my freedom right now. There's nothing wrong with that."

There was if the woman you were dating was pregnant.

"You're immature, Griffen," I said. He was entitled to his feelings and he might have been perfectly justified, but he was immature. "I suddenly have to grow up too and accept that my life as a single woman without a care is over. But the situation is what it is and I'm accepting it. I'm not pretending it doesn't exist by just ducking out."

"Abortion is legal in this country, Sarah," he snapped. "You have something called a *choice.* There's no such thing as 'ducking out.' It's called making a choice. And *I'm* immature? I'm not the one who's going to have a baby that I can't even take care of. You make shit money, you have a roommate, you're not even particularly maternal, Sarah."

"Is that why you haven't fallen madly in love with me over the past two months, Griffen?" I asked through gritted teeth. "I haven't mothered you?"

"Forget it," he said, and stood up. "Look, I said what I came to say. I'll do my share financially. But this is your choice and you're making it. I'm choosing something else."

"So you're not interested in any news about the pregnancy or ultrasound results or pictures?" I asked. "You just want to know when I need half my co-payment from you?"

"What's an ultrasound?" he asked, his expression nervous. "Is that to test if something's wrong with the baby?"

So he *was* interested. "You see the baby on a monitor, hear the heartbeat, get a little picture. The doctor checks to see that everything's okay. My appointment's next Thursday at Lenox Hill Hospital. Twelve-thirty."

"Do you have someone to go with you?" he asked.

"I was hoping you'd come with me," I replied, grabbing my jacket and bag. "But I could ask my sister, I guess. Ally would kill to come with me to an ultrasound."

He gestured to the door and I led the way out. We stood in front of the coffee lounge, looking everywhere but at each other.

"Well, like I said, call me if you need anything, Sarah."

"Like money."

He nodded. "Yeah."

"I have insurance, Griffen. There really aren't any expenses until the baby's born."

"Well, um, call me if you need anything," he said again.

I nodded.

And he walked away.

That was getting to be a habit of his.

The moment Griffen turned the corner and disappeared, my legs gave out. Really. Right on Second Avenue. If there hadn't been a telephone booth in front of me, I might have fallen. Hanging on to the top of the phone box for support, I dropped a quarter in the slot and dialed Lisa's number, but of course the pay phone ate my money. I dug out my cell phone. Lisa said she'd call Sabrina and we should meet at her place right away.

For a half hour I sat on her couch, hyperventilating,

then I stared at the ceiling. I was going to be a single mother. I wasn't just a this or a that anymore. I was a single-mother-to-be.

I'm going to have a baby alone.

Lisa and Sabrina calmed me down with "You don't know what the future holds, wait and see," but we all knew what we were really thinking: that I'd better face reality and fast.

How did you face reality, exactly? How did you go from terrified, albeit somewhat happily, to accepting your life as it was?

"Check this out," Sabrina said, handing me this month's *Smart Woman* magazine, which was a major competitor of *Wow*. "I saved it for you."

I opened to where she'd bookmarked: It was an *Are You Ready For Motherhood?* quiz.

"Okay, question one," I said. "It's New Year's Eve and your four-month-old has her first cold. Do You: A) Hire a baby-sitter and go out and party till 5:00 a.m. B) Stay home and care for the wee one. C) Ask your mom to watch the baby (after all, what were she and your father going to do anyway?). D) Bring the party to your place and ask everyone to keep it down.

"*A,*" Lisa said. "It's New Year's Eve. You can't make the baby better just by staying home and suffering along with it. No, maybe *C,*" she amended. "Yeah, *C.* If it's your mom, then at least you know the baby will be in capable hands."

"Not my mom," Sabrina said. "She wasn't exactly mom of the year."

My mother had been. God, she was wonderful.

"But I agree," Sabrina added. "Definitely *C.* Better a mom than a teenager."

"I think I should say *B,*" I said. "But I want to say *C* also."

Then again, I didn't have a mother. The baby would have only me.

Only me. Only me. Only me.

We finished answering the questions and took our scores. We all scored in the *Don't Go Anywhere Without a Condom!* category, but at least I came in on the high end, just a few points below *You're Ready But Need a Reality Check.*

"Speaking of a reality check," Sabrina said, "what about Puerto Rico? We haven't talked about it in weeks."

Puerto Rico. I'd forgotten all about it. Sabrina and Lisa and I had birthdays in consecutive months—Lisa was September, I was October and Sabrina was November, so we'd decided to celebrate the big twenty-nine (Sabrina was turning twenty-eight) with a fun trip to an island, if we could afford it. Before I knew I was pregnant, Ally said the plane fare could be her gift to me this year, but I'd have to take care of everything else, like the hotel and meals and drinks.

"I don't know," I said.

"But it's only the first trimester," Lisa said. "You're allowed to fly, aren't you?"

I could, but hanging out on the beach and drinking virgin piña coladas had lost its thrill. All I wanted to do was read baby books and come up with articles that would wow Ms. Wow so I could get promoted.

"It's probably our last chance to do anything fun," Lisa said. "Soon you won't be able to do much at all, Sarah."

I glanced at Lisa. "I know, but…I just don't think I should waste my money on a vacation when I have to price cribs and stock up on diapers and baby food. It seems like an irresponsible thing to do."

"Would you mind if we went?" Sabrina asked.

"Of course not," I said, and burst into tears. "I'm super hormonal, don't mind me," I added.

Sabrina put her arm around me. "Of course we wouldn't go without you," she said. "I'm sorry, Sarah. I don't know what's wrong with me. I guess it's your life changing and I don't know how to handle it. It's not like you cut off all your hair and need help making it look good while it grows out. You're going to have a *baby*."

"Speaking of virgin piña coladas," Lisa said. "How about I make us a batch?"

Lisa came back a few minutes later with a pitcher and margarita glasses, and the three of us talked for hours about womanhood, singlehood and babyhood like we were guests on *Oprah*.

Whenever I needed to talk to my mother, I went to Katz's Deli on Houston Street, a few blocks and one avenue from where I grew up. The huge, old-fashioned deli had been like a home away from home for as long as I could remember. My mom, Ally and I had gone every Sunday afternoon for stuffed corned beef and pastrami sandwiches and Dr. Brown's cream soda, and every day after school I had stopped in for a potato knish.

The three of us would sit at our table and talk about our weeks and school and work and who said and did what, and we'd walk home hand in hand, my mother between us. Katz's was a tradition, my mother always said, and traditions were important. For a long time after she died I couldn't bear to go on Sundays, but then one Sunday I did go, and Ally was there, slumped over the table and crying, her head against the Formica as she sobbed, and the long-employed counter clerks let her cry it out and shushed people who tried to ask her what was wrong.

Ally had also avoided Katz's for years, but had started going once a month or so about five years after our mother's death. I'd graduated from college in Boston and returned to New York to find a job in publishing, and Ally had graduated from law school in California and came back with a husband, but we started going to Katz's again regularly, as though it were expected, even though we never discussed it or arranged it. We'd talk about whatever and get into fights, and then we both got busy and one of us would say we couldn't make it and then we both stopped going altogether, or at least, I did. And then a couple of years ago, when a guy I fell in love with hard and fast broke up with me and I wanted my mother more than anything, I started going to Katz's to talk to her. I'd sit at a table facing the wall, pick at my pastrami, tears streaming down my face, and eventually, I'd feel her there with me.

Now, as I sat staring at the corned beef on rye and sour pickle that I'd had a craving for a second ago, I wondered what my mother would think of me being pregnant and alone. I tried to imagine what it must have been like for her with a newborn and a six-year-old, no husband and no job skills. My mother had been a winner of local beauty pageants and a sometime catalog model (she was only five foot five and too short to become a fashion model), and she'd been working as the "car and boat girl" at trade shows when she met my father. She'd been a housewife, and then she started drawing amazing portraits of Ally, and when my father left a month after I was born, she got a job as a secretary that paid pretty well, refused what I once overheard her describe as "guilt money" from my father for a better apartment and she made do.

You'll be fine, she would tell me now. *You're smart, you have a great career going, I raised you to be strong and independent. You'll be fine and so will your baby.*

Strong and independent. I wondered what she would think of me ending up on Daddy's doorstep.

You do what you have to do, she'd always said. *As long as it doesn't compromise you or make you feel funny about yourself.*

Being at my father's didn't make me feel funny. I rarely saw my father and Giselle—he was Mr. Meeting and Giselle had study groups—and as much as I tried to play with Madeline, she was often asleep by the time I got home from work. Despite wanting never to share a bedroom with Ally again, I actually liked the close quarters, liked hearing Zoe's quiet *oms* during her yoga sessions and Ally's clicking on her laptop keyboard. Every night, when I turned the key in the door to my father's apartment and smelled the familiar vanilla potpourri that my father liked so much, and then walked into my room to find my sisters sprawled on their beds, reading or working or thinking or sleeping or not even there at all, but their sweaters or nightgowns on the beds, I would feel safe.

I picked up my pickle and bit into it and started telling my mother, quite silently, of course, that Zoe wasn't such a bad egg, after all.

11

Ally

For a date with a man who could potentially one day become my husband and the father of my child—my first date in thirteen years—I'd gone mega shopping. A black lacy Miracle bra and matching garter (for me, not him), seamed black Donna Karan hosiery that felt like satin and a killer black suit with a short skirt and a cropped jacket that I'd gotten in Paris last year. Add my three-inch black leather pumps, some red lipstick and a spritz of Chanel No. 5, and I was ready. Ready to sit across from another man, a handsome man, and flirt my ass off.

Not literally, of course.

I'd been thinking the past two weeks about what I'd do if I clicked with someone. I mean, *really* clicked with someone. The kind of clicking that makes you want to have that third glass of wine, invite him back to your place (or have him invite you back to his place, in my case), listen to some Marvin Gaye and then fool around on the sofa and see where it leads.

Thirteen years ago, when I first met Andrew, you didn't

go home with someone you just met. You didn't sleep with anyone on the first date or the second or maybe even third. You carried condoms everywhere you went and you worried about catching something. When Sarah told me that she slept with Griffen on their second date, I'd been shocked. And when I found out she didn't use a condom, I'd lectured her for a half hour. *"Diaphragms aren't one hundred percent effective!"* I'd yelled. *"And they're zero percent effective against chlamydia, herpes, AIDS and God knows what else is running around out there!"*

For once, Sarah hadn't defended herself. She'd simply said, *"You're right."*

Sex. Who was having sex so fast, anyway? Not me. At least, I didn't think so.

Thirteen years I'd been with Andrew. And for the first time in twelve and a half years, Andrew Sharp wasn't sharing my bed. Two weeks had passed since the hammock incident. Since the vasectomy claim. Two weeks. And I hadn't heard a word from him.

How was that possible? How did he go from asking my forgiveness and telling me he loved me to apparently being quite happy to have me gone?

"Men don't always know what they want," Kristina had said yesterday. "Maybe he's having a midlife crisis."

A midlife crisis at thirty-six? And what was he in crisis about? His wife who'd been doing everything she possibly could to keep him happy and interested for eleven years? His work that paid him three hundred grand a year? His friends and family who thought he was the greatest thing since the wireless Web?

I'd finally broken down and confided in Kristina about the breakup of my marriage. I went to work every day, barely able to concentrate and therefore relying on the associates more, and one of them, an idiot with an entitlement complex, the kind of guy who called all women *honey* (except judges, who could hold him in contempt), made a mistake that had cost me two hours to fix. I'd screamed bloody murder at him. Funwell, the senior partner, had called me into his office to tell me that I seemed on edge lately and was something wrong at home?

The idiot! I wanted to grab him by his veiny, bulgy neck and squeeze!

But I calmly told him no, everything was fine, expressed the appropriate concern for the client and the case, and then fumed to Kristina. I needed to vent to someone, and I wasn't ready to share the breakdown of my personal life with my family. I didn't know if I'd ever be ready.

Just telling someone had made me feel better. Kristina had shut her office door, pulled me into her arms for a long, comforting hug, then handed me a Godiva chocolate and insisted on taking me to lunch.

"The best revenge is to go sleep with the hottest guy you can find," she said over salad niçoises and white wines. "Once you see that there are men out there, men to play with, men to fall for, men to marry, you'll feel a lot better. Andrew Sharp is not the be-all and end-all."

"But I thought he was," I said. "Now I'm at square one again, and it's scary as hell. That part of my life was settled, and I was hoping to move on to the next chapter—having a baby."

"You can do that with someone else, Ally. You're not even thirty-five. My older sister had her first baby at forty-one. You still have time."

Time. For what? To get over being betrayed, lied to, in terrible ways by the man I loved? The man I thought loved me? How do I get over my marriage and my husband enough to fall in love with someone else?

"No one says you have to fall in love, Ally," Kristina

continued as if reading my mind. "You just want to put yourself out there to see that you are a desirable, lovable woman who any man would be honored to have. You want to feel good about yourself, and it's very easy to do when a good-looking guy is fawning all over you."

Kristina thought FindAMate.com was the greatest idea she'd ever heard. After I'd filled out my profile, I'd gone chicken about sending e-mails to the men I liked; it had taken days for me even to compose an e-mail. But thanks to her encouragement, I'd called back eight of the men with whom I'd been corresponding.

I'd begged Kristina to keep the news of my failed marriage to herself.

"Your marriage didn't fail, Ally. *Andrew* failed you. And a separation and divorce are nothing to be ashamed about. You do know that, right?"

I did. I did know that. So why did it feel so embarrassing?

And why hadn't Andrew been calling to beg me to come back? Was he dating Marnie? Other staffers at Hot-Bods? Other women? Was he glad I was gone?

Who the hell cares!

Do not cry. Do not ruin your makeup! Andrew Sharp betrayed you. He is not the man you married. He is not the man you loved. He is a lying bastard.

I'd been repeating those words over and over and over these past two weeks. And FindAMate.com had become like a drug. Lonely? There were hundreds—thousands!—of profiles to read, thousands of men whom you could potentially meet. Feeling unattractive? There were thousands of men who could look at your photo and find you beautiful and exciting.

And instead of feeling awful about my marriage, I felt hopeful. I felt hopeful about the future.

You can get pregnant through your early forties. Can. Maybe…

My sister had her first baby at forty-one….

And now there was every chance I could meet some great new man, have a whirlwind courtship, and find love. Real love. That was what I wanted. Not a fling. Not some guy to make me feel good. I wanted the real thing.

"You don't think it's too soon?" I'd asked Kristina. "Shouldn't I be taking yoga or going to Machu Picchu or something?"

Kristina snorted. "You don't need to find yourself, Ally. You need to get laid, and good. You need to find what you're looking for. You already know who you are."

She was right. I was aware that I was moving a little quickly, but what was I supposed to do? Mope in my father's living room? Veg and watch Sarah's belly grow?

Instead, I had eight dates. With eight potential new loves.

How exciting it all sounded! I'd spoken briefly to all eight men by telephone. I'd actually spoken to twelve men, but four sounded like such duds that I'd nipped them in the bud.

I pulled out my Palm and clicked on *Thursday, 7:00 p.m.* and double-checked that my seven o'clock date's name was indeed Jeffrey and not Rick, who I thought was my nine-thirty. When you scheduled eight dates for as many days, you tended to mess up the names. Yes, Jeffrey was up first.

He was first for a reason. He was a doctor and also separated. We'd e-mailed back and forth a few times, long, flirty, honest e-mails about what we did for a living, our marital status (which I'd come clean on after he spoke openly about his separation), how hard it was and how wonderful it would be to sit across from an attractive person and feel hopeful. We'd connected.

Last night, I'd dreamed that Jeffrey was delivering our baby. In the dream, he'd morphed into an OB/GYN, my new husband and the father of our six-pound, eight-ounce bundle of joy. I'd woken up smiling, despite Sarah's snores and Zoe's ridiculous sunrise yoga routine.

There was indeed something about having eight dates set up in a week's time that made a person feel proactive. Last night, with tonight's date waiting in the wings, I'd been actually happy. That Andrew hadn't called to beg me back barely registered. That I was sharing a room with my sisters barely registered. That I was subjected to yet another question from Giselle about rosebud arrangements barely registered.

I was moving my life forward. I'd been wronged, and I was taking charge! Full of action. Not sitting around crying. Not feeling sorry for myself. I wanted love and a baby, and I was taking good steps toward my goals.

I'd thrown out *How To Spice Up Your Marriage* and bought *How To Find a Good Man: A Three-Month Plan.* During those moments when images of Andrew's ass rising and lowering came to mind, I'd repeat a mantra from *How To Find a Good Man* and feel comforted.

Number one on the list of what a good man didn't do: cheat.

Number one on my list of hot prospects: the hot doctor whose wife had cheated on *him*. Her excuse, Jeffrey had told me during our hour-long conversation, was that he was never home and she'd been driven to cheat with a friend of his. One of the reasons why he was so glad to hear I was a corporate attorney was because I clearly understood a sixty-hour work week. We'd shared horror stories. We'd laughed. We'd connected. I couldn't wait to meet him.

And if for some strange reason Jeffrey didn't work out, there were seven more where he came from.

My dating itinerary for the week:

Thursday: 7:00 p.m.: Jeffrey. 35. Doctor (surgeon). Upper West Side. 6' 2", 190. Dark brown hair. Hazel eyes. Would recognize him by his scrubs. (All right, he could change for a date, for God's sake, but what did I know about doctors and their clothing? Maybe they all ran around in scrubs.) Enjoyed tennis, ethnic food, antiquing and football.

Friday: 9:30 p.m.: Rick. 39. Stockbroker. Upper East Side. 6', 200. Wavy blond hair. Blue eyes. Writing a novel for the past ten years.

Saturday: 12:00 p.m.: Ralph (which according to him was pronounced Rafe, à la Ralph Fiennes. And according to him and his picture, he looked a bit like Ralph Fiennes too). Lived on Long Island and owned a restaurant in Chelsea. Enjoyed gourmet cooking, mountain climbing and "all New York City had to offer." (Just about every guy's profile said that.)

Saturday: 6:00 p.m. Bill. 41. Bergen County, New Jersey. Divorced. Bought and sold companies. 5' 11", 190. Dark hair, slightly receding. Dark brown eyes. Considered very handsome. Enjoyed working out, good conversation and was looking for a woman who knew what she wanted. (I did! I did!)

Monday: 7:00 p.m. Ted. 40. West Village. Divorced. Lawyer. 6' 1", 200. Light brown hair. Blue eyes. Scandinavian look. Enjoyed films, restaurants, being in love.

Tuesday: 7:00 p.m. Mark. 32 (my only younger man—not that he knew that). Upper West Side. Curly dark hair. Dark eyes. Often compared to a cute Al Pacino. Loved Central Park, extreme sports, running.

Wednesday: 7:00 p.m. Jonathan. 37. Hudson Valley.

Tall, dark and handsome. Investment banker. Reddish hair, blue eyes. Looked a bit like Kenneth Brannagh. Owned a gallery in Soho.

Thursday: 9:30 p.m. Rafael. 36. Hot, hot, hot.

I smiled. And then I glanced at my watch and frowned. Jeffrey was now fifteen minutes late. I was sitting on an uncomfortable stool in the Oyster Bar of Grand Central Station, albeit a stool that managed to show off my legs the way a table would not. I looked around the huge restaurant. No sign of a tall, handsome man in scrubs.

He was now twenty minutes—

Ooh la la.

A *very,* and I underline *very,* good-looking man in green scrubs rushed in and surveyed the bar, where I was sitting. Mmm-mmm! Jeffrey was everything his profile and his picture promised he'd be.

I smiled and tried to catch his eye. He glanced at me for half a second, then resumed his perusal of the people sitting at the bar. Looking a bit confused, he eyed a cute redhead who was sitting alone, but her long hair must have assured him that she wasn't his date because he immediately began his sweep of the bar. There were only three women sitting alone—two redheads and a brunette senior citizen. Why was he having so much trouble finding me?

When he eyed me again, now with the same confusion, I waved at him.

He rushed over. He had the most amazing green eyes. With flecks of gold. Long, dark, silky eyelashes. "You're not Ally, are you?"

"The very same," I said in my best Kim Cattrall-Samantha Jones voice.

He wasn't smiling. In fact, he looked a bit miffed.

"Is something wrong?" I asked.

"Didn't your profile say you were twenty-nine?" he asked.

Oh. I almost forgot about that.

"And?" I asked, holding any edge from my voice or expression.

Don't get angry. Maybe he's about to pay you a compliment.

"Honey, if you're twenty-nine..." And then he shot me one of those *Don't bullshit the best bullshit artist there ever was* looks.

Asswipe!

But you *did* shave a few years off your age in your profile, I reminded myself.

"I've always enjoyed the beach a little too much," I said, again in my best Samantha Jones voice and accompanying smile. "The sun is a killer on the skin. But I don't have to tell you that, Doctor."

He didn't return the smile. "C'mon, honestly. You're what—thirty-five, thirty-six?"

"I'm twenty-nine!" I snapped.

"Look, honey, you're the one who lied on your profile. Shaved off a few years, sent in a younger photo. Happens all the time. The problem is that when you lie, you're wasting someone else's valuable time. And as a doctor, I don't have time to waste. I'd expect a lawyer to understand that, but I'm sure you lied about that too. What are you, a manicurist or something?"

Jerk! But my nails *did* look good. "Satisfy my curiosity for a moment, will you, *Doctor?* Let's say I am thirty-five or thirty-six, which I'm *not*—" and that was true for another month "—so what? You liked my photo, you liked my e-mails, you liked me on the phone. *You're* thirty-six. What, you can't handle a woman your own age?"

He rolled his eyes. "Look, lady, I just got out of a bad

marriage—or did you forget that from our telephone conversation? I'm not looking to jump into another one so fast. So if I meet someone and it gets serious, I want to date for a couple of years, then get married, then start a family. You'd be too old for that."

I gasped. Literally.

"I'm thirty-four," I snapped. "I'm plenty young to have a child. Two or three if I want! So fuck you."

"You'll never get the chance," he snapped back and walked out.

"You're thirty-four?" the woman a seat over asked me. "You look a little older. I swear by Botox. Really, you have to try it."

"You're not my type," Rick said with his mouth full the moment I introduced myself. He finished chewing. "I hope you don't mind my honesty. And I hope you don't mind that I ordered something to eat," he added, swiping a chicken shish kabob into dipping sauce. He had sauce on his chin. "You *were* a little late."

After the nightmare in Technicolor I experienced yesterday with Jeffrey, I'd decided to take the upper hand and arrive ten minutes past the meeting time.

Apparently, arrival time had little to do with upper hands.

"I'm not your type?" I repeated. *"What?"*

"Want a piece of chicken?" he asked, gesturing at the plate before him. Now he had sauce on his fingers. "You're a little too type A."

I raised an eyebrow. "I only said hello. How the hell can you tell what type I am?"

"How you phrased that last question is a dead giveaway. But I can tell just by how you look—the suit, the too-severe hairstyle. You're type A."

Moron. Although, technically, he was right.

"We spoke for twenty minutes on the phone a few days ago and we spoke again last night. Couldn't you tell my *type* from our conversation?"

"You didn't sound type A on the phone," he said. "You sounded nervous. I liked that."

"Oh, so you like nervous women," I said. "Makes you feel more like a man, is that it, you wuss?"

"Look, I was just being honest. If you're going to be like that, maybe we should just cut this short."

Good idea, prick.

Next.

The trouble was, I was afraid of Next. My first foray into dating was about as bad as it got, which, then again, might not be such a bad thing, since it could only get better.

Right?

I stared at the little alarm clock on my bedside table. It was 4:00 a.m.

Maybe if you didn't lie off the bat, Ally. Maybe if you approached dating honestly. Dr. Jeffrey might have been a jerk, but he had reason to be upset. How would you have liked it if a bald, overweight insurance salesman had shown up and said, *Well, you wouldn't have liked me as I am so I said I was a tall, dark and handsome doctor.*

Oy.

But I didn't want to be thirty-five if the men I wanted wanted a twenty-one-year-old.

Did you want a man who wanted a twenty-one-year-old?

What I wanted was some sleep!

I was now wearing a tight, colorful Betsey Johnson dress with a flouncy hem. My hair was slightly wind-blown to avoid the "severe" look, and my lipstick was sheer and glossy.

I didn't look like a lawyer. I looked like a good-time girl.

I didn't look like anyone in the Candle Café restaurant on a Saturday at noon, but that was okay. I had a hot date.

Thanks to jerks one and two, I'd decided to go with something a little less aggressive, a little more feminine. Even though I was about to confess that I was about to turn thirty-five, I felt twenty-nine. I looked twenty-nine.

Ralph had a star next to his name in my Palm. And he earned another when he sat down across from me at my table, on time. Over fresh-made vegetable juice, which I'd never had before in my life, we discussed: Where we grew up. How many siblings we had. Last book read. The violence of *The Sopranos.*

And then he looked at his watch. A Cartier, I noticed.

"Oh, man, is it one o'clock already?" he said. "I'm meeting a friend."

I'd spent almost three hundred dollars on a dress, eaten some sort of vegan appetizer at the juice bar (I hadn't realized the Candle Café was a vegetarian restaurant), had the kind of conversation you might with a stranger in an elevator and then been dismissed after an hour?

It wasn't because I wasn't twenty-nine, which hadn't even come up.

"Ralph, I don't mean to put you on the spot, but I'm new at this dating thing, and I'm just trying to figure out why some dates are, well, duds. Can you enlighten me a little bit? Why are you cutting this short?"

"Uh, I don't know," he said. "No chemistry, I guess."

"Ah, that makes sense. No chemistry. Can't place blame for that."

He gnawed his lower lip. "And, well, you did make fun

of the menu. I'm a vegetarian, and I'm not militant or anything, but that sort of bothered me. And you did sort of ask me a lot of questions, like you were interviewing me to be your husband."

Asswipe!

"I would hardly be interested in you for the position of husband," I said. "We just met."

"Well, that's how you came across. Look, I have to go. It was nice meeting you. Good luck! Take care!" And then he hightailed it out of the restaurant.

Had I interviewed him? I didn't mean to. Or maybe I did. I just asked a few questions that I thought would let me know whether or not we were really suited to each other. I didn't ask his exact salary or anything, just where he intended to be in five years, that sort of thing.

Nothing that a prospective father-in-law wouldn't ask.

Oh God. I had to calm down. *You have to calm down.*

What the hell was wrong with me? I couldn't even interest one guy into moving on to dinner, let alone a second date.

Andrew, meanwhile, was busily dating every blonde in New York City and Long Island. Kristina had seen him nuzzling a Heather Locklear look-alike in the Blue Water Grill last night.

I had a very hot date on Saturday. I would not interview him. I would not make fun of the menu. I would not be bitchy.

He didn't show up.

And I'm giving up.

12

Zoe

My father thought a macrobiotic wedding reception would be the height of trendy, potentially worthy of a write-up in *In Style* magazine.

The bride and groom, the bride's baby and mother and the groom's three daughters were waiting in the reception area of Cater To Me, the fifth caterer we'd been to in as many days. Giselle, her mother, Sarah, Ally, the caterer—who'd burst through a set of double doors just in time to hear my father's pronouncement—and I turned to stare at my father in horror. At the sudden silence, Madeline, in her umbrella stroller, covered her face with her hands and let out a shriek.

Giselle laughed and wheeled the stroller back and forth. "He's joking, everyone!"

"You didn't think I was serious, did you?" my father asked, grinning. "You guys don't know me at all! I'm a total carnivore!"

Ally looked like she wanted to punch him.

Sarah just looked sad.

We *didn't* know him at all.

I crossed my arms over my chest, a habit I tried to break in all my clients. "Dad, the last time we had dinner, you said you were a *vegetarian*."

"Well, honey, that must have been a long time—" He caught himself. "Ah, there's the caterer! Hello, there. We're the Archweller-Solomon party."

Sarah glanced at me. *So you don't have a relationship with him either,* I could hear her thinking.

I knew my sisters had always thought I had some sort of Daddy's Little Girl relationship with my father. Ha. Bartholomew Solomon was an equal opportunity father: if he was going to ignore his daughters from his first marriage, he'd ignore his daughter from his second, too. The last time I'd had dinner with my father was right before he'd broken the news to me that he'd left my mother for my friend. We'd met for lunch once or twice several months later, but the broken record kept skipping on the age-is-just-a-number routine, and my father and I had drifted even further apart than we'd been.

Bartholomew Solomon seemed to not even realize that his three daughters had been living in his apartment for three weeks now. Three weeks. Not a weekend. Not a week. Three weeks. Gee, Dad, do you wonder why a married woman is suddenly living with her sisters in a small bedroom in your apartment? Gee, Dad, do you wonder why Sarah fell asleep at the dinner table last night? Gee, Dad, do you wonder why I always look like I'm going to cry?

Last night at a rare family dinner (we all happened to be home at around the same time), while Sarah was dozing during the soup course, my father sent Zalla for the wedding bulletin board, which now held photos of bow ties.

"It's too bad Andy's not here, Al," he'd said. "Your husband knows a good bow tie."

Silence from Ally.

"So when's the Andymeister due back from—where is he? France, right?" my father asked.

No, Dad, don't you listen? He's in Switzerland *and* Japan simultaneously.

"Yes, France," Ally said, pushing a cherry tomato around on her plate. "Paris is his favorite city, so he's extending his trip for a week to do a little sightseeing. I've already been three times and this is such a busy time at the firm, so I opted to stay home."

Ally then changed the subject to which bow tie she liked best. As she went on and on about how the right tie could make or break a tux, Sarah and I glanced at each other. We both knew there was something very wrong in Ally's marriage.

Many times over the past week, I'd woken up to the sound of sniffling. It was Ally crying. I was so tempted to go over and ask her what was wrong, if she wanted to talk, but I knew the response I'd get. She'd snapped me away so many times, I was afraid to even approach her.

I glanced at Ally now. She was twisting her wedding ring and staring out the window at a brick wall.

"A may-crow-bee-ahtic vedding receepshun," the caterer said with a forced chuckle. "Goood vun! Three quarters of ze guests vould not show up! Okay, folks, right thees vay," he added, leading us into a tasting room. A bunch of little plates were set around a long wooden table. "Here ve have our famed cheeken cordon blue, our avard-vinning fil-et mignon, and our cheef's speciality—swordfish."

We all picked and nibbled the forkfuls on our little plates and cleansed our palates with orange slices.

"I vill leave you alone to deescuss," the caterer said, and whooshed out of the room.

Every chicken dish tasted the same, no matter the sauce or what it was stuffed with. Same for every steak and fish dish.

"What do you think, Ally?" my father asked.

"Nothing special," she said. "I'd pass."

"I like the swordfish," Sarah said. "The other caterers all had salmon. Swordfish is different, unexpected."

"You're not even supposed to be eating swordfish," Ally snapped at Sarah. "The mercury levels are very high."

Sarah rolled her eyes. "I don't think one forkful of swordfish is going to hurt—"

"Since when is fish unhealthy?" Giselle's mother interrupted. "I've been cooking a niçe filet of sole or flounder for Giselle's stepfather three times a week for twenty years now. The man is healthy as a horse. I'll tell you what the real danger is—these stupid health fads. That's what'll kill people."

Giselle's grumpy mother talked nonstop. No wonder her husband had opted to stay home in California.

Sarah walked slowly over to Ally and nudged her in the ribs with an accompanying *shut-up* look.

"Zoe, what do you think?" Giselle asked me. She was forever trying to engage me in conversation and I was forever leaving the room. "The caterer we saw at noon had a better chicken dish, but the filet mignon here is out of this world. Do you agree?"

"I liked them all fine," I said.

"No one loves a good piece of filet mignon better than you, Zoe," she said. "I remember the time we went to—"

"They're all good," I interrupted.

"You must have a preference, Zo," my dad said. "You're my steak reference point. C'mon, what do you think?"

"It's hard to get excited about a piece of too-tough steak when your mother is God knows where doing who knows what!" I yelled.

Everyone turned to stare at me, including the two other parties. I felt my cheeks burning. I was acting like a five-year-old. I hadn't meant to burst out with that. I wasn't even thinking of my mother at that moment.

Or maybe I was.

"I'm sorry, Dad," I said. "I'm just a little stressed out at the moment."

"That's okay, hon. But really, Zo, your mother's fine. I'm sure she's at the Statue of Liberty right now, asking if there's an elevator up to the chin." He laughed, then rubbed my shoulder. "She's fine, Zo. Your mother has always been able to take care of herself."

I fake glanced at my watch. "Is it two already? I'm supposed to meet someone." I wasn't lying—well, not completely. Daniel and I had arranged to meet at three in Bloomingdale's to hunt for my mother. We didn't really expect to find her, but Daniel thought the looking would make me feel better.

"Von more feesh to try," the caterer said, carrying a platter with little plates. "Zish particular feesh eez am-a-*zing!*"

With everyone's attention back on the food, I slipped out the door.

I found Daniel at Bloomingdale's Estée Lauder counter. Joy was behind the counter, slathering moisturizer on his cheeks.

"This moisturizer is me," he said, making faces into the mirror. "Yes, it is definitely me."

"Daniel, I'm *working,*" Joy said. "If you're going to joke around, you're going to have to leave."

He eyed me at the next counter. "I'll let you work, my sweet. We're on for tonight, right?"

"I'll have to let you know, okay?" Joy said. "I might have to work late." A woman approached and starting asking about eye shadow, and Daniel made his way over to me. Joy did not follow him with her eyes.

"Maybe you should introduce me as your friend, make her a little jealous," I suggested.

"I thought about that," he said, "but I don't like playing games. She likes me or she doesn't, right?"

I was impressed. "Right."

"Okay, let's look for Madame Solomon," he said. "Should we split up or search together?"

"Let's look together," I said, surprising myself.

He smiled. "You just can't get enough of me, can you?"

Actually, I couldn't. I'd begun to need Daniel the way I needed coffee or a hug, and there weren't many hugs coming my way these past few weeks.

"She left another message on my machine in California saying she was fine and taking a fondue course," I told Daniel. "She said she's been taking tours. She's been to the Aquarium at Coney Island, the Statue of Liberty, up and down Fifty-seventh Street, the Lower East Side and Central Park. She sounded great, like she's been having fun."

"She didn't say anything about your father?" he asked.

I shook my head.

"So maybe she's over it," he said. "Maybe she just needed to feel like she was doing something. Maybe flying here was enough. Maybe she bought a voodoo doll, stuck a few pins in it and felt be—" Daniel froze. "I don't believe it, but there she is!" he said, pointing. "She's trying on lipsticks at the Bobbi Brown counter. Unbelievable. I never expected to actually find her—I just thought a look-for-your-mom session would make you feel better."

I turned to where he was staring, and there indeed was my mother, puckering her dark red lips in a display mirror and blotting them. I couldn't believe my eyes.

"Girls, that salesclerk was helping *me,*" she was saying to a gaggle of teenagers vying for attention at the counter as I ran over. "Where *are* your manners?"

"Mom?"

At the sound of my voice, Judith Gold Solomon whipped her head around so fast that she accidentally dabbed the woman next to her with the tube of lipstick.

"I'm so sorry!" my mother said. "I'm sure they have something to get that out with," she added, gesturing behind the counter. She put down the tube of lipstick, grabbed my arm and pulled me into the crowd, darting her gaze back to see if the lipstick-stained woman was chasing after her.

"Mom, you're not going to get arrested for getting a little lipstick on someone. Slow down," I said.

She pulled me into the wallets and day-planners section. I glanced around for Daniel and found him sniffing a fragrance with an eye on us. I nodded and turned to my mother.

"Mom, I have been worried sick about you for three weeks! Where have you been?"

"Dear," she said, "I told you my plans. I'm fine. I've been leaving you messages every few days."

"Where have you been staying?" I asked.

"You remember my friend Sasha?" she said, rubbing a cashmere scarf against her arm. No, I did not remember a friend Sasha. "Oh, how nice this feels, Zoe." She rubbed the fabric against my cheek. "Sash is going through a divorce, so when I called her to let her know I was in town, she asked if I wanted to stay with her. We've been having a grand time. Taking cooking courses, going on tours, visiting plastic surgeons to discuss some nipping and tucking. We even went out at night a few times to a popular theme bar and flirted!"

She was having fun. "So you're not going to destroy Dad's life, after all?" I asked.

"Well, I didn't say that, dear," she said with a laugh. "Oh, there's Sasha now! Sash!" she called. "Hold on, dear, and I'll bring her over and introduce you."

Like a fool, I let her go. She disappeared into the crowd and never came back. Ten minutes later, she called my cell phone to say she had to run to her yoga session and that she'd call in a few days. She was fine, she said again, and added her customary *Toodles, dear!*

"Don't worry, Zoe," Daniel said, slinging an arm around me. "We found her once, we'll find her again. Your mother has always been incredibly predictable."

"For everyone but me," I said.

"C'mon. Let's go get a late-afternoon margarita."

And with one eye peeled for a fifty-year-old woman in a Britney Spears video outfit and a faux-fur leopard-print coat and knee-high boots, I let Daniel lead me away.

"My mother's beginning to look less like Morgan Fairchild and more like Michael Jackson," I said as Daniel returned to our little table with two frozen margaritas and a bowl of tortilla chips and salsa. "She's had so much plastic surgery I can't even recognize her anymore."

Daniel laughed. "She looks good, though. I have to say, she really does look like she's in her late thirties."

"But she's not. She's fifty. And what's the point of trying to look ten or twenty years younger when you're not?"

"If it makes her feel better, why not?" he said. "One day, she'll come to her senses. Or she'll meet a new man who'll like her just the way she is. But right now, this is what she needs to do. People do this kind of thing all the time. They go crazy because they have to, and then a couple of months later, they're themselves again and telling anecdotes that conclude, 'Do you believe I did that?' I think she'll be fine, Zoe."

"It just makes me feel so…I don't know. So out of control myself, I guess."

He looked at me, then stood up and pulled his chair around the table right next to mine. "I'll catch you," he said.

If he hadn't stuffed a tortilla chip laden with salsa into his mouth at that moment, I might have kissed him on the lips.

"Daniel, that is so immature," Joy snapped, her eyes darting around in embarrassment. "Stop it."

As I sat at the bar at Favia Lite, an Italian restaurant near Bloomingdale's that served very good low-fat food with the calories and fat grams printed right there on the menu next to the prices, munching my "personal pizza for one" and eavesdropping on what Daniel feared was his last date with Joy, I realized what the real problem was between them. Daniel was very funny, and Joy was devoid of a sense of humor. It wasn't just that she didn't appreciate his humor; she was truly lacking a funny bone.

Which made me wonder why he liked her so much. Yes, she was very pretty, as women who sold cosmetics in Bloomingdale's invariably were, and, yes, she had a great body, but she was stiff and boring and—

And I was jealous.

Oh God, I was jealous of her. Because Daniel liked her, was crazy about her, spent his waking hours fantasizing about her and his sleeping hours dreaming of her.

But why would he like someone so unlike him, someone so not funny, so not fun?

And why would I be jealous, anyway? This was Danny Marx from high school, class clown, king goofball. And yet, as he sat there with Joy, those puppy-dog eyes of his on her, I wanted to pick up her chair, carry it back to Bloomingdale's and come back and take her place. I wanted to be sitting across from Daniel, the object of all that energy and intensity.

I wondered what he was like in bed.

I looked at Daniel; he was alone at the table. I glanced toward the rear of the restaurant, and there was Joy, heading into the bathroom. Touching up her heavy makeup, most likely. Meow, I thought. Your claws are coming out, Zoe.

Daniel walked over to me and ordered two bottles of Bass Ale for his table. "This is going as bad as can be," he whispered. "She's in the bathroom. I have about five minutes to save the relationship before she makes an excuse to leave and then never returns my phone calls."

"Well, maybe that's not the worst thing that can happen, Daniel," I said.

"It would be from where I sit."

"Why?" I asked. "Why do you even like her, Daniel? She's not particularly nice. She has no sense of humor. She's critical of you. What's to like?"

"Whoa, Zoe, judgmental much?"

"I'm just saying—"

"Yeah, I hear what you're saying. And I think it's a good

thing these critiques are on the house, because I'd probably want my money back."

"Daniel—"

"Look, you're done with your pizza, so why don't you just save yourself the agony of watching the rest of the date?"

"Daniel, I didn't—"

But Joy was coming out of the bathroom.

"Just go, Zoe," he whispered, and headed back to his table with the two bottles of Bass.

Shit. Shit. Shit.

As he sat down, he pulled his chair so that it was facing away from me and blocking my view of Joy.

I paid for my pizza for one and left and promptly burst into tears the second I hit the air.

Midnight: Toss. Turn. Toss. Turn

Saturday, 9:00 a.m. to Sunday, 11:00 p.m.: Called Daniel. Got machine. Left message (four, to be exact).

Sunday, midnight: Figured I'd blown it.

"I wanted to throw little pebbles at your window so you'd come out and talk," Daniel said, "but I didn't know which was your bedroom window and I didn't want to wake up your sisters."

God, it felt good to hear his voice. I clutched my cell phone against my ear and tiptoed out of my bedroom and into the walk-in closet in the hallway. I sat down on a cardboard box and moved the tail end of a long sweater off my head.

"I'm sorry about calling so late," he added, "but I didn't want another day to go by. You know you're not supposed to go to bed angry, and I've gone to bed angry for the past three nights."

Mrs. Guttleman would approve.

"I'm glad you called, Daniel. I'm so sorry about the other night. I was out of line, and I shouldn't have—"

"Ah, forget it," he said. "You were right. I just didn't want to hear it."

"No, I had no right—"

"Actually, you had every right. I think we've become really good friends, Zoe. And that's what I'd want a friend to do—tell me the truth."

Friends.

What the hell was wrong with me? Now that wasn't enough? When I didn't necessarily want more, either? I'd spent the weekend driving myself—and my sisters—crazy trying to figure out my feelings.

"Go to his apartment," Sarah had suggested when I'd come home from the restaurant in tears.

"No—she shouldn't throw herself on him," Ally insisted—and she repeated it twice the next day. "She's called and left too many messages as it is."

"Sometimes a little groveling is good," Sarah had pointed out as we were getting ready for bed last night. "What I would do for a little groveling from Griffen."

"She didn't do anything wrong," Ally said. "She told him the truth. If he can't take it, oh well and who wants him anyway?"

I did.

So why did that feel so strange? Did I want to be Daniel's girlfriend? Did I like him because he was unavailable? Did I like him because he used to like me and now liked someone else?

We might as well have been back in high school for all I was acting and thinking like a thirteen-year-old.

"And, anyway," Ally had said as she rubbed body lotion on her elbows, "what's the point? He has a girlfriend."

Deep sigh.

"Yeah, but a girlfriend who doesn't like him!" Sarah pointed out.

"And that's why he likes her," Ally said. "Because she doesn't like him. If Ms. Unfunny did like him, he'd have told her long ago to develop a sense of humor and then get back to him."

"Why do we do this?" I'd asked. "Why don't we like who we're with? And why are we with them in the first place if we don't like them?"

"Because sometimes we're just with the wrong people and it takes a while to figure it out," Ally said very quietly.

Sarah and I had looked at Ally then, waiting for her to say something about herself and her husband, but she didn't.

I'd been with Charlie for over a year when he wasn't the one. I'd known all along, but something had kept me with him. Because it was safe? Because I got to have a boyfriend who couldn't hurt me?

I was giving myself a headache.

Once Sarah and Ally had fallen asleep, I had lain awake staring at the ceiling. I'd crept out of bed to take *But I Don't Know How To Be Pregnant!* off Sarah's chest (she was on the last chapter), and I pulled Ally's law journal out from under her cheek and put it on her bedside table.

Neither had stirred when my cell phone rang. Ally and Sarah could sleep through anything.

"So what happened with Joy?" I asked Daniel. "Did you break up?"

"Yup. It was pretty ugly."

"Oh, Daniel, I'm really sorry."

"Nah, it's for the best," he said.

"So how'd she do it?" I asked. "Did she make some bad excuse and leave?"

"Actually, I broke up with her."

"You broke up with her?"

"Zoe, the woman has no sense of humor. I can't date someone who doesn't watch *Seinfeld* reruns."

I laughed. "I love *Seinfeld*."

"I know. It's too bad you'd never go for me. We'd make quite a good couple."

"Why don't you think I'd ever go for you?" I asked.

"Zoe, I already told you—I have self-esteem. You don't need to build up my ego. I know full well you wouldn't go for me. I'm not your type."

"What's my type?"

"George Clooney. Brad Pitt."

"And who are you?"

"I'm their sidekick, the funny one who never gets the girl."

"Actually, that's the one who always gets killed."

"That's right."

Tell him how you feel. Tell him how you feel.

But I couldn't. Because if I let myself feel what I felt, I'd be in trouble. A few months down the road, once he got to know me or once he was used to me, comfortable, he'd see me for who I was, see all my flaws, and a few months later, he'd be gone and I'd have my first broken heart—at the hands of a boyfriend, anyway.

"So when are you leaving for Thanksgiving?" I asked, dreading the thought of him flying home to L.A. for a few days. I felt as though I'd just gotten him back, and now he'd be gone again next week.

"Actually, I'm not," he said. "I have to work on the Friday after Thanksgiving, so it's a Swanson's turkey TV dinner for me."

I smiled. "Or you can have Thanksgiving in the Zone," I said. "No stuffing or potatoes, but all the turkey you want."

"Ooh, I get to meet the famous and infamous Solomon sisters? Can't wait," he said.

Me either.

13

Sarah

"Impromptu staff meeting!" called Astrid's assistant.

Shit. Shit. Shit. Usually our staff meetings were at 3:00 p.m. I thought I'd have a good hour or two to work on story ideas before my ultrasound appointment.

The editorial staff of *Wow Woman* magazine, six of us in all, sat around the scarred wooden table in the conference room, waiting for Astrid. Danielle sat directly across from me, as she always did. It took me a year to figure out she did so in order to spy on my reactions. Finally, Astrid swept into the room and announced that she'd killed two stories in the February issue and two articles had to be written overnight.

"All right, everyone," Astrid said, snapping off her eyeglasses. "In the next five minutes, I want two great story ideas and volunteers to write them."

"How about an article on how to tell if you're pregnant?" Danielle suggested.

Astrid slowly moved her gaze from her watch to

Danielle's gauzy maternity shirt. She stared at the crocheted neckline. "Danielle, the *Wow Woman* reader isn't interested in a full feature article on *pregnancy*. That's what *Power Pregnancy* magazine exists for. If you'd like to write something up on pregnancy, feel free to suggest it for our Health Page's sidebar." Astrid then went on to reiterate for the hundredth time *Wow*'s mission statement and promise to our female readers and asked if anyone had any *relevant* ideas for emergency article replacements.

Wait a minute. Why wouldn't the *Wow* reader be interested in the signs of pregnancy? What if Lisa hadn't been so obsessed with taking pregnancy tests? I'd been so sure it was simply PMS I had. Not that I'd ever thought about it, but I was sure I would have figured that pregnancy means no period and therefore no PMS symptoms. Who would have thought the symptoms would be so similar?

There had to be countless young women who'd benefit from some basic information. After all, there was article after article about sex. And one of the potential outcomes of sex was pregnancy.

"People," Astrid snapped. "We're down two articles. Get your thinking caps on!"

I was about to back up Danielle, but then realized I could potentially give myself away. I wasn't willing for anyone to even think I might be pregnant, or I could forget about the promotion. I had to cough up something good.

"Um, Astrid, have you ever heard of the Dating Diva?" I asked.

"The Dating Diva? Why does that sound familiar?"

"She was written up in *L.A. Magazine* last year. She's a relationship guru who critiques people's dates for a living. She gets paid like two hundred bucks an hour to tell people to stop talking about politics or their mother on their first dates, stuff like that."

Astrid's eyes lit up. "That's fabulous! I love it! Sarah, find out who her agent is and see if we can get an exclusive—"

"Astrid, she's my sister," I said.

Danielle looked like she wanted to murder me.

Astrid's eyes lit up even more. She even clapped, three times fast. "Fabulous!" she said again. "Absolutely fucking fabulous! Have her call me and we'll talk. I'd love her to do a series of articles, even a column." Astrid froze. "If she can write. Oh hell, who cares. We'll do an as-told-to or have someone do a profile if she can't write."

"I'll have her call you," I said.

Suddenly it occurred to me that I had no idea if A) Zoe could write. And B) if she'd be interested. I had a feeling, though, that she would be.

"Fabulous," Astrid said again. "Okay, people," she snapped. "We're still down two articles!"

"How about 'How To Tell If It's Too Soon in a Relationship for Sex,'" I suggested. "I could write the article and do a fun sidebar list of 'If he does this, it's too soon.'"

"Great, Sarah!" Astrid exclaimed.

I glanced at Danielle. Now she looked like she wanted to cry.

"I'm very impressed with you today, Sarah. Very impressed. I want the article on my desk by 9:00 a.m."

Shit. Shit. Shit. The *great* was great and the *very impressed* even better, but between the ultrasound appointment today and then a trip to a bridal salon with Giselle and a family meeting tonight to choose between bow tie number two or number five, I'd never be able to research and write up an article by nine tomorrow morning.

Then again, how much research did I need to do? *It's too soon to have sex if you get pregnant and the father of your baby says to call if you need anything....*

Astrid's assistant came up with "How To Handle Your Meddling Mother," and we were dismissed.

I stopped in *Wow*'s tiny kitchen for a much-needed caffeine boost, then remembered I could have only dull decaf.

"I should report that fucking bitch to HR," Danielle whispered to her friend, a copy editor. She was standing by the coffeemaker. Her friend nudged her, and she glanced up at me with worried eyes, then turned around and grabbed a filter.

"Didn't hear a thing," I assured her. "I'll make a pot of decaf. I'm too wired for caffeine today. I'll bring you a cup when it's ready, if you want, Danielle."

She stared at me for a moment. "Okay. Thanks."

She wouldn't report Astrid. It wasn't something you did. What you did was what Astrid said or you got sacked. Granted, *Wow Woman* wasn't *Vogue* or *Elle* or *Glamour,* but it was reasonably popular and had been growing in ad revenue ever since Astrid took over as editor in chief in 1998.

When I stopped by Danielle's cubicle with two mugs of decaf, I found her trying to hide the fact that she was crying.

"I am going to report her!" she whispered, tears running down her cheeks. "That bitch just stopped by a minute ago to hand me back an article I wrote—my own pregnancy journal. She says it's not relevant for *Wow* and then stared at my bare feet and asked me to 'please put on your shoes.' She has no right to treat me like that. Women *would* be interested in an article about pregnancy, and what the hell does she care if I don't wear my shoes in my cubicle?"

"I agree," I said.

She tucked a lock of her short blond hair behind her ear. "Give me a break, Sarah. My loss is your promotion."

"Not if I'm pregnant too," I whispered.

She stared at me. "Really?"

I nodded. "And you know what I think we should do? I think we should write an article about how pregnant women are treated in the workplace, interview a bunch of recent moms, really do it up. We can offer it to Astrid, and if she won't take it, we'll submit it to the competition."

She beamed. "I could interview everyone in my Lamaze class!"

"Let's do it!" I said. "We'll shove it in Astrid's face!"

"So when are you going to tell *Acid* that you're pregnant?" she asked.

"A few minutes before I go on maternity leave."

She laughed. "By the way, Sarah, congratulations," Danielle said. "Um, if you have any questions about anything, you know who to come to."

I nodded and headed back to my desk, aware that if she were really the asshole I always thought she was, she would have asked me a few questions, namely, *Who's the father? That guy you've been dating for the past couple of months? How are you going to manage?*

How I was going to manage was still beyond me. But the seven new e-mails I received in the past twenty minutes from Ally—links to pregnancy Web sites—would at least take care of the info factor. Amazing. The woman was clearly having serious marital troubles, yet she still found time to send me links about the importance of taking prenatal vitamins and how prenatal yoga classes would make delivery all the easier.

I picked up the phone and called Ally's cell. She answered on the first half ring as though she were waiting for an important call. "Ally," I whispered, "I have an ultrasound appointment at twelve-thirty, and I thought if you were free for lunch or could get away from the office, maybe you could go with me."

"Of course I'll go!" she said, and I could tell I made her happy.

I whispered the address and we hung up.

I wasn't used to calling Ally when I needed the support of a friend, but Lisa had a nasty cold and Sabrina was away on a buying trip and Griffen was going on with his life as though the woman he'd been dating weren't pregnant.

Had been dating. Weird. I was so focused on the subject of the baby that I hadn't even realized I'd been dumped.

Ally was in the waiting room of the Lenox Hill Fetal Maternal Clinic when I arrived. She was flipping through *Time* magazine. No, she was pretending to flip. She was actually staring at the pregnant woman next to her. Ally was looking at the woman's belly with the kind of longing I reserved for Häagen-Dazs chocolate chocolate chip ice cream and caffeinated coffee.

Last I heard, she and Smarmdrew were trying to have a baby. I thought Ally would make a great mother. A little overbearing, yes, but a devoted mother.

"You show up late to your own ultrasound?" she said when she saw me. "Sarah, when are you going to grow up?"

"Ally, when are you going to lay off?" I said in the same inflection.

I was *five* minutes late. But only because Danielle began telling the copy editor in the cubicle on her left about her own ultrasound appointment, which I assumed was for my benefit, and I'd sat in my cubicle, eavesdropping. She'd found out she was having a girl, and her husband wanted to name the baby Rosalind after his mother, but Danielle hated both the name and her mother-in-law.

Danielle had made me laugh for the first time in my history of knowing her.

"Five minutes, Ally," I said. "Doctors keep you waiting for a half hour, minimum, so I'm technically twenty-five minutes early."

"Are you going to show up five minutes late to pick up your child from day care? Are you going to show up five minutes late for his basketball games? Her ballet recitals? How about your own delivery? Are you going to show up late for that?"

"Being late is how I got into this condition," I joked.

She shook her head. "Go let the nurse know you're here. Bring your insurance card."

What was I, five? "Ally, I've been to a doctor before."

Signed in, insurance card handed over, I took a seat next to Ally. There were five other women sitting in the upholstered chairs. Each one was with a man.

My eyes went straight to every woman's ring finger. Every woman had a wedding ring.

I put my ringless hands to my sides and fidgeted. Why did I suddenly feel embarrassed that I didn't have a ring? Women chose to be single mothers all the time.

But you *didn't choose to be a single mother. Your ringless finger announces to the world that the father of your baby doesn't love you.*

That was stupid. *Remove that thought pattern from your brain this second, Sarah!*

But it was there.

The women around the room were in various states of

pregnancy. The blonde across from me—she looked to be around five or six months along—was talking about how nervous she was about having amnioscentesis. I didn't even know what that was. The blonde to my left had her head on her husband's shoulder. He was staring straight ahead, like a zombie.

You never know what's going on in people's homes or marriages, Sarah, Ally had said more than once when I'd complained last year that everyone had a boyfriend or a date to the company Christmas party or a perfect life but me. *A couple walking down the street holding hands and looking for all the world like the happiest people on earth could be mourning the loss of their baby,* Ally had said. *Or maybe the man beat her up the night before. Or maybe they are happy. But don't think that couples are happy just because they're a couple.*

Sometimes I thought Ally was the most cynical person I'd ever known, and then sometimes I thought she was the wisest. It usually depended on my mood. Right now, when I assumed that everyone thought the worst about me, her Ally-isms were comforting.

She and Smarmdrew always looked happy enough. He was a touchy-feely type and always had his arm around her shoulder or he'd sneak up on her in the kitchen and pinch her butt. But I always applied Ally's own pronouncement to her own marriage. Yeah, they always seemed happy at the rare times I saw them together, but that didn't mean they were.

"Do you know what to expect when we go in?" Ally asked.

I nodded. "I read one of the articles you e-mailed me."

She glanced at me. "Good. It should be very exciting. You get to see the baby, even if it's just a tiny little speck at this point."

I smiled. "I know. I'm so nervous!"

"I'm glad you invited me, Sarah," she said. "It means a lot to me. I know we don't always get along or see eye to eye, but you do know that I'm one hundred percent here for you, right?"

"I do know that," I said. "And thanks, Ally."

It was true. She was overbearing, domineering, bossy, impossible, annoying and incredibly judgmental. But she was there. And she always would be. She was there the way my mother would have been there. And, sometimes, knowing that made my mother's loss a little easier to bear. I supposed that Andrew fulfilled that need for Ally. Maybe that was why she got married so young. I had Ally, and Ally needed an older sister too, so she got married.

Finally, my name was called. Ally and I shot up and followed the nurse.

"Sarah—"

I whirled around and there was Griffen, his hands stuffed in his pockets.

I was surprised. Very surprised.

"Uh, Ally, this is Griffen. Griffen, my sister Ally."

They said awkward hellos and we all trailed after the nurse. I noticed Ally give Griffen the once-over, as though checking to see what the baby might end up looking like.

The baby looked a little bit like a mouse.

On the monitor, the technician pointed out the baby's head and stomach, which both looked the same. Everything was fine and good and where it should be, the woman informed us. And then we listened to the heartbeat.

I glanced at Griffen. He was staring at the monitor, at the *zzzz*'s of the heartbeat, which sounded very loud and fast.

"Wow," he said, looking quite awestruck.

"Yeah, wow," I breathed.

"Wow," Ally added.

A doctor came in and gave us the stamp of health. I was ten weeks pregnant and due in May.

"A Taurus," Ally said with a smile. "Like Mom."

I smiled back.

"Like me," Griffen said, biting his lip.

That's right. His birthday was May 12.

"Here," the technician said, printing out still images of the ultrasound. "Keepsakes." She handed one to me, one to Ally and one to Griffen.

Griffen glanced at the little black-and-white photo, then folded it and tucked it into his jacket pocket. "I'd better get back to work," he said. "Um, bye, Sarah. Nice meeting you, Ally."

Ally nodded and Griffen practically ran down the hall.

"Did you know he was coming?" Ally asked as the technician wiped the jelly off my slightly rounded tummy.

I shook my head. "I was shocked to see him here. From the way our conversation went last week, I never expected to hear from him again. He doesn't want anything to do with me or the baby." Tears stung the backs of my eyes.

Ally slung her arm around me. "It's still very early, Sarah. He came today, and that's a very good sign."

"A good sign of what? That he wanted to make sure I was really pregnant at all?"

She handed me my pants and socks. "Hey, I'm the cynical one in this family, Sarah. I have a feeling he needed to really see the baby, hear it, in a hospital setting, to believe in it. Once it really sinks in, he may change his tune."

Optimism from Ally was worth quite a lot. If she believed, I could too.

★ ★ ★

"Which is the head and which is the body?" Zoe asked, turning the grainy photograph of my ultrasound upside down and sideways.

The three sisters Solomon were in a Mexican restaurant near the bridal salon Giselle and her mother had dragged us to in order to photograph potential gowns. Ally and Zoe and I had all made excuses to leave at exactly the same time, found ourselves breathing sighs of relief outside the salon on Madison Avenue and having exactly nowhere to go. Zoe had suggested getting a bite to eat, and Ally, with a "My appetite is miraculously restored now that I'm out of wedding gown hell," agreed.

"Any way you hold the photograph," Zoe added, "you can't tell which is which."

Ally laughed and pointed out which end was up. "These pictures were taken only seven hours ago, so they're already very outdated. The changes to the fetus in just one day are incredible."

"Wow," Zoe said. "It's just amazing. Giselle once showed me Madeline's first ultrasound picture, and I couldn't believe that big, bouncy baby girl was once a teeny tiny little thing like this. Isn't it amazing that this little creature is going to be a walking talking little person very soon?"

"You're scaring me," I said with a smile. "I've only read up through twelve weeks of fetal development. Baby Solomon doesn't even have knees yet."

"Baby Solomon?" Zoe repeated. "So you're going to give the baby your name?"

"Looks that way," I said. "Unless Griffen magically wants to be 'and daddy makes three.' "

Zoe turned to me. "But he did show up at the ultrasound appointment. That has to be a sign of things to come."

"That's what Ally said, but I don't know. 'Wow' was about the only thing Griffen said during the entire hour. That and 'Nice to meet you, Ally.'"

"Well, at least our nephew's father has manners," Ally commented.

Except for his habit of walking away. "I can't even speculate anymore about what Griffen's going to do or say. It's enough of a brain-drain to think that this—" I gestured at the photograph with a tortilla chip "—will be a Madeline or a Matthew one day."

"Speaking of Madeline," Ally said, "I think she should stay at home when we go on wedding hell outings. Maddy-Waddy vomited on my shoes twice in one hour."

As our entrées arrived, I wondered why Ally was suddenly anti-Madeline. Ally had zero interest in Giselle, and Giselle had long ago given up on trying to engage her in conversation, but Ally could never get enough of Madeline. She always wanted to hold her and sing to her. But tonight's after-work wedding gown hunt seemed hard on everyone, not just the baby. We didn't even have to watch Giselle try on dresses; she wanted only to select a bunch she liked and photograph them so that she could figure out what style wedding she wanted. The dress was the showpiece for everything else. If she liked a modern dress, she'd have a modern wedding. If she liked an antiquey dress, she'd have an old-fashioned wedding. Maybe if she chose a transparent dress, she could have an invisible wedding!

There was something about watching an excited bride-to-be pick out wedding gowns that made you even more aware of how far from the altar *you* were. I'd sat on a stool and wondered if people used the word *illegitimate* anymore. Ally had practically ripped apart the headpiece she was "looking at." And Zoe had stared out the window onto Madison Avenue, every now and then adding a "very nice" when Giselle asked for her opinion.

It was interesting that the three of us felt compelled to go on these little trips; it was as if each of us felt we had to go in lieu of rent or something. Or perhaps we simply thought our crankiness about choosing china patterns and wedding gowns and rubber chicken would make our own love-life issues a bit too apparent. Ally still hadn't mentioned her husband's name once. Zoe stared at a wallet-sized photograph of a good-looking guy every now and then, but without expression. And I spent my nights thinking up baby names for boys and girls, rejecting anything that didn't sound musical with both Solomon and Maxwell.

The waiter arrived with refills of our drinks, three more Sprites in honor of my inability to consume margaritas.

"How about a toast—to the new addition-to-be to our family," Zoe said, and we raised our glasses and clinked.

A couple passing by smiled at us in midclink, and I realized we probably looked like three friends or possibly sisters (not that we looked that much alike, except for the eyes; we all had the Solomon almond-shaped dark blues), out for a fun night together. This was the first time the three of us had gone anywhere alone together. And it was nice. If I didn't have to write a two-thousand-word article on sex and relationships by the crack of dawn, I'd even suggest a movie after dinner. It wasn't every day (or any day) that Ally and Zoe could be in the same room, let alone sitting right next to each other, without one of them (usually Zoe) stomping away hurt.

Brainstorm. "Are you guys in the mood to help me plan out an article I have to write by tomorrow morning?" I asked my sisters. "If I don't get started now, I'm screwed. I can't keep my eyes open past ten o'clock anymore and I can't have caffeine to help me."

"What's the topic?" Zoe asked.

"How you know it's too soon to have sex in a new relationship," I said. "And let's not use me as an example, Ally," I added fast. I knew my older sister too well.

"Okay," Ally said, forkful of refried beans in her hand. "It's too soon to have sex if you don't know where you stand."

"Only if you *care* where you stand," Zoe said.

"Yeah, but you can't care where you stand on the third date," Ally countered.

"Who has sex on the third date?" Zoe said. "That's *way* soon."

Ally and I stared at her.

"In fact, my boy—my *ex*-boyfriend made me wait," Zoe said. "His last girlfriend was two-timing him, and he got so burned that he wanted to take things slowly in the intimacy department. It took him three dates to French-kiss me, a month before he went near my bra, and it was two months before we slept together."

"How long were you together?" I asked.

"A year," Zoe said. "So maybe he had something there."

A year. I slept with Griffen on our *second date.* I even initiated it. Well, not sex itself so much as sexuality. He'd walked me home after the movie, I invited him up for a nightcap, and a glass of wine later, we were liplocked on the couch. Of course, Jennifer walked out in her bra and teeny-tiny underwear (*"Oh my God, Sarah, I am so sorry. I totally didn't know you were even here. Oh my God, if I'd known you had a guy here, I would never have walked out like this. Giggle. Giggle. Oh hi, there. You must be Griffen. Really, I never would have walked in half-naked if I'd known Sar had a guy here. She never does. Oops, I mean, well she's no slut, huh! You two have fun, see you in the morning, singsong, singsong.")*

I was not exaggerating.

Something about Jennifer's little cutesy routine worked, though, because Griffen and I both rolled our eyes in unison and shared a laugh, a real laugh, and I'd felt better than I had in forever.

And then he leaned closer to me and kissed me. A sweet kiss, with tenderness, that he turned hot real fast. And then I took his hand and led him into my bedroom and closed the door.

And unbeknown to either of us, sperm met egg.

I dipped a tortilla chip in salsa. "How about, it's too soon for sex if you don't know how he'd react if you got pregnant?"

"I don't know, Sarah," Zoe said. "No one really knows how they're going to react. You couldn't have said for sure how you'd react. Even married couples don't necessarily react well to a pregnancy. What if it's unplanned?"

That was true. "I think I should skip the pregnancy angle anyway."

"Consequences of sleeping with a guy too soon are important to mention," Ally said. "Let's say you don't know someone's sexual history and end up with chlamydia?"

"Good one," Zoe said, pointing a chip at her.

During dinner on that second date, I'd asked Griffen about his previous relationships, not so much for sexual history but because I was curious and wanted to know what his track record was.

"What would the Dating Diva say about that question?" he'd asked. On our first date, I'd told him about Zoe and what she did for a living. He was impressed that someone could make such good money telling people to stop talking about sex and politics on a first date, essentially what they already knew if they'd been socialized in this country.

"The Dating Diva would say there's nothing wrong with a provocative conversation about experiences," I told him.

He tapped me on the nose. "Unless one party of the conversation would rather not discuss his experiences."

I'd turned red. "Oh. Okay. I didn't mean to pry."

He softened. "I've had a few relationships, one serious that didn't work out a few years ago."

I wanted to ask five more questions, but I held my tongue. He hadn't asked me about my history, which consisted of three prior relationships, none lasting longer than six months.

Ally grabbed a tortilla chip. "It's too soon for sex if you don't know some basic information about his family, his prior relationships, his work and his values."

I didn't know anything about Griffen when I slept with him, except that I found him gorgeous, sexy, smart, funny, his own person, creative, interesting and kind. I knew he worked as a producer in television. I knew he grew up in Brooklyn. I knew he had a brother who worked in the White House as some sort of congressional aide. I knew he liked red meat. Black coffee. Violent guy movies. Pop culture. Breasts. Running. Talking about current events. Sex.

And I'd thought he liked me. The way he looked at me while we were making love seemed to say what was in his heart and head. Was I a naive idiot? Did all men look like they were in love while they were having sex? Maybe. I'd slept with four guys, the first guy only once, and the other three regularly enough for a few months. No one had ever looked at me the way Griffen did.

And I had never felt about anyone else the way I felt about him.

I couldn't describe why he overwhelmed me. I was wildly attracted to him, yes, but not just physically. Our chemistry was unlike any I'd ever felt. We could talk about anything and did. We could disagree and did. We laughed a lot. We could kiss for minutes on a street corner. We were in sync. We were friends, lovers and, I thought, on our way to becoming the mythical soul mates.

"Well, Zoe, let's say you decided to make a play for Daniel," I said. "Because you're such good friends already, would you immediately sleep with him? Or would you wait until your romance was more settled first?"

"Good question," Zoe said. "I'm not sure."

"Because you don't really know how you feel about him," Ally said. "You want him, but you don't."

"No, she just wants him at arm's length," I said.

"Then it's definitely too soon to sleep with him," Ally said.

"I'm glad I asked," Zoe said, winking at us.

"Speaking of you, Zoe," I said. "I told my boss about you this morning, and her eyes lit up at the idea of you writing an article or even a column about being the Dating Diva. She wants you to call her if you're interested."

"You're kidding!" Zoe practically shouted. "That sounds amazing! I will call her."

"This Dating Diva thing is a scam," Ally said with a wink at Zoe. "You're making a shitload of money by telling people what they already know."

"What they already know?" I repeated. "Who knows *anything?* If I knew anything about when it was too soon to have sex, I might not be pregnant."

"Yeah, Sarah, you might not be pregnant," Zoe said quite seriously. "Look, I know being single and pregnant might not be how you planned things, but being pregnant is quite a blessing, quite a beautiful thing."

"I'll second that," Ally said. "On the one hand, in your situation, there's a lot to work out. But on the other, you're damned lucky, kid."

"A toast to me, then," I said with a smile, raising my glass. We clinked. "Okay, so how about it's too soon to sleep with someone you're not in love with—that takes the guesswork right out of— No, that's unrealistic. You could be very interested, very attracted, and that could be reason enough. It takes a long time for real love to develop."

"That's why single people have sex and married people don't," Ally said. Then she blushed and hurried to say, "Not that my marriage is an example. I'm just *saying.* When you're in love, you're blinded by romance. You have sex four times a day. It's why people who marry after two weeks end up divorced a minute later. You're in love with newness, the mystery, the zing. Once you're living daily life and putting up with his obnoxious friends and being nice to his overbearing mother at family functions, the in-love part tends to recede and the love part takes over."

That did make sense.

"Take you and Griffen," Ally went on. "Let's say you're living together, changing diapers, picking up his socks from the living-room floor, he's pulling your long hairs out of the bathroom sink. The baby's crying. When are you going to have sex then? That's real life. Dating isn't."

"So are you saying it's too soon to have sex if you're not ready to move in with the guy?" I asked.

"If you get pregnant, then yeah," Ally said.

★ ★ ★

When I arrived at work the next morning, Griffen had left a message. *Beep:* "Um, Sarah, it's Griffen. I tried you at home, but your roommate said you moved out like four weeks ago. Where are you living? Is everything okay? Um, I have to go out of town on business for a story this week, but, uh, I told my parents the big news, and you're invited for pumpkin pie on Thanksgiving at their house if you can make it. They're really anxious to meet you. Uh, give me a call back when you have a chance."

As if calling him back wasn't the most important thing on my to-do list.

"Why *is* it?" Ally asked that night. "I mean, I'm happy for you that he called and that he told his parents and that they want to meet you. But you haven't been the most important thing on *his.*"

"You don't know that," Zoe said, twisting herself into a painful-looking yoga position. "I wouldn't be surprised if he's thought of nothing else but you and the pregnancy. And telling his folks is a big deal."

"What I'm saying is that I don't think Sarah should count on Griffen or get all hopeful about his involvement, even if he told his parents. This isn't a fairy tale."

No kidding. Even Cinderella got her own room.

14

Ally

My mother-in-law wanted to know, via telephone from Cincinnati, why Andrew was bringing home another woman for Thanksgiving.

"Because he's a lying, cheating—" I stopped when I remembered that I was talking to Andrew's mother, not that she'd ever been particularly warm and fuzzy to me. As Mrs. Sharp went on and on about forgiving and forgetting and compromising and what Dear Abby would have said, I held my cell phone at arm's length and seethed.

"No, there's no chance of reconciliation," I told her. "No, I don't think there's anything he could say or do."

So Andrew was bringing someone home for Thanksgiving? Which just happened to be my birthday this year? And whom could he have possibly met in a month, five weeks, that he liked so much he was bringing her to meet his parents—for a major holiday?

"You superwomen try to do it all, and what happens?" Mrs. Sharp went on. "You implode. You try to do it all, having a high-powered career and taking care of a house and a husband, and what happens? The house falls to pot and the husband is tempted away into the arms of another woman. But don't blame yourself, Ally, dear. I'm sure this Valerie person cooked her way into Andrew's heart. All a man really wants is a good hot meal waiting for him at the end of the day."

Remember that she's seventy-four. Remember that she's seventy-four. Remember that she's seventy-four.

"Mrs. Sharp, with all due respect, I don't agree with a word you just said."

"Well, Ally, *that's* your problem. You do a lot of arguing—I guess it's that career of yours. Arguing is what you do for a living, isn't it? Well, dear, maybe if you'd done a little less arguing and a little more *agreeing,* Andy wouldn't have had to look elsewhere. He would be bringing *you* to our Thanksgiving celebration."

It was too bad that cell phones didn't have cords. I needed something to strangle and Mrs. Sharp was in Ohio. A little too far away for neck squeezing.

"Mrs. Sharp—" I had been calling her Mrs. Sharp for thirteen years. "During eleven years of marriage to your lying, cheating son, I've been subjected to your overcooked turkey, limp, tasteless vegetables and ridiculously outdated views on life. So if Andrew is bringing his latest floozy to the family Thanksgiving, I can only hope they both choke on a turkey bone. Happy holidays, *dear.*"

I threw my cell phone against the wall and sank down on my bed. My legs were shaking. *This Valerie person. This Valerie person.*

And suddenly my sisters were staring at me, their mouths hanging open to the floor. My heart had been beating so fast during that little conversation that I hadn't even heard them come in. Sarah was clutching one of those two-pound hollow chocolate turkeys you found in drugstore candy aisles during the holidays. The head had been gnawed off.

"Chocolate has traces of caffeine," I said, and burst into tears.

Sarah zoomed to one side of me and Zoe to the other.

"Ally, what happened?" Sarah asked, tucking a piece of my hair behind my ears the way my mother used to.

"I left Andrew," I blurted out. "That's why I moved here. He's been cheating on me. I caught him in the act myself."

"Oh no," Zoe said.

"Oh yes. In my own house," I said. "And then I found—"

"You found what?" Sarah asked, taking my hand.

"And then I found a vasectomy bill—"

The tears came fast and furious, and I covered my face with my hands.

"Oh, Ally. I am so sorry," Sarah said. "I know how badly you've been wanting a baby."

"He had a vasectomy and didn't tell you?" Zoe asked.

I nodded. "We've been trying—or so I thought—to have a baby for *five* years. And then I found the five-year-old claim form—"

Sarah leaned my head on her shoulder and Zoe rubbed my shoulder. I told them what happened, starting with Mary Jane jumping on Andrew's back and ending with my flurry of nightmarish blind dates from FindAMate.com.

"I can't even interest a man in getting past drinks and appetizers," I said. I'd gone on three more nightmare dates from hell before I canceled the two remaining. "I'm a bitch."

"Ally, you're not a bitch," Sarah said. "You're wonderful. You're you, and I don't know what the hell I'd do if you didn't exist exactly as you are."

"Really?" I asked. "You don't think I'm the bitch queen of the eastern seaboard?"

"Well, sometimes you are," she said, grinning. "But someone's gotta tell people what's what."

"Telling people what's what is exactly why I'm suddenly single *and* unable to interest a man in a conversation," I pointed out.

"I doubt that," Zoe said. "*Not* telling people what's what—that's what keeps people single."

"What do you mean?" Sarah asked.

"When you don't lay your cards on the table," Zoe said. "When you're not you and the *youest* you, you're holding back. And when you hold back or when you act like you think you should to make someone interested, you end up with someone you're not comfortable with or with someone who thinks you're one way when you're quite another."

"That's true," I said. "But how I *am* doesn't seem to interest anyone."

"Is there something in particular you think you're doing wrong?" Zoe asked.

"Well, I guess I could stop telling everyone that I'm twenty-nine," I said. "I was going to fess up, but the dates were all such duds that I couldn't bear to make things even worse."

"You could definitely pass for twenty-nine," Zoe said. "Absolutely."

"I think we're going to get along fine after all," I said to her, and she smiled.

"Are you sure you should be dating so soon, anyway?" Sarah asked. "*Wow Woman* would probably advise a good therapist and a painting class or a vacation."

"I know it's too soon, but I don't care," I said. "I need to do something that will make me feel attractive again, even if it's external. Yeah, yeah, I know I'm supposed to get that crap from myself, but right now, I need a man to make me feel the opposite of how Andrew made me feel last month."

"I can understand that, Ally," Sarah said.

"But I'm such a total washout as a single woman that I feel worse now," I confessed. "I met Andrew when I was twenty-one, married him at twenty-three. I don't know how to be single."

"Hey, you don't know how to be single and I don't know how to be pregnant!" Sarah said. "We're a good match."

I laughed and yanked her long ponytail.

"You know, Ally, I *do* critique dates for a living," Zoe said. "I'd be happy to give you the Dating Diva's best work, on the house."

Nooooo way. "I don't know if I could handle that," I said. "You, sitting at the next table, watching me acting like an idiot, watching me get rejected? I don't think so."

"Ninety percent of my clients tell me they forget I'm even there the minute the date arrives," Zoe assured me. "They're too wrapped up in the date or the moment to remember me. And it's not like I'll be sitting there staring at you and making myself obvious. You won't even know I'm there."

"Go for it, Ally," Sarah said. "If you're dating, you'll forget all about Andrew. Plus, you'll be too busy with all your men to harass me about eating chocolate and learning to put on a BabyBjörn."

I wanted to put on a BabyBjörn. And if getting a critique of my dating skills took me a step closer to wearing my child on my chest, I'd do it.

"You guys are right. I don't have what I want, and I have to start going after it! Proactive all the way. I have no husband, no baby, and I can't even handle a date, so— Oh God, what am I talking about. My life sucks!"

"*Your* life sucks?" Zoe said. "How about waiting for your client's date to show up and it turns out to be your own boyfriend?"

Now it was my and Sarah's turn to stare at Zoe with mouths agape.

Zoe gave us the details. "Oh yeah, and let's not forget that my mother is missing in New York City, planning our father's destruction."

"Big whoop," Sarah said. "I'm single, pregnant and, drumroll please…homeless!"

"I had a feeling that's why you moved in here," I said. "What happened with the roommate?"

"A big diamond ring," she explained.

"I don't know, sister dears," I said. "I still think I win the life sucks award."

"No—I do," Zoe said."

"No—it goes to me," Sarah said.

"Sorry, kid," I said. "But you're pregnant. The baby makes anything you're going to go through worth it. And you're not homeless, Sarah—you're here. And if you weren't here, you'd come live with me. You'd never be homeless."

Sarah bit her lip and threw her arms around me. I couldn't remember the last time she hugged me like that.

"Actually, my life isn't so bad either," Zoe said. "Even though Charlie and I broke up, I couldn't make a decision about him anyway, so life took care of it for me. *And* my mother will probably go home eventually. And I sort of like someone else, a little, anyway."

"I guess mine could be worse too," I said. "I'm going to be an aunt. I'm getting a free critique from the famed

Dating Diva and I make a shitload of money for doing what I love, even though I hate who I'm doing it for."

Sarah broke off the chocolate turkey's plump body and gave it to me. She gave Zoe the legs and popped the neck in her own mouth. And for the next half hour, we sat on our beds, eating cheap, bad chocolate as Zoe told us all about her last phone conversation with Daniel, I told them all about finding Andrew in the hammock with the Pilates instructor and Sarah read us the page on fetal development, week eleven. Then we spent the next half hour making fun of my father and his stupid bow ties.

I'd changed my profile on FindAMate.com. I was now thirty-five, as of next week, anyway, and separated.

Neither of which seemed to have any effect on Rupert Jones, a landscape architect. Thirty-six, also separated, and also a Westchester émigré living in a terrible, tiny sublet on the Upper West Side. Like me, there was zero chance of reconciliation with his spouse. Rupert Jones and I had a lot in common, not including his calm demeanor and love of landscapes. *I could teach you to smell the roses,* he'd said on the phone during one of our two conversations. *And you can teach me how to send back overcooked steak in a restaurant.* We both liked the same music, we both loved Arnold Schwarzenegger flicks and we both had been cheated on.

Rupert Jones wasn't my type. But he was absolutely appealing. Tall and lanky with a professor's beard and intelligent, warm brown eyes, he showed up on time, wearing a date outfit and a smile. He'd even brought me a little present, a blank journal with a tapestry cover, since we'd discussed the importance of writing down our feelings during a maelstrom. I liked Rupert.

But acting natural was a bit of a problem with Zoe sitting three feet away, her notebook open and pen at the ready. I was already a nervous wreck, and every time Zoe's hand moved, it distracted me. Every time she touched pen to paper, I was tempted to run over to her, grab her notebook and read it.

I'd thought I was doing pretty well with Rupert, but Zoe's fingers were flying. What the hell was she writing? I thought she was supposed to be invisible!

"You're even prettier in person," Rupert said, filling my water glass from the carafe on the table. "I didn't think that would be possible, but here you are."

I beamed. I'd uploaded another photo, a recent one. "Thank you," I said.

Zoe's hand went wild.

What was she writing? What could I possibly have said wrong? I'd accepted a compliment the perfect way, with a simple *thank you*. I didn't go into a two-minute monologue about how the photo was old or awful or how unphotogenic I was.

Zoe's hand was still going wild.

"Do you see someone you know?" Rupert asked. "You keep craning your neck to see around that big guy."

"I thought so, but no," I said. "I'm sorry—I hope I'm not being too rude."

Again I craned my neck around the very large man blocking my view of Zoe's notebook. She was sitting two tables over and had a view of us, but my view of her was partially blocked. I only saw part of her hair, her right foot and her hand.

Rupert leaned back and looked in the direction I was staring.

"Rupert, I really am sorry," I said. "It's just uncanny how familiar she looks. Maybe it *is* who I think it is." What, what, what was she writing!

Our drinks were served, and we settled into a conversation about where we grew up. Rupert was also a native New Yorker. And he'd also gone to Stanford for graduate school. That gave us quite a bit to talk about. And despite the lack of conversation about marriage, separation, cheaters and other dating no-no's according to *How to Find a Good Man: A Three-Month Plan* and Zoe, her hand was still whizzing over her notebook!

"Would you mind if I did go over and see if she is who I think she is?" I asked Rupert.

Excused, I went over to Zoe. "What are you writing!" I whispered. "I haven't broken one dating dictum! Let me see that pad!"

"Ally," she whispered back, "I'm writing all the *great* things you're doing. Not all critiques are negative. Some are reflective of how well a date is going. I thought it would be nice to write down just how well you *are* doing, so you'd know just how absolutely fine you are on a date."

Oh.

"Why don't you head back to Rupert?" Zoe said. "He seems to like you so much he probably misses you."

I smiled. "I like him too. Isn't he nice-looking? And he's so smart and soft-spoken. Not like the opinionated loudmouth I was married to for—"

I froze. The opinionated loudmouth I was married to for eleven years was sitting across the restaurant, feeding soup to a blonde who used a little too much hair spray.

That lying, cheating—

"Ally? What's wrong?" Zoe asked. She looked in the direction of my glare. "What's the matter?"

"Do you see that man in the navy shirt and navy tie?" I gestured with my chin. "The one with the ugly blonde?"

Actually, the blonde was quite pretty.

"Who is he?" Zoe asked.

"My husband," I said.

"Oh shit," Zoe said. "Are you okay?"

"I'll be okay after I march over to his table, dump his plate on his head, punch the woman he's with and mash his face into the floor!"

"Ally, lower your voice!" Zoe hissed as gently as she could. "Rupert will hear you."

I'd forgotten Rupert. And the more I stared at Andrew cutting bites of something that looked like ravioli or gnocchi and sliding his fork into Blondie's mouth, I forgot Rupert again. By the time Andrew took his finger and dabbed away some red sauce on the side of Sluttie's mouth, then stuck his finger in her mouth and she licked it, I'd forgotten where I was.

"I'm going over there," I said. "I'm going to mash his face in his goddamn dinner!"

"Ally, calm down this second!" Zoe hiss-whispered. "There's an alternative."

"Oh yeah? What?" I asked, watching Blondie's shoeless foot slip up Andrew's pant leg. "Punch the slut first, then rub his face in his dinner?"

"You could simply ignore them and enjoy your date," Zoe pointed out. "Ally, this is a guy you've been very excited about meeting. A guy you spoke to for two hours on the phone twice. A guy who made you feel that there's a whole new world open to you if you want it. And that's before you even met him. And now that you have *met* him, you've been having a great time. Are you going to let Andrew take this away from you too?"

Damn. Damn. Damn. She was right.

"Okay. You're right, Zoe," I said. Deep breath. Deep breath. Deep breath. "You're absolutely right. He took away my marriage, my dreams for a baby, everything. Why should I let him ruin a very good date, too? My first good date after six duds."

Zoe nodded. "That's right. So forget about Andrew, go back to Rupert and give great date!"

Of course I had to take one last look before I turned to go. I was rewarded with watching Andrew offering his date a long velvet box.

My blood boiled. And before Zoe could grab my arm, I stomped over to Andrew's table.

"If I were you, Andrew," I said, "I'd save my money for what you're going to owe me in the divorce, you lying, cheating scum!"

Andrew and the blonde stared at me, mouths agape for a moment, then Andrew shook his head as though I were Mary Jane jumping on the dinner table.

"*Excuse* me," Blondie said. "We're having a nice dinner. Why don't you go back to wherever you came from."

"Why don't you mind your own business," I retorted.

"Oh, but I am," she said. "And you're interrupting my dinner with my boyfriend."

My husband was someone's boyfriend.

"Andy's told me all about you and your bad attitude," she continued. "It's no wonder he left you for a woman like—"

"Valerie..." Andrew began.

Ah, so this was This Valerie Person.

"Oh, no, *Andy,* let her continue," I said. "I'm fascinated. A woman like what? A woman like you?"

Valerie took a bite of her salmon as if to show she was hardly fazed by my presence. "You're not worth it. I'm quite done."

"Then you won't be needing this," I said, picking up her dinner plate and turning it upside down on her head.

The salmon slid along her lacquered hair and adhered halfway, near her ear, which poked out a bit. Rice tumbled over her in every direction, along with some asparagus, which hit the table and the floor. Valerie jumped up and screamed. Real screams.

Everyone in the restaurant was staring.

"I want her arrested!" Valerie yelled, tears streaming down her face. "I'm pressing charges! This is a silk dress! I'm pressing charges! Call the police!" she screamed at the waiter, who was simply staring, his mouth open.

"Val, honey, calm down," Andrew said, his eyes darting around in embarrassment as he stood up with his napkin and began dabbing what smelled like mustard sauce off his date's face. "Let's all just calm down."

"I want the police!" Valerie shrieked. "Someone call the goddamned police!" Blondie ran screaming and crying in the direction of the bathroom.

Andrew was shaking his head. Zoe had her hand plastered over her mouth.

And Rupert was staring at me. Everyone, actually, was staring at me.

The maître d' came rushing over with a cell phone in his hand. "I want you all out now! Out right now! Or I will call the police and have you all arrested! You pay first, then you leave!"

"Hey, what did I do?" Andrew said. "I was enjoying a nice meal until this lunatic dumped my girlfriend's plate on her head."

My husband had a girlfriend.

Suddenly I felt very sick. Very tired and very sick.

"Ally?"

I turned around and there was Rupert, looking quite disappointed.

"Are you with this woman?" the maître d' asked Rupert.

Rupert nodded.

"Out now!" he shouted in Rupert's face. "All of you!"

Andrew threw some bills on the table and stomped over to the ladies' room. He called Valerie's name, and she came out crying hysterically. He led her past a throng of tables outside and into a cab.

"Out now!" the maître d' shouted at us again. "Pay first, then leave!" he screeched.

Rupert pulled out his wallet and handed the man a hundred-dollar bill, about eighty dollars too many for the two drinks we'd had. Zoe was half-hidden behind a very large Ficus tree, gnawing her lower lip.

"Did you dump that woman's dinner plate on her head?" Rupert asked me.

"Why, did you see that?" I asked.

"Look, I don't need this," he said. "I realize you're going through the early stage of separation and it's tough stuff. I'm going through the same thing. But if I saw my wife on a date with another man, I'd have enough self-control not to attack the guy."

I was about to say *Well, bully for you,* but Zoe was shaking her head back and forth in a very serious way.

"I'm sorry, Rupert," I said. "I—"

"I'm not interested, Ally," he interrupted, and walked out.

As Zoe and I left the restaurant, I got two thumbs-up and a *"The homewrecker probably deserved it"* from two women sitting near the door.

"I don't know about that," Zoe said as we walked up Lexington Avenue. "Why is the *woman* the homewrecker? The spouse who *cheated* is the homewrecker."

"You're absolutely right," I said. And she was. "I should have dumped Andrew's food on *his* head."

Zoe shook her head and laughed, and we walked in silence for a block or two, enjoying the cool November night air and watching two cabdrivers argue out of their windows right in the middle of Lexington Avenue. Suddenly Zoe stopped dead in her tracks. "No, forget that thought," she said, and kept walking.

"Huh?" I said. "What thought?"

"For a second I was thinking that I should apply that rationale to Dad and Giselle, but I realized it doesn't apply. Giselle *is* a homewrecker."

"What's different in the situation?" I asked.

"Because Giselle *knew* my father was married," Zoe explained. "She willingly went for a married man."

"Okay, that's true. She knew he was married. But, and I'm playing devil's advocate here, Zoe—she met him and fell in love. Was she supposed to say you're married, so sorry, you're not available, see ya?"

Zoe nodded hard. "Yes. That's exactly what she should have said. And she might have added, 'And you're my *friend's* married dad, so really see ya.' Why go on a date with a married man in the first place? Why set yourself up to fall for a married man? To ruin his marriage? To hurt his children?"

"Oh God, Zoe. If I spent a minute being angry at your mother for breaking up my parents' marriage, I would be a walking volcano."

"Um, Ally, you sort of are. Or are you forgetting your recently demonstrated inability to control your impulses?"

I glanced at her and had to laugh, though I could see she was quite serious. "Okay, maybe you're right." We walked in silence for a few minutes. "I suppose it was a lot worse that Giselle was your own friend," I continued. "I can't imagine how that must have felt. What are you even doing here, picking out china patterns and tasting salmon and mashed potatoes and watching Giselle twirl around in wedding gowns? Are you really that worried about your mother?"

"Well, I was. I mean, I came because of my mom, and I guess I ended up sticking around because there's no real reason to go home. Charlie and I are kaput, and you and Sarah and Dad and even my mom are here. It's nice to be around you all, even if no one's ever home at the same time. And then there's Daniel, who's become a really good friend—more, maybe."

"So, was Charlie right?" I asked. "Did you want to break up and waited for him to do it?"

"I guess," she said. "Maybe I was just clinging to the relationship because it kept me safe. Involved but not involved with my heart and soul, you know?"

"Or maybe you were clinging to the relationship because you did love Charlie," I pointed out. "At one point. Maybe you needed something to shake things up to make you realize that your feelings had changed. Take me, for instance. If I hadn't caught Andrew fucking another woman, I wouldn't have realized that I didn't love him. I would have just thought that it was long-term marriage, that I did love him but that the passion was gone or whatever. But when the dust settled, I realized I didn't love him. That we didn't love each other."

"Then why did you get so upset in the restaurant?" she asked. "Was it just the anger at his lies?"

"I think so," I said. "To find out your whole life, your marriage, is a lie. That your husband isn't who you thought he was. That he's been lying to you, making a fool out of you— I've always thought I was pretty smart, and it turned out I'm an idiot."

She squeezed my hand. "I think you're plenty smart,

Ally. I also think you should call Rupert and try to explain things. He seemed like a nice guy—maybe he'll be willing to start over. It was quite an experience to share with someone on a first date."

I smiled. "Rupert and I can tell our children that Mommy dumped a plate of fish on someone's head during her first date with Daddy."

Zoe laughed and linked her arm through mine. "And Auntie Zoe was a witness."

"Uh, Zoe, you're not going to mention this little dating disaster in the article you're writing for *Wow,* are you?"

"Your dating secrets are safe with me," she said.

We swerved out of the way of a teenager on a skateboard going fifty miles an hour down the sidewalk. "You know, Zoe, Giselle *did* get her comeuppance—I mean, look who she's marrying."

She grinned. "Very good point. And Dad will probably leave Giselle in fifteen years for a younger woman! Maybe an eighteen-year-old!"

"A friend of Madeline's," I offered.

We both cracked up. And arms linked, we headed home.

Zoe

This was a Thanksgiving of firsts. For the first time in my life, I was having Thanksgiving dinner without my mother—and with my father and his fiancée. For the first time in ten years, Ally was having Thanksgiving dinner with her father. For the first time ever, Sarah was having Thanksgiving dinner with a sudden distaste for turkey and sudden craving for cheddar cheese, which Zalla had rushed out to buy for her.

And also for the first time, I'd brought a male guest to Thanksgiving. Daniel, looking absolutely irresistible, sat on my left, to my father's right, and pretended great interest in the Zone diet, which my father was waxing on about ad nauseum.

"It's like Barry Sears says, Daniel," my father pontificated, his forkful of dark-meat turkey, skin and all, pointed at Daniel, "*carbohydrates* are the real culprit. Not fat. Carbohydrates. And—"

Oh God. Oh God. Oh God.

My father was halted in midsentence by the sudden appearance of my mother, in a skintight red dress that flounced about her knees, and a long, slinky faux fur leopard-print coat, in the entrance to the dining room.

"Mr. Bart," Zalla said, "Mrs. Judith Solomon is here."

My father smiled. "I see, Zalla, thank you."

"Funny," my mother said, "and both funny ha-ha and funny strange, anyone would think that this woman—" she pointed at Giselle's mother "—was the bride-to-be, and that the four young lovelies at the table were your daughters, and that this little cherub—" she made a kissy face at Madeline "—was your granddaughter."

Giselle smiled pleasantly, as she always did. Daniel squeezed my hand in support, and I squeezed back. *Do not let this turn into World War Three,* I chanted silently.

"So this is the ex-wife?" Giselle's mother asked, forkful of turkey laden with cranberry juice on its way to her mouth. "That's some getup," she added, looking my mom up and down, disapproval smacking her lips.

Again Daniel squeezed my hand.

"Giselle, June, Madeline, this is Judith, Zoe's mother," my father said. If he was the least perturbed by his ex-wife's appearance, you'd never know it.

"Oh, I've met the blushing bride, Bartholomew," my mother said with a smile. "Are you forgetting that she and Zoe used to be friends? Where did they meet? That's right—in a college class, doing what young people their age do."

"Mom—"

"Zoe and I were having lunch one day last year when we ran into Miss Archweller," my mother interrupted. "Amazing how I didn't call her young friend the next day to arrange a date!"

"Mom, enough—"

"No, dear," my mother said, "it's not enough. But I'm

through giving a flying fuck. I came to give you this, Bartholomew." She took off her wedding ring and walked over to my father. We all stared, waiting to see what she would do.

What she did was drop the ring with quite a plop onto my father's pile of no-carbs stuffing.

Giselle's mother gasped. "Look, lady, there's a two-year-old at this table, if you haven't noticed. If you can't watch your dirty mouth, you'll have to leave. In fact, I suggest you *do* leave."

"My dear woman," said my mother, "I've noticed *all* the children at this table. Zoe, honey, I'll call you tomorrow about setting up a lunch. Nice to see you again, Ally and Sarah. You're both looking lovely. You take care now, everyone. Happy Thanksgiving! Toodles."

And then she whished out of the room, Zalla trailing behind her.

My father fished the ring out of his stuffing with his salad fork and set it on his napkin.

"Shall I clean it?" Zalla asked, hurrying back to his side.

"I really don't know," my father said, looking quite perplexed. "All right, everyone—" Big smile. "Let's make a toast! No, I have a better idea. Let's go around the table and say what we're thankful for."

That was my dad. Able to change an uncomfortable subject in ten seconds despite the fact that my mother's wedding ring sat gleaming with goo stuck to it twelve inches from his hand.

"I'll begin," he continued. "I'm grateful that—"

"Dad," I interrupted. "I'll take the ring. Maybe Mom will want it back."

"I doubt it," Ally said.

"Do you believe that woman?" Giselle's mother snapped, shaking her head. "The nerve of some people!

Waltzing in here like she's Elizabeth Taylor. Well, she's not! Who *does* she think she is, that's what I'd like to know!"

"So what's this stuffing made out of, anyway?" asked Sarah, always the diplomat, looking from my father to Giselle. "Vegetables? Soy? It's just delicious!"

"Who she is, Mom, is Zoe's mother," Giselle said very quietly, and all eyes swooped to her. "And she deserves our respect." All of a sudden she jumped up, tears in her eyes, and fled the room.

"Oh, for heaven's sake," my father said. "Now look what happened!"

"Poor Dad—you'll have to deal with your upset fiancée!" Ally singsonged. "Or maybe you'll just finish your carbs-free stuffing first. And it's not delicious—it's absolutely disgusting!"

He looked at Ally with the honest confusion of someone who had no idea what the hell she was talking about. "Ally, is something wrong?"

"Is something *wrong?*" she repeated.

"Yes, is something wrong?" he asked, his blue eyes, recently lifted (well, the eyelids), flashing concern at his eldest daughter.

"Why would anything be wrong?" Ally retorted.

"Well, for starters, you just snapped at me and practically accused me of acting like my upset fiancée was a nuisance to me. As though I would be more interested in my meal than in making sure she was all right."

"That *is* what I think, Dad," Ally said. "But that wouldn't make 'something wrong.' That's just the status quo."

Sarah and I were volleying our gazes back and forth from our father to Ally. It's what we thought too, but neither of us had ever said it aloud.

He wiped his mouth with his napkin, then stood up. "Well, Ally, you would be wrong, honey. Quite wrong," he added as he headed out of the dining room. "Giselle, sweetie?" he called out, running up the staircase.

"Oh, and happy birthday, Ally!" Ally called after him. "I can't believe I forgot to say happy birthday to my own daughter even after Sarah reminded me this morning! But you're still wrong, honey—I'm a very sensitive person!"

Giselle's mother looked at Ally like she was crazy. "The person who should be getting some respect around here is your father, young lady," she snapped at Ally. "That man is a godsend."

Ally chuckled, and June scooped up the toddler and harrumphed out of the room.

"I think I'll skip the Zone birthday cake, if you guys don't mind," Ally said. "I'd really like to just get the hell out of here."

"Why don't you and Sarah come have drinks with me and Zoe?" Daniel asked. "My treat."

"Thanks, Daniel," Ally said, "but I've got a hot date. I might as well be unfashionably early."

I winked at Ally; after some doing, she'd finally convinced Rupert Jones to give her a second chance.

"Sarah, this is the big meet-the-parents, right?" I asked.

She nodded. "I'm a nervous wreck!"

"Good luck to both of you," Zoe said. "Happy Thanksgiving."

And suddenly it was just Daniel, me and a lot of food left at the table.

"Ally was right about the stuffing," Daniel whispered. "It isn't delicious at all."

I laughed. "I'm glad you're here, Daniel," I said, squeezing his hand. "Things can get pretty tense around here."

"Why don't you go *un*tense things," he suggested. "I'll

wait right here. I promise not to eat all the stuffing or whatever's in that bowl," he added, pointing at what I was pretty sure was solid tofu.

"You mean with my father?"

He nodded.

Knock. Don't knock. Knock. Don't knock.

I knocked.

Giselle opened the door. "Your dad's tucking in Madeline," she said.

"Actually, it was you I wanted to see," I said. "I promised Ally I'd walk Mary Jane for her before I left, and I was wondering if you'd like to come with me."

Five minutes later, Giselle and I were walking down Park Avenue, Mary Jane scampering ahead of us and sniffing every tree plot.

For a moment, walking with Giselle felt so natural. During the six or seven weeks of our budding friendship, we'd taken so many walks together.

Mary Jane lifted a leg and the two of us stopped. "I don't really know what to say, Giselle."

"You don't have to say anything, Zoe. I know it's going to take time. And I also know you may never forgive me. I hope you do. But I won't expect it."

"That's the key word," I said. "*Expecting.* My whole life I expected my father to leave my mother, leave us. It was like living in a constant state of worry. And then he leaves after twenty-five years—for you. Do you have any idea how weird that was for me?"

She nodded and her eyes filled with tears. "I can imagine, Zoe."

"Just when I started to think commitment meant something, boom. It's a joke."

"What do you mean?" she asked.

"I never trusted in commitment," I explained. "But then Charlie came along and I started to think it could mean something. And then, boom, my parents' marriage falls apart. Twenty-five years down the drain."

She nodded. "But you know, I don't think it's so much a matter of being able or not able to commit, but of being with the right person. Something stopped you from saying yes to Charlie, and I'm not so sure it had anything to do with your father."

"Maybe, maybe not. It doesn't really matter anymore."

"Yes or no, Zoe," she said. "It doesn't matter because from the looks of things tonight, you are with the right guy. If you'd said yes to Charlie, you wouldn't have been free for Daniel. It's as if something inside you kept saying, 'Don't stop here. This isn't the end of the road.' "

I shrugged. "I don't know."

Mary Jane scampered along, and we resumed walking. "One day, Zoe, I hope we can be friends again. I realize it may never happen, and we might never get past the truce you're willing to agree to, but I really hope so."

"Well, I guess if I want my father in my life, I need to accept that the two of you love each other and are getting married. It's what my mother—"

Interesting. I'd been about to say that it was what my mother needed to accept so that she could move on. I hadn't realized that I was as blocked as she was, that I was holding on to something very heavy that wasn't mine.

I took a deep breath and added that thought to the five hundred others swirling around my mind. For the past couple of weeks, ever since I'd spoken to Sarah's boss on the telephone, I'd been writing the article for *Wow Woman* in my head. Every time I thought I knew exactly what I wanted to say, a *but* came to me and I had to amend what

I'd mentally written. Dating, romance, love, marriage. People trying to have relationships with other people. Why was it so hard?

"Can you just tell me one thing, Giselle?" I asked, and she nodded. "What the hell do you see in my father? Why are you in love with him? I mean, I spent my life waiting for him to leave us for another family. Why would you trust him?"

"That's a good question," she said. "And I guess it's not about trusting him so much as trusting, period. I've been left, Zoe. You know that. My father left my mother when I was very young. Madeline's father wasn't even there *to* leave. But I do trust your father. I trust him because I love him. And I love him because he makes me feel incredibly happy. When I'm with him, I'm the most peaceful I've ever been in my life. I feel the most me. And I feel the most hope. Does that make sense to you?"

The Snoopy dance.

"It's like how I feel about Daniel," I said in so low a voice I wasn't even sure I said it aloud.

"I could tell, you know," she said. "I saw it in the way you look at him, how comfortable you are with him. And I saw it in him too. Where is he, anyway?"

"He's waiting for me at the apartment. I left him in front of the tuxedo bulletin board and the wedding cake bulletin board."

"Why don't you go save him," Giselle said. "I'll finish walking Mary Jane."

"You sure?" I asked.

She took the wad of newspaper and plastic bag and crammed them in her jacket pocket. "So I'll see you at the engagement party on New Year's Eve?"

I nodded. "Let's just hope you don't see my mother there."

She smiled. "Zoe, I don't know your mom very well, but I have a feeling there was a lot of symbolism in her giving back her wedding ring—and on Thanksgiving, no less."

I looked at her and realized she was right. My mother was done fighting.

And it was time for me to stop too.

"For someone who untensed things, you sure do look tense," Daniel said as he unlocked the door to his Upper West Side apartment. "I think I know what you need. Have a seat in the living room. I'll be right there."

As he disappeared into his tiny kitchen and began making quite a racket with bottles, glasses and plates and the sounds of a knife hitting a cutting board, I sat down on the red velvet sofa and realized I was beginning to trust that he did indeed know what I needed. "I'm in your hands," I said.

He poked his head through the kitchen doorway and shot me a grin and wiggled his eyebrows à la Groucho Marx, just as he'd done when I'd arrived in New York almost two months ago.

"You have to hand it to your mom, Zoe," Daniel said as the whoosh of a cork popped. "She knows how to make an entrance, a speech and an exit in less than five minutes."

"Drama's her specialty," I agreed, checking out Daniel's digs. His apartment was a one-bedroom in a brownstone off Columbus Avenue. Guy-furnished, but nice, very Crate & Barrel and Pottery Barn, with a lot of individual touches. He liked the color red.

"Voilà," he said, carrying a silver tray into the living room. There was a bottle of wine, cheese and crackers and a tiny pumpkin pie. "For someone who just had Thanksgiving dinner, I'm starving."

I laughed. "Me too. I've been hungry for almost two months now."

"Open up," he said, waving a cheese-laden cracker in front of my lips. I opened, and he placed the cracker square on the middle of my tongue.

"Sexy," I joked.

He smiled and popped his own cheese 'n' cracker into his mouth, then poured us each a glass of red wine.

"To full stomachs and untensing," he said.

"Hear, hear," I seconded, and we clinked.

As if on cue, Murray, his mutty-looking gray tabby cat, jumped up and sprawled between us, his furry head hanging over the edge. I scratched and the cat purred. "Now there's the definition of untensed."

"Twist away from me," he said, clenching and unclenching his fingers in the air. "I'll give you my special massage."

The moment his hands touched my neck, I tensed.

"Uh, you're supposed to melt, Zoe. Not stiffen."

"I guess I have a lot on my mind," I said. "I'm glad I talked to Giselle, but the conversation left me unsettled. I'm not even close to accepting her in my life."

"You're not supposed to be close. Talking to her was only supposed to be a start. That's what it's all about, Zoe. Starts. They're the hardest."

I nodded and took a sip of my wine, then took my mother's wedding ring out of my pocket and cupped it in my palm. Tiny bits of vegetable stuffing squished.

"Here," Daniel said, "gimme." He took the ring into the kitchen. I heard water running. "Sparkling clean," he said, handing it back to me. "You know, I still had a better meal in the Zone than I would have had you not invited me to your family's Thanksgiving. It would have been just me and Murray, sharing a frozen Swanson's TV turkey dinner, just like the Fonz before Richie insisted he come to the Cunninghams' Thanksgiving feast. That episode was on Nick At Nite last night. Did you see—"

Suddenly I was all over him. I pressed myself against him and kissed him, passionately, and after what I sensed was a second's hesitation, he pressed me back against the couch with his body, squishing Murray, who slithered out from under me and jumped down, and took over.

"I expected you to be a talker," I said to Daniel. I lay naked on his bed, half-covered by a sheet, staring up at the ceiling, relaxed, sated and just slightly, truly slightly, uneasy.

"I know when to shut up," he said, turning on his side to face me. He stroked my cheek with the tip of his finger.

"I don't know what this means," I told him, pointing a finger from him to me. "I don't know how I feel about *anything.*"

"That's okay, Zoe," he said, those warm brown eyes on mine. He kissed my neck and trailed a line of kisses across my collarbone. His silky hair swept against my skin. "You don't have to know how you feel. You just have to *feel.*"

And as Daniel slid on top of me, the weight of him deliciously against me, I took his advice and felt.

Sarah

Once again, I stood in front of a full-length mirror, trying on clothes for a date with Griffen. After-Thanksgiving-dinner-dessert-to-meet-the-future-grandparents-of-my-child meant a reasonably nice outfit. But now, not even the skirt Ally had bought me a size too big fit anymore. What was I going to wear? I slid through the clothes in the closet. I could forget about borrowing any of Ally and Zoe's clothes; they were both skinnier than I was when I wasn't pregnant.

Everything I owned had been flung in frustration onto the floor. I picked up my trusty stretchy long black skirt and squeezed into it. My stomach and my butt puffed out in a very unattractive way. I could forget about formfitting clothes.

There was a knock at the door.

"Come in, I'm decent!" I called, surprised that Ally and Zoe hadn't yet left for their own respective after-Thanksgiving-dinner plans. Both my sisters had learned to knock when the door was closed, since I was self-conscious about undressing in front of them. I still wasn't used to my rounded belly, and no one was seeing it until I got comfy with it.

"Hi, Sarah."

I whipped around. It was Giselle.

"Uh, hi, Giselle."

"Can I come in for a sec?" she asked.

"Of course."

She sat down on the edge of my bed and twisted one of her wild blond curls around her finger for a moment, then let it spring away. "I've already talked to Zoe, and I was hoping to find both you and Ally in here. I wanted to say how sorry I am about what happened at dinner. Thanksgiving is a very special holiday, and I'm just so sorry it got ruined."

"It wasn't ruined, Giselle," I said. "Really. And it certainly wasn't your fault. And c'mon, what is Thanksgiving without family angst?"

She smiled. "Don't I know it. You've gotten to know my mother, after all."

I laughed. "She's something."

"She's something, all right," Giselle said, making a face. "You know, your dad's told me a lot about your mother. She sounds like she was a wonderful person."

I took a deep breath, as I always did when I was suddenly reminded of my mom. "She was. She loved Thanksgiving. She used to cook the most amazing feasts. I don't think she'd deal well with the Zone."

Giselle laughed. "Your dad does it to make me happy. If I can't eat carbs, he doesn't want to eat carbs. That's support."

"Is Dad okay?" I asked. "Ally gave it to him pretty good."

"He's fine," she said.

"Why can't you eat carbs?" I asked.

"Look at me." She held out her arms on either side of her body. "I'm twenty-five pounds overweight and a big girl to begin with."

"But you're gorgeous," I countered. And she was. "You look fabulous. You don't look overweight at all. I, on the other hand—" I grimaced into the mirror "—can't fit into any of my clothes and I have a hot date."

"Pregnancy will do that to a gal," she said with a gentle smile.

I whirled to face her. "How'd *you* know?"

"Once you've been pregnant yourself, you can usually tell. Plus, you can't live with a pregnant person and not know it. Falling asleep in our most uncomfortable chair in the living room at seven-thirty at night is a dead give-away. As is passing up coffee and all alcoholic beverages and asking Zalla if there's any butterscotch syrup to pour on your toast."

"Why do I crave that?" I asked. "Am I crazy?"

"I used to crave pistachio nuts," Giselle said. "That helped me gain fifty-five pounds when I was pregnant."

"Wow. I read a typical weight gain is twenty-five to thirty, but I've already gained ten pounds and I'm only eleven weeks along now."

"Sarah, I hope you know that you can always come talk to me about the pregnancy or babies or the father of the child—anything. I've been through quite a bit in that department. And if you don't want your dad to know you're pregnant, I'll respect that."

"Thanks, Giselle. I really appreciate that. All of it. I'm not ready to tell Dad yet. I'm not sure why, but I'm not."

She nodded. "So for this hot date, why don't we raid my closet? I'm sure the clothes I've put away as my 'when I drop a few pounds' outfit will fit you just fine now."

Very much relieved, I followed Giselle like a happy puppy.

It was amazing how comfortable clothing two sizes up was. And as I waited in the living room for Griffen, who was picking me up at any minute, I didn't have to constantly squirm and tug at the way-too-tight-around-the-ribs-and-tummy black leather jacket that Ally had bought me only six weeks ago for my birthday, because Giselle had brilliantly moved the buttons. I hadn't even known you could do that.

Giselle had dressed me in a stretchy black knee-length skirt that didn't pull on my tummy, a slightly loose, slightly long black cardigan sweater, and with my knee-high black leather boots, I looked both perfectly stylish and perfectly slightly pregnant.

I'd known Giselle was nice, but I hadn't realized how nice. As she'd plucked things from the back of her closet, creating *yes* and *no* piles for me, she'd told me about Gunther, whose real name was Harold, a wannabe rock star whose band put out a record that flopped in the U.S. but was something of a minor hit in Europe, where he'd set up shop. They'd been seeing each other for a few months when Giselle had discovered she was pregnant. Harold-Gunther denied he was the father.

"We only did it a few times," he'd said, like a thirteen-year-old, according to Giselle, and that had been the last she'd seen or heard from him.

I shook my head. "I don't understand how someone could not care about his own baby—baby-to-be," I said as Giselle had nixed a ruffly sheer shirt with a camisole under it. The hem of the camisole ended right above my belly, drawing attention to it. "Griffen doesn't want anything to do with the baby," I confided in her, and then I burst into tears and she'd pulled me into a hug.

"If he doesn't want anything to do with you or the baby, then why is he having you meet his parents—on such a major holiday, no less?" Giselle asked.

That was a good point, and one that kept me company until Griffen rang the doorbell at eight o'clock.

I pulled open the door, and there he was, looking gorgeous and nervous. He smiled somewhat awkwardly at me, asked if I was ready, and off we went, walking to the subway in near-silence, except to talk about whether we liked white- or dark-meat turkey better, how he didn't like cranberry sauce because he'd grown up mistaking it for horseradish, and whether or not we thought it impolite for men to disappear into the living room with their plates midway through dinner for football, which he'd reported that his father and uncle had done this afternoon (we both agreed it most certainly was rude). As we headed down the steps into the subway station, he took my hand and said, "Careful," and his hand felt foreign instead of comforting.

Our train came in as we reached the track, and we sat down on the hard orange seats, Griffen's thigh against mine, which felt comforting instead of foreign.

Pregnant women are horny! said *But I Don't Know How To Be Pregnant!* That was one of the few things about pregnancy I did know—or learned fast. I'd spent many a night thinking about Griffen, about the nights we'd spent together.

He opened his knapsack and took out a very large, very smushed red gift bag. "Here," he said, handing it to me. "For you."

Surprised, I took the bag and set it on my lap. This time

there was white tissue paper puffing out. "Is Thanksgiving a gift-giving holiday in the Maxwell family?"

"Hardly," he said. "I just wanted to get you a little something. I didn't know which one to get you, so I got them all."

I pulled out *What To Expect When You're Expecting, The Girlfriends' Guide To Pregnancy* and *But I Don't Know How To Be Pregnant!*

"I hope you don't have any of these already," he added. "I couldn't believe how many books on pregnancy there were at Barnes & Noble. I figured I had a good chance of getting you some you didn't have."

I couldn't hold back the laugh. "Nope, I don't have a one of these."

"Good." He smiled at me, somewhat nervously. "You're looking really good, Sarah. Are you feeling okay?"

"Yeah, and thanks. You look good too, Griffen."

And he did. So good.

"I bought these for myself," he said, and pulled out of his backpack, *The Guy's Guide to Fatherhood, Fatherhood 101* and *My Boys Can Swim!* "I've started reading this one," he said, flipping through *Guy's Guide.* "Did you know that newborn babies sleep twenty hours out of the day? Or that babies go through eight to ten diapers a day?"

"You *have* been reading," I said. "Me too."

"A lot of it sounds pretty scary. Colic, for instance."

I nodded. "But it lasts for only three months. Though that probably feels like forever at the time."

"I've been reading up on everything a baby needs," Griffen said. "For the first day alone, you need a ton of stuff, like a car seat and a crib or bassinet and enough diapers and clothes."

Okay. Hold on here. "Griffen, I'm a little confused. I

thought you didn't want any part of this," I said. "Have you changed your mind?"

The train screeched to a stop. "This is us," he said, taking my hand.

Saved by the stop. My question was on the tip of my tongue, but the station was too noisy for us to talk.

"Did you like growing up in the city?" he asked me as we emerged out of the station and into the cold night air. "I did and didn't. I had Prospect Park right there—" he pointed "—but it's not having woods to play in. That'd be nice for a kid."

I glanced at him. I sensed I should just let him talk, and he did, telling me all about Park Slope and how it used to be a normal neighborhood but had turned into million-dollar brownstones and even more expensive than Manhattan. Just when I couldn't take it any longer and was about to repeat my question, we arrived at his parents' house, a two-family on the outskirts of Park Slope in a working-class neighborhood. The Maxwells occupied the bottom floor and two twentysomethings lived upstairs and paid way too much rent, according to Griffen, which provided his parents with a nice income now that his accountant father was retired.

"Do I look okay?" I asked him on the top step to the house as he pulled open the storm door.

He turned to look at me, really look at me, and after a moment said, "You look great, Sarah. You really do. Pregnancy glow and all that, I guess. Not that you didn't look good before too, I mean."

I smiled. "Thanks. You look good too, Griffen."

And he did. Very good. The contrast of his black leather jacket with his silky light blond hair…those pale brown eyes, that Roman nose, those lips….

"Look, before we go in, maybe I should warn you

about my parents," Griffen said. "They're not exactly thrilled that you're pregnant."

"You're telling me this now?" I asked. "So I can have, what, two seconds to prepare for the fact that your parents hate me?"

"No, no, no—it's not that bad," he rushed to say. "They're just old-fashioned. It's more a 'not married' thing than anything else."

"Phew," I said. "You had me worried there for a moment. At least your parents and I will have something in common."

He stared at me with the same someone-just-punched-me-in-the-stomach expression as he had when I told him I was pregnant. "Are you kidding or not?" he asked. "I'm not sure."

Could he look any more nervous and uncomfortable? What was I, a leper?

"Um, I guess," I said.

He eyed me, clearly trying to figure out whether the I guess went to "I'm kidding" or "Not," then gave up and rang the bell.

"Why doesn't he use his key?" I heard a grumpy-voiced man call out. "Did he lose it?"

"I don't know, Bert. How am I supposed to know?" responded a grumpy-voiced woman.

Oh God. Oh God. Oh God. I knew this type. These were not going to be the polite-let's-have-tea-and-madeleines-and-not-even-bring-up-the-fact-that-you're-pregnant parents that I'd expected. These were in-your-face, ask-you-questions kind of people.

The door opened, and a heavyset fiftyish woman with Griffen's blond hair opened the door. A heavyset, fifty-ish man was behind her, smoking a cigar.

"Dad, the cigar—" Griffen said, gesturing to me.

"What?" his father asked.

"Bert, put out the cigar. The girl's pregnant!"

Bert grumbled and disappeared down the hall.

"Mom, this is Sarah, Sarah, this is my mother, Marlene Maxwell."

Marlene Maxwell. It must have been quite a glamorous name in her day.

Marlene Maxwell looked me full in the face, and after the nice-to-meechas, led us into a living room I didn't expect. Pale yellow leather couch and matching loveseat, with chrome legs and a glass coffee table, pale yellow filmy drapes shot with white silk string, blond wood bookcases, wall to ceiling. The faces and voices didn't match the furniture.

I sat on the yellow leather loveseat and Griffen sat down next to me. His mother sat across from me on the sofa, and her husband came rushing into the room, smelling like cigars.

"In my day, you could smoke in the house with a pregnant woman and babies," Mr. Maxwell said.

"Things were *very* different in our day," Mrs. Maxwell said to her husband with a none-too-hidden harrumph in her expression.

"You have a lovely home," I said to change the subject. That and because I was supposed to say it.

"Thank you, dear," Mrs. Maxwell said, folding her hands on her lap. Then she unfolded them, then folded them.

It was so strange that I made her nervous. *I* was the one who was supposed to be nervous. And I was. The house was warm, and as I was always overheated anyway, my cleavage was beaded with sweat. So much for the spritz of Gucci Envy that Giselle had given me for good luck.

Mrs. Maxwell handed me a plate of pumpkin pie, and

I did what I always did when nervous and handed food: I started stuffing my face.

"You're very pretty, dear," Mrs. Maxwell said. "Isn't she, Bert?"

"What?" Mr. Maxwell said, eating his pie as though he hadn't eaten in days.

"Never mind," Mrs. Maxwell said, smoothing her skirt over her knees. "So, Sarah, how far along are you, dear?"

"Um, thank you," I said, "for the compliment. And I'm twelve weeks now. I can't believe the first trimester is over. I'm still not quite used to the idea of being pregnant."

"Well, I suppose you're out of the danger zone," Mrs. Maxwell said with a sigh.

Was she unhappy about that?

"In my day, you didn't announce a pregnancy until you were at least three months along," she added.

"I don't understand that," Griffen said. "If, God forbid, Sarah had lost the baby, wouldn't she want sympathy?"

God forbid? Interesting.

"You're carrying high," Mrs. Maxwell said, effectively changing the subject. "It's a girl."

"Mom, she's not even showing," Griffen said, smiling at me and shaking his head.

Mrs. Maxwell smacked her lips. "She's showing a little. A mother knows. It's a girl. Girls are harder to raise than boys."

"Well, whatever sex the baby is, I'll be thrilled," I said.

"All that matters is that the baby's healthy," Griffen added. "And according to the doctor at Sarah's ultrasound, all is well. Here," he said, handing his mother the ultrasound photo.

Mrs. Maxwell looked at the picture, turning it upside

down and sideways the way Zoe had. "I just can't believe this," she said, and burst into tears.

"Mom?" Griffen said. "Are you okay?"

"I just don't understand this," she said. "She's going to have a baby, but you're not even dating?"

"We're just at a funny point," Griffen said. "I found out that Sarah was pregnant and I needed some time to think, so we haven't been seeing each other."

A funny point?

Silence.

"Are you getting back together? Are you getting married?" she asked. "You make such a lovely couple, don't they, Bert?"

"What?" Mr. Maxwell asked, staring at his stubbed out cigar. "Yes, the pie was very good."

Mrs. Maxwell rolled her eyes, then got up and walked to the windows. She let out a deep breath. "Well, what's done is done. There's no sense in being upset about it."

"Mom..." Griffen said.

"I'm just saying that I'm coming around to the idea," Mrs. Maxwell continued. "At least there's no stigma in a child being illegitimate. Years ago there was, but now, what with all the sex and violence on television, anything goes."

"First of all, Mom," Griffen said, "no one uses the word *illegitimate* anymore. There's nothing illegitimate about a baby having parents who aren't married."

"And how would you know, Griffen?" Mrs. Maxwell asked. "Do you have unmarried parents? How about you, Sarah?"

"Mom, I thought you wanted to meet Sarah. That's why I brought her here. If you want to interrogate her or make her uncomfortable or insult her, we'll leave."

"Oh, so now I don't get to see my grandchild?" she

said, her voice rising. "Do you hear this, Bert? They're going to keep the baby from us."

As Griffen shook his head in utter amazement, I was struck with the thought that his mother was much worse than my father. Perhaps clueless and always jovial was better than crazy.

"Marlene, no one said anything about the grandchild," Mr. Maxwell said. "Do you see a baby here?"

"Always siding against me," Mrs. Maxwell snapped at her husband.

"Mom, there's nothing to side against. No one's keeping the baby from anyone. We're here so that you two and Sarah can get to know each other, that's all."

"Grandparents have rights," Mrs. Maxwell said. "There was a case on television, on *Law and Order,* I think it was, about this terrible woman who didn't like her mother-in-law, and the court gave the grandmother visitation rights."

"So you want this baby in your life even though it's *illegitimate?*" Griffen asked with a wink at me.

"Of course I do! This is my grandchild! My first. Oh, I do hope the baby gets your eyes, Sarah. Such lovely blue eyes. Both my boys got their father's brown eyes. Not that there's anything wrong with your eyes, dear," she added to Mr. Maxwell, who was busily scraping the last bite of pie off his plate.

"What?" Mr. Maxwell asked.

"Nothing, dear," his wife said. "Have another slice of pie."

And as Mrs. Maxwell heaped another slice of pumpkin pie on her husband's plate and Griffen smiled at me, I was absolutely sure his family just might be almost as neurotic as mine.

★ ★ ★

"Make yourself comfortable," Griffen said as we walked into his apartment. He turned on a lamp, and the living room I spent so much time in between August and October lit up before me. "Let's see...I have wine, Coke, coffee—everything you can't have," he added as he opened and closed cabinets and the refrigerator. "I'll run out and get you something."

"Griffen, it's Thanksgiving. Everything's closed. And water is just fine. You have that, don't you?"

He nodded. "That I have."

I sat down on his sofa and hugged a throw pillow against me. He came into the living room with two glasses of water and sat down next to me. Our thighs were touching.

"It's going to take them a while to get used to it," Griffen said.

"That's to be expected," I said. "You've known for six weeks now and you're still not used to it."

He took a deep breath and stood up and paced for a minute, then sat back down. "I'm sorry, Sarah. I am really, really sorry." And all of a sudden, he burst into tears. He covered his face with his hands and cried.

"Griffen, it's okay," I said, placing my hand on his shoulder. "It's okay."

He dropped his hands on his thighs and leaned his head back against the back of the couch, letting out another deep breath. "God, I'm an asshole. An idiot."

"Griffen, talk to me," I said.

He turned to face me. "I was scared out of my mind, Sarah. I still am. But the way I just bailed on you when you told me—" He covered his face with his hands again. "And the things I said to you that day in the coffee bar—

I don't even know how to apologize for that. What could I possibly say to make up for that?"

"Griffen, it's okay, really," I said. "I've been fine. I am fine."

And I was. I wasn't a mess. I wasn't falling apart.

"I need you to know that I haven't just been going on with my life as though you're not pregnant, Sarah. I didn't just walk away and wash my hands. It wasn't like that."

"What was it like?" I asked.

"You, the baby, it's all I've been thinking about. What it means. What it's going to mean. How I feel."

"And how do you feel?" I asked.

"I don't know. I don't even know what I'm thinking about. I just know that I've missed you, Sarah. And that I'm scared to death of being a father."

"It's okay to be scared, Griffen. I sort of still am too."

"I've lain awake nights thinking about you walking around with this," he said, "going through this alone—"

"I'm not alone," I said. "I have my family. My sisters have been a great support system."

As I said it, I realized how much I meant it. I *didn't* feel alone anymore. My sisters *were* a great support system. I didn't know what I would have done without them this past month.

"I'm glad they were there for you," he said. "And I'm so sorry I wasn't. If you'll let me, I'd like to start being there."

"Meaning?" I asked.

"Meaning I don't know. I've thought a lot about what you said about me being immature, that the situation is what it is. Just like you need to step up to face that your life is going to change, so do I."

"But, Griffen, I'm happy about the baby. I *love* the baby. I *want* the baby. I needed to face the reality that my life is going to change and that I might very well be a single mother, but I never had to accept that I'm going to have a baby. Do you know what I mean? You were all set to break up with me when you thought I was pressing you for a *commitment,*" I reminded him.

"I know," he said. "But I also didn't know you were pregnant."

"So now that you do, now that you've *digested,* you suddenly want me?"

He took a deep breath. "Honestly, I don't know what I want. That's the truth."

"So, I'm here because…?"

"Because you *are* pregnant with my child. Because I do have feelings for you."

"What feelings?" I asked. "Are you saying you want to be friends? Are you saying you want us to continue dating? Are you saying you want to get married? What?"

"Sarah, all I know is that I like you—a lot," he said. "I know I was having a great time getting to know you. I know I find you intelligent, funny, warm, sweet and interesting. I know I like being with you, hearing what you think."

"So you want to be friends," I said.

He leaned close to me and kissed me on the lips. "I've wanted to do that since I picked you up a few hours ago."

"So you want to be more than friends," I said. "I don't think I'll make the best fuck buddy in my condition, Griffen."

"Sarah, that's not what I'm saying."

"What *are* you saying?" I snapped. "Because you're going to need to be clear. I'm pregnant, Griffen. I'm having a baby. I'm not looking for uncertainties right now. If you want a relationship with me, great. If you're not sure of anything, then I'd prefer we were simply friends."

"I am sure of a few things, Sarah," he said. "I'm sure

that I have strong feelings. I'm sure that I can be a good father to our baby. I just think that we need to get to know each other in this new context. Before, we were just seeing each other a couple times a week, going to the movies, having fun. Now, we're going to be someone's parents. We have a lot of work to do, Sarah. I think we can do it together. I'm just saying that everything is different and we need to start all over again."

I took his hand and placed it on top of my belly. He leaned his head on my shoulder, and we sat like that for a very long time.

"So, Ally, how about a nightcap?" Rupert asked as we left Gastronomica.

"Sounds great," I cooed in my Samantha Jones voice.

He squeezed my hand. "And I just happen to have a great bottle of Chianti and some incredible smoked Brie. Unless you'd prefer to go to your place."

My place was a little crowded at the moment with two sisters and a dog. And after that scene with my father at the table, I doubted that he'd want to find me fooling around with a date in his living room. *Do not think about your father. Do not think about family fights. Do not think about Andrew. Do not think. Just go with the flow.*

That was very good advice-to-self, especially because it was my birthday, which my father had forgotten until this morning, when Sarah had asked him if he and Giselle would like a special Zone cake made out of God knows what so he could join in the festivities for my birthday. *"It's Ally's birthday?"* I'd heard him ask. *"That's right. How could I forget? It's always on Thanksgiving!"*

Uh, no it's not, Dad. Unless Thanksgiving is always on November twenty-second, you turkey.

Speaking of food, to get Rupert to agree to this second date, I'd had to promise twice on the telephone that no turkeys, cranberry sauce, stuffing or pumpkin pie would land on anyone's head. I'd been so excited about the date, a birthday date for me, no less, that I'd spent an hour dressing two hours in advance, praying during the dinner from hell that I wouldn't spill cranberry sauce on my sweater. I'd originally planned to wear a sexy little black dress, but Zoe had shaken her head and said jeans and a sweater, which I couldn't imagine wearing on a date, but Zoe insisted it was after-Thanksgiving-dinner wear. I arrived at the café in my vintage Levi's, a cream V-neck cashmere sweater, and a pair of low-heeled suede boots, and Rupert was wearing the same thing, only his boots were leather and a white T-shirt peeked out of his V-neck.

There was something about wearing the exact same outfit that broke the ice, and in moments we were clinking to Thanksgiving and new beginnings and swapping family-dinner horror stories. (Mine won worst story, by the way.) And suddenly it was nearing midnight, pumpkin hour for no reason at all since we both had the next day off, but you couldn't have more than two glasses of wine on a date without worrying Mr. Potential that you were a major lush. (This, per Zoe and the stupid book I was reading on hooking a man.) And so I suggested we get going, which per both again the woman was always wise to initiate. And suddenly I was invited for a nightcap. Score one for Zoe and the book. Actually, score a few for Zoe.

Rupert's apartment was a small one-bedroom in a Tribeca skyscraper. Decor consisted of a black leather couch, black leather chair, black, white, and red print rug and a glass coffee table. A white roller shade covered the windows. The tiny galley kitchen contained a microwave, a coffeemaker and a freezer full of frozen food (discovered during my grand tour of the apartment). In the bedroom were a bed, also black and white, a dresser and a treadmill, which took up almost as much room as the bed.

"The furniture I collected over the years remained in the house," Rupert said, "which remains with the wife, so I bought some guylike stuff and that was that."

"I like it," I said. *And I like you....*

As Rupert brought over the Brie and a plate of crackers and the wine, I knew I was going to sleep with him.

It's my birthday and I'll have sex if I want to, sex if I want to, sex if I want to...

He sat, he poured and I pounced. I put my hand directly on the zipper of his jeans and looked him in the eye.

He jumped in his seat, spilling the glass of wine in his hand. "That was unexpected," he said.

I dabbed at the tiny drops of wine on his thighs with the napkins, pressing with a bit more pressure the closer I got to his zipper.

"But not unwanted," I cooed, leaning close.

"Ally, why don't we have some wine, talk a bit."

"Because I have a better idea," I said, and straddled him. I felt him stiffen, in *every* area, and pressed my chest against his. "Was there something you wanted to say?" I breathed in his ear.

"Actually, there is," he said, gently pushing my shoulder away from him. "I don't think you're ready for this. I don't think *we're* ready for this."

I felt my cheeks burning. "You're not attracted to me?"

"That's not it," he replied. "I said that I don't think *we're* ready, not that I'm not interested."

Oh God. Why was I so bad at this? Why couldn't I figure out how to date someone? Why did I need my twenty-six-year-old sister to dress me and tell me how to behave?

"Maybe I should just go," I said. *You're an idiot, Ally! An idiot!*

"Maybe you should have a glass of wine," he said. "And a piece of this incredible cheese."

"Look, Rupert, maybe I'm just not ready to date, period. I'm clearly a big washout—" I grabbed my jacket and my purse and stood "—so if it's all the same to you, which I'm sure it is, I'd really just like to slink home."

"Actually, it's not all the same to me, sorry. Mmm!" he said, as he slipped a sliver of cheese in his mouth. "Deeelicious."

I gnawed my lower lip. Should I stay or should I go now? I started singing in my head.

"I just don't know how to recover from that embarrassing little episode," I confessed.

"So, Ally, seen any good movies lately?" he asked, patting the cushion next to him. "You don't strike me as a sports fan, or I would have said, 'How about those Mets!'"

"Actually, people say that when they want to change the subject, not start a conversation," I pointed out.

"Well, I'm trying to do both," he said, handing me a glass of wine.

Oh, what the hell. Things couldn't get any worse, could they? I took the wine and sat down. He smiled. "I did see a movie recently, Rupert. A serial horror film about a woman who caught her husband cheating on her with her Pilates instructor, right in her own backyard, literally, mind you."

"That does sound scary," he said. "What happens next?"

"Well, the day after, when she came home to confront

him, she found an insurance claim form for a vasectomy in her husband's desk, when she thought they were trying to have the baby she wanted so much."

"Oh, Ally," he said with such feeling that tears welled up in my eyes.

"And so this woman," I continued, "her life as she knew it a lie, goes sort of temporarily insane."

"And dumps a plate of food on her husband's girlfriend's head?"

I smiled. "You've seen this movie!"

He nodded. "That part was almost funny, actually."

"In fact, the woman was on a first date with a wonderful man when she did that. Someone kind and smart and sweet and good-looking. Someone she could really talk to. She really regrets that this guy saw her at her worst."

"Well, then she can only go up from there," he said.

I smiled again. "Actually, the film gets scarier. Then she actually gets this wonderful man to agree to a second date, and what does she do? She forces herself on him."

"This is just my opinion, Ally, but I got the sense he enjoyed that little moment."

"Really?" I asked.

He nodded. "That's what's so great about the movies. Different people see totally different things, and afterward you can discuss it all quite reasonably and passionately and logically."

"Jeez, what does a psycho woman have to do to get you to never want to see her again?" I asked.

"She'd have to turn into my soon-to-be-ex-wife."

I laughed and he slipped a Brie-laden cracker between my lips.

"Today's my birthday," I told him, mouth full.

"Happy birthday," he said and kissed me on the lips. "Mmm, those cracker crumbs on our lips are pretty tasty."

"Then maybe you should have some more," I said.

He tipped my chin up with his hand and kissed me again, gently, then he pulled back. "Just a sec," he said. "I'll be right back."

He disappeared into his bedroom and returned with a short red candle on a glass dish. He lit it. "Make a wish, Ally."

I smiled and thought for a second and made my wish. And then I blew out the candle.

The next morning I went to visit my house. That was Rupert's suggestion, actually. After gorging on cheese and switching from wine to good old Coca-Cola, we talked until two in the morning about everything from marriage and separation to hopes and dreams to children to work, and in the end agreed that despite how crazy things could seem, everything would be all right.

I was beginning to believe that. I was also beginning to believe that the reason I'd clung to my marriage, been so oblivious, was because I'd felt so alone in the world. My mother was dead, my father was clueless and didn't know his firstborn child's birthday, my sister Sarah lived in another universe and my half sister Zoe basically didn't exist.

My clueless father aside, I wasn't alone. Sarah didn't so much live in another universe as she was simply a different person than I was. Younger and different. And Zoe did exist—much to my benefit. I'd lost a marriage and a dream and gained two sisters I didn't even know I had.

"And you haven't lost the dream to have a baby," Rupert had said last night. "Babies, I should say. You're still capable of having children, Ally. And if you aren't or if having a child with a man you're romantically involved with simply doesn't come to be, there are alternatives."

Alternatives. That seemed to be the key word to the future. Alternative ways of thinking, of behaving, of being.

It was what made me knock on my father's den door this morning to apologize for last night. The moments the words "I'm sorry" were out of my mouth, my father pulled me into a hug.

He sat down on the leather sofa and patted the cushion next to him. "Ally, didn't you see the movie *Love Story?*" he asked, tucking a piece of my hair behind my ear. "Love means never having to say you're sorry."

Oh Lord. "Dad, you don't really believe that, do you?" I said, sitting down next to him. "I mean, it's the stupidest thing I've ever heard. In fact, I believe that's what Candice Bergen said in the sequel."

He laughed. "I don't believe it either. I know there are sorries to be felt and said. But I do like to just forgive and forget and put things behind me and move on. That's what keeps a person happy, don't you think?"

"Honestly, Dad, I don't know. No, I do know. And the answer is *no.* I don't think that's what keeps a person happy. I think talking things out is what keeps a person happy."

"Sometimes, though, Ally, talking is just talk."

What did that mean? "Dad, haven't you been curious as to why your three adult daughters are living in your house?"

"Of course, Ally. But I respect your privacy."

"Or you're not really interested," I said. "I'll go with 'not interested.'"

"Sweetheart, I'm always interested. I guess I'm the type of person who figures that you'd come to me if you wanted to talk to me. If you wanted me to know why you were here, you'd tell me. If not, then I want you to feel comfortable knowing you're always welcome, for as long as you want, and have a place to be where no one's pestering you."

It was true that his lack of questions, lack of prying, had been a huge plus.

"Honey, when you stayed longer than a week, I knew there was trouble in your marriage. I know all about that subject."

I stood up and walked to the window and toyed with the curtain. "You know about *leaving,* Dad. That's different."

"Ally, I didn't just walk out on a great marriage to your mom. It wasn't like that."

"What was it like?" I asked. "She loved you and you left."

"We did love each other, Al, that's true. But there were still problems. There always were, from the beginning. We thought being in love would conquer all, but it didn't."

I dropped down on the sofa again and leaned my head back. "I thought the same thing with Andrew. I don't even really know when we fell out of love. I was so focused on having a baby that nothing else mattered to me. I didn't even realize I didn't love him until—" I took a deep breath. "I caught him cheating on me. That's what happened."

He pulled me close against his side. "I'm sorry, Ally. I'm very sorry."

"I was too. But I'm getting over it, slowly but surely, and picking up my life."

"Of that I have no doubt. Your mom would be so proud of you, Ally. You do know that, don't you?"

I leaned my head on his shoulder for the first time since I was very little and we sat like that for a long while, until Mary Jane's barks threatened to wake up Madeline. And as we sat, I realized that I loved my father and always had.

I didn't like him; I never had and I probably never would, but I could love him anyway.

"I think it's time for me to go, Dad," I said. "I mean, go-go. Go house-hunting. I'm ready to move on."

He smiled. "I never liked Andrew Sharp. Not thirteen years ago and not now."

"Really?" I asked. "You always acted like you adored him. Slapping him on the back, engaging him in conversations about the stock market."

"For you, Ally. Because you liked him, and that was enough for me."

"But why pretend?" I asked. "Why not just avoid him? Why the act?"

"How would you have felt then?"

"I probably would have been angry," I said.

"And you wouldn't call or come visit," he said. "And then how would I have felt?"

"Honestly, Dad, I wouldn't have thought you'd notice or care."

"You really think I'm a shit, don't you?" he asked.

"I *used* to think you were a shit," I corrected. "Now, I see everything differently. Including myself. Being here these past six weeks has done me a world of good."

"I'm glad, Ally. Because no matter what, if I forget your birthday, if I don't ask questions, if I don't know the first thing about what's going on with you, I love you."

I still wasn't sure how to reconcile the three, but I was beginning to realize that it didn't have to be a condition. "I love you too, Dad," I said.

The drive from the city to Great Neck had been bumper-to-bumper as usual, but for once I hadn't been in a rush. I listened to the radio and sang along. I thought about Rupert. I thought about Sarah, about Zoe. I thought about the conversation with my father. I thought about work, about that idiot Funwell. And instead of filling with rage, I laughed as the image of Funwell, his jowly neck and roly-poly body, came into mind. To hell with Funwell. To hell with Andrew. And to hell with rushing.

Now, as I pulled into the driveway of the house I had shared with Andrew for eleven years, Tara and her husband and baby Allison were just coming out their front door.

"I've been gone for what, six weeks?" I called out as I headed over to say hello. "And Allison has already changed so much!" Allison smiled wide to reveal a sharp-looking little tooth in her lower gums. "I've missed you, sweetie."

"Oh, shoot," Tara said. "Ally, would you mind holding her for a second? I forgot her bottle."

The moment Allison was in my arms, I knew without a doubt that I would have a child. That I wanted a precious bundle in my arms for the rest of my life. Whether that bundle was my own baby or a five-year-old from a foster home or another country didn't seem to matter. What I wanted had been put into perspective, somehow.

It was what I'd wished for last night, before I'd blown out the candle. A child of my own.

"I'll take her, Ally," Allison's father said. "I want to get her settled in the car seat so we can take off."

And as he took the baby, I realized that my heart was still full instead of feeling hollow with the emptiness that usually followed whenever it was time to give Allison back.

And then I went into the house, happy with the knowledge that Andrew and This Valerie Person were probably stuck on Mrs. Sharp's green plastic-covered couch in

Cincinnati, clutching their stomachs in pain over her awful cooking and personality.

And then I began to pack what was mine.

"I completely disagree with you," Astrid O'Connor said, handing me back my article with a snap of her wrist. "I've starred in the margins where I think you're quite wrong."

My article was covered in little red stars.

"First of all, Zoe, the title is awful," she said, leaning back in her leather chair behind her desk. "'The Dating Diva Was a Dating Dope'? I don't think so. All wrong." She shook her head, so delicately it barely moved, and folded her hands on the desk in front of her. She reminded me of the teacher's pet in elementary school.

"But it's the truth," I said. "I was a dating dope and I gave dopey advice."

"That's where we disagree," she said. "You gave *excellent* advice. You'd like to tell our readership, however, that you're going to give them *dopey* advice."

I leaned back in my chair and glanced at my article. All four pages were marked up with red stars and *absolutely not!* every second line. "I have no idea what you mean, Ms. O'Connor."

She shook her head again and pressed her intercom. "Sherry, come in here for a moment, and collect Sarah and Diana too."

Uh-oh. Was she bringing an audience for a vetting session of my article?

In moments, Sarah and two other young women entered and stood by the door, their arms crossed over their chests. They all looked so nervous. I couldn't imagine working in this kind of environment every day with a witch like Astrid for a boss. I waited for Astrid to say something—we all waited—but she was staring at one of the staffer's shoes. And staring. And staring. The staffer stepped back behind Sarah until she hit the wall and banged against it. Astrid then turned her attention to me.

"I've called you all here because I'd like you to listen to Ms. Solomon's article on dating. After she reads it, I'd like your opinions on how you feel *Wow*'s readership will respond." She smiled, a satisfied, smug smile and nodded at me—once, as though she were sending me to my death.

Was this school? Read aloud? Part of me wanted to storm out of her office and tell her to go blow. The other half wanted to defend my article and get it published. A monthly column was my ticket to grad school.

"We're waiting, Zoe," Astrid said.

I cleared my throat. "The Dating Diva was a Dating Dope," I began, reading my headline. "My job is to critique people's dates. To tell men and women exactly what they're doing wrong. Why that hottie didn't call for a second date. Why she won't return his calls. Why he suddenly remembered a dentist appointment a half hour into dinner. Let me give you a scenario. Jill and Joe are at a café for a first date. Jill is talking nonstop about her job as a customer service representative for a credit card company. Joe is squirming, staring at his watch, but Jill doesn't notice. She keeps talking. Joe makes an excuse to leave. Jill wonders what she did wrong to turn him off. The Dating Diva would have told Jill to talk less, listen more. To learn social signals of boredom. To give good date. But that was before I realized that Jill shouldn't have to change to appeal to anyone. If Jill is passionate about her job and wants to talk about it all night, I'm sure there's a guy out there who wants to listen—"

One of the staffers started clapping. "I'm so sorry for interrupting!" she said. "But that is so awesome! The same thing happened to me last Saturday night!"

Astrid stared at the young woman. "Why don't you elaborate, Diana."

"Well, I was on a first date with this really cute guy who I met at a bar, and I was telling him all about my job here at *Wow,* how much I loved the magazine, how excited I was when I got my first chance to write an article since I'm only an assistant, how much I've learned in only six months out of college, and John—that's his name—he listened for about five seconds, and then his attention started wandering. Instead of asking me questions or even breaking in to tell me about *his* job, he just checked out the people in the restaurant, stared at his watch, even flagged down the waiter to order another beer."

"Well, if he ordered another beer, Diana," Astrid said, "he clearly wanted to prolong the date. That should have been a sure signal to you that he wasn't bored in the least."

"I don't know about that, Ms. O'Connor," I said.

Four pairs of eyes swooped to me. Apparently, no one ever contradicted the great Astrid O'Connor.

"You can't really know what's going on in another person's mind," I explained. "Maybe he was interested. Maybe he's an alcoholic. All that really matters is how Diana felt while she was talking about something important to her, something she feels passionately about, while he was more interested in the restaurant's wallpaper and getting a drink."

"Diana, we did a piece in last February's *Wow* about signs that your boyfriend may have a drinking problem," Astrid said. "I think you should read it. You don't want to get involved with a man with a drinking problem, no matter how cute he is."

"Um, Astrid, I didn't say he was an alcoholic," Diana pointed out.

"Dear, you've just touched on one of the first hallmarks of those with drinking problems—denial," Astrid said, tapping her pencil against the desk. "All right, Zoe, continue, please."

Sarah rolled her eyes and shook her head with a devilish smile. I knew what she was thinking and I agreed: I could walk out. I could send the article to the other women's magazines. But I wanted it published in *Wow* solely because Astrid *didn't* agree with my point of view. I wanted her to suck it up. And so I read on, to more cheers and claps from Sarah and her co-workers.

"Well, Zoe," Astrid said when I finished, "I've always thought the young women who work for *Wow* reflect the readership, as they come from all walks of life, from all parts of the country. Since you've managed to engage them with your point of view, I've decided to run the piece as is."

"As is, Ms. O'Connor," I said. "That's the whole point."

19

Sarah

Perhaps choosing the week before Christmas to shop for my baby registry wasn't my most brilliant idea. Baby Bonanza was packed. With pregnant women. With bored and miserable-looking men. With little kids running wild pushing kid-sized shopping carts. With overworked and exhausted-looking salespeople.

"Griffen, we can come back next month," I said, staring at the three-page checklist of everything a new baby needed that I received at the registry counter. "I figure even walking into Baby Bonanza is tough on a guy, let alone during Christmastime."

"No, no," Griffen said, a brave smile on his gorgeous face. "I'm ready. And see, the store is smart, they give the guy something to play with." He aimed the registry gun at me.

I laughed. "Okay, you're a trouper. Let's start with the stroller department."

There were at least fifty or sixty strollers. And for some reason, they were all navy blue.

Ten minutes later, I'd narrowed my choice down to twenty of them.

"Which do you think, Griffen?" I asked.

He shrugged.

"Let's check one of the books," I said, and pulled *But I Don't Know How To Be Pregnant!* out of my tote bag. "Aha! This says that urban dwellers need a sturdy stroller, like that one," I said, pointing. "But to beware buying one too heavy or big because you'll need to schlep it into a taxi and crowded shops and restaurants and—"

Griffen adopted the expression I usually reserved for documentaries about war or sports, and I read silently. He began aiming the registry gun at various items and posing like a cop about to break down a door.

Fifteen minutes later, I'd narrowed it down to three strollers.

A half hour later, I'd made my choice. "Okay, Griffen, you can zap at this one."

"Oh, I wouldn't get that one," said a very pregnant woman wheeling a toddler in a stroller. "It won't fit through supermarket checkout aisles."

The last time I shopped in a supermarket was when I made dinner for Griffen a week into our relationship (the one week I wasn't pregnant)! I tended to eat out or order in. I explained this to the woman, and she laughed.

She added a cackle. "Honey, you're in for a rude awakening," she said before wheeling herself away.

"What did she mean by that?" Griffen asked.

"I guess mothers shop in supermarkets more than single people," I said.

"Well, it'll still be just you," he said, "So, it won't really—"

He very smartly shut the hell up. But I'd heard him loud and clear. It would be just me. He was here, he had been here for the past three weeks, but he was here to a point.

Since Thanksgiving night, Griffen and I got together two or three times a week, after work and on a weekend afternoon. What he was doing with his weekend nights, I had no idea. I'd meet him at his place, and he'd order in anything I craved, which for the past two weeks had been Pad Thai and chicken burritos. And then we'd read our baby books together and watch some TV or a movie on cable. He researched Lamaze classes for me. I practiced prenatal yoga in his living room. He rubbed my feet. I tried to teach myself how to knit. He began childproofing his apartment.

And three times, we'd both fallen asleep in his bed, fully clothed, and I'd woken up with him spooned against me, his hand on my belly. He kissed me on the cheek. He held my hand when we walked outside after it snowed. His arm was often around me in a protective way.

I'd gone from wanting him to needing him out of pure panic to not needing or wanting him, to wanting him, to loving him. Really loving him.

I didn't know what was going on. On one hand, nothing was going on. And on the other, something was. Maybe it was just a lack of anger on his part. There certainly wasn't anything going on in the romance department.

"What's a onesie?" Griffen asked, scanning the checklist. "This says you need at least twelve onesies."

I explained onesies and sleepers and what a receiving blanket was.

"And what exactly do you do with a bulb syringe?" he asked.

I laughed. "When the baby has a cold and can't blow his own nose, you have to—"

"Okay, stop right here," he said. "I think I get the picture. You'll be handling nose issues, right?"

"Sure. Especially since you'll be handling diaper issues," I said.

He looked at me. "Um, but—"

"Diaper changing is usually the dad's job," I said. I figured he didn't know any better.

"Really?" he asked, wrinkling his nose. "But I don't know how to change a diaper."

"We'll learn at the baby-care class I'm signing us up for."

He bit his lip. "Baby-care class?"

"Griffen, you do want to learn how to care for a newborn, don't you?"

"Yeah, of course, but I mean, the baby's going to be living with you, right?"

Maybe it was a good thing that he was reminding me of how uninvolved he actually was. A lack of anger or "getting used to the idea" wasn't the same as *involved*. I needed to be careful, to be on guard. We weren't a happy family shopping for our baby registry. We were separate.

"Let's move on to the infant car seats," I suggested.

A half hour later, I chose my car seat. Registry gun in hand, Griffen zapped the wrong one.

Fifteen minutes later, he zapped the wrong bouncy seat. A half hour later, the wrong playpen.

"Griffen, if this is a little too much for you, I totally understand," I said. "We can go. I can come back with my sisters or my friends or Danielle from work. Any of them would love baby registry shopping. Really. I know this probably isn't a guy's idea of a fun Saturday afternoon."

I wondered if a father in love would enjoy an afternoon in Baby Bonanza. Based on the expressions of the men trailing behind women, that didn't seem to be the case.

I pretended great interest in a display of crib mirrors so that he wouldn't see that I was perilously close to tears.

I mean, the baby's going to be living with you, right?

"Griffen, my father and his bride-to-be are having an engagement party on New Year's Eve. I don't know if you have plans, but, it would be great if you could come. You could meet my dad and my sisters, and—"

"Uh, I'm really sorry, but I made some tentative plans for New Year's Eve," he said. "So I don't know if I'll be able to make it."

"Oh."

The symbolism was important to me. If we spent New Year's Eve together, we would be starting off the new year together, regardless of how "un" things were between us. Unformed. Unsaid. Unanything.

Twenty minutes later, he zapped at the wrong crib.

"Griffen, let's just go," I said.

He took the checklist and put it down on top of a changing table, a very nice one, and then put the registry gun on top of that. And then he put his arms around me and pulled me into a hug.

I melted against his body and hugged him back. "Oh, Griffen," I said. "This feels so good." And then I looked up at him and kissed him on the lips. Passionately.

He pulled back and dropped his arms as though I'd zapped him on the groin with the registry gun. "Um, that changing table is really nice," he said rather nervously, pointing at an armoire. "And I really like that onesie," he said, gesturing at a Winnie-The-Pooh diaper stacker.

He wouldn't be coming to the engagement party. He wouldn't be spending New Year's Eve with me.

I grabbed the registry gun, pointed it at his chest and zapped.

Griffen took a deep breath and mouthed *I'm sorry. I'm really sorry.*

I burst into tears.

"Oh, honey," said a very pregnant woman. "It'll pass, really. Your hormones go crazy, make you cry right in the middle of the changing table aisle, the frozen food aisle in supermarkets, at work, on the street, wherever. And then a few months into being a new mama, your hormones go back to normal."

"Whew!" Griffen said. "It's just hormones!"

"Right," I said, trying desperately to smile. "It's just hormomes."

Smiles frozen on both our faces, we continued on, zapping at one of everything.

I wasn't sure if it was the meatball parmagiana hero I'd had for lunch or morning sickness, but for the third time this week, I'd been overcome with nausea and had to run to the bathroom at work. Perhaps it was all the snacking. Christmas was four days away, and the amount of holiday cookies, cakes, chocolate and other edible treats in the office was amazing. Writers, agents, advertising agencies and God knew who else sent goodies by the sackful, and I couldn't resist.

When I came out of the stall, there was Astrid, freshening her trademark dark red lipstick. She eyed me in the mirror.

"I've just had a brainstorm, Sarah," Astrid said. "I'd love to do an article on bulimia for the June issue, just in time for bathing-suit weather. Women get very insecure at the start of summer, and a warning on bulimia would be a wonderful public service. Why don't you do some research and let me see your notes."

"Bulimia?" I asked. "Didn't we just do an article on eating disorders for the April issue?"

Astrid capped her lipstick tube. "Sarah, I want you to know that I understand. The weight gain, being single, the open position for senior editor—it's a lot of pressure for a young woman. But I think once you do some research, you'll see that binging and purging are not the answer, that it's not about food—it's about our underlying emotional issues. I went through a brief bulimic period in college, so trust me, I understand. Don't get me wrong—I applaud your motivation to be thin. Thin is definitely—and always will be—in."

What an idiot. The woman thought I was bulimic, but actually approved of my supposed quest to be thin.

"Astrid, I'm not bulimic."

"Sarah, denial is the hardest thing to conquer in an eating disorder," she said, smoothing her blonder-than-blond hair in the mirror. "Once you accept that you have a problem, you'll be thin in no time."

"I doubt that, Astrid," I said. "In fact, I'm pretty sure that in time, I'll be getting a lot bigger."

"Confidence is—"

I couldn't take one more word of wisdom from this asshole. "Astrid, I'm not bulimic—or overweight for that matter, not that it's any of your business. I'm *pregnant*."

She froze for a second. "Pregnant! Well, congratulations, Sarah. You and your husband must be quite thrilled."

"I'm single, Astrid. Don't you remember adding that to the mix of why I'm under so much pressure?"

She blushed for a second. "That's right. It's Danielle

who's married. Well, well, both of you pregnant. Isn't that something. Must be something in the water!"

"Speaking of Danielle and both of us being pregnant," I said. "We've been working on an article—on our own time—about how pregnant women are treated and mistreated in the workplace. And since you've stated over and over that *Wow Woman* readers wouldn't find information about pregnancy relevant, we're planning on submitting it to *Glamour* and *Elle* and *Smart Woman*. I just wanted to be on the up-and-up about it."

She colored for just a second and adjusted her jacket. "Well, of course I think *Wow* readers would be interested in *any* subject that deals with women's rights. I'd love to read it and be granted first consideration."

"Great," I said. "I'll leave a copy in your in-box."

She smiled her fake smile and left the bathroom, but her sickening perfume overpowered me, and I had to clutch the sink for support. I heard the door whoosh open and I thought it was Astrid again, but it was Carol, the copy editor.

"Sarah, Danielle's water just broke!" she said. "Help!"

I ran back to Danielle's cubicle, and there she was, sitting on the floor with her legs spread. There was no puddle of water, at least that I could see.

"Okay, Danielle, I've called Mark," Carol assured her. "He's heading to the hospital now."

"Sar-ah, can…you go…ahhhhh…ahhhhh…with me," Danielle asked in between pants. "Pleeeeeeease. Ahhhhhhhhhhhhhha!"

"Carol, tell Astrid I'm taking Danielle to the hospital, and if she's curious, no, we're not coming back today."

Someone was holding the elevator for us. In moments, I had a moaning Danielle in a speeding taxi.

"Don't leave meeee…ahhh!…ahhhhhh, Sar-ahhhhh,

please!" Danielle scream-panted. "Our families are both so far away, and no one expected me to go into labor a month early," she rushed on. "Ahhh! Ahhhhhhhhh!"

"Is she going to have the baby in the cab?" the taxi driver asked nervously, his eyes darting to me and the road.

"Just drive, buddy," I said. "Fast. But be careful!"

"Sar-ahhhh," Danielle moaned. "Mark is…ahhhh! Ahhhh! Going to be a…a..aaaaaaaaaaaaa…a wreck…in the delivery roooooom ahhhhhh! Staaaaaaaaaaay, pleeease!"

And so I did.

Once she was more comfortable, the effects of her epidural working nicely, I told her all about my bathroom conversation with Astrid and that I wouldn't be surprised if a huge bouquet of flowers arrived for her tomorrow morning from *Wow.* Danielle beamed in between contractions.

At three o'clock in the morning, Danielle Ann gave birth to a baby girl, six pounds, twelve ounces. Her husband got a little faint from all the screaming, so I took over as videographer. I wouldn't have to buy *But I Don't Know How To Give Birth!* after all.

"Attention, everyone!" Astrid announced the next day at *Wow*'s staff meeting. "I have some big announcements to make. First, I'm thrilled to report that Danielle gave birth very early this morning to a healthy baby girl!" Astrid tried to adopt a warm and fuzzy expression, but she failed. "Okay, listen up," she said with her trademark snaps for attention when everyone started buzzing about the weight and length and how many hours Danielle was in labor. "I'm also thrilled to report that Danielle and Sarah wrote a truly fabulous exposé on how pregnant women are treated in the workplace, and that we will absolutely publish it in an upcoming issue."

My mouth dropped open.

"In fact," Astrid went on, "after sharing the article with Human Resources this morning, Sarah, I decided that you should even go a little farther, interview a few other pregnant women at many different types of workplaces."

Ah, so Astrid and the powers-that-be were scared of our little article. They should be.

"Sarah, come see me after the meeting and we'll discuss the revisions I want," Astrid added, fake smile on me. A moment later she was back to her usual witchy self, yelling at Carol for a fact-checking error (in front of everyone, of course) and killing a story she'd approved yesterday, her favorite thing to do.

After the meeting, I practically skipped to her office.

"My star writer!" she exclaimed. "Have a seat, Sarah. Would you like a glass of water?"

I was going to milk this for everything it was worth. "Yes, actually, I would. With a twist of lemon. Cravings!"

She smiled tightly and buzzed her assistant.

"Sarah, I'm pleased to announce that I'm promoting both you and Danielle to senior editor. For now, the two of you will share the job. You'll perform the duties of the job until she returns from maternity leave, and then she'll handle it when you go. Once you're back, the job will be defined for two people."

Yes! Yes! Yes!

"In fact," she said, "I was thinking that you and Danielle—once she's back from her leave—would like to do columns on the pregnant woman's perspective—married and pregnant, single and pregnant. Just an idea, of course."

She looked absolutely sick, and I realized none of this

was her idea. Our article had made her nervous enough to show HR, and they'd been nervous enough about potential lawsuits and bad press to give us the moon.

"That sounds great, Astrid. Wow, my own column!"

"Yes, just great," she said, pulling at the collar of her shirt.

As Astrid twittered on about pregnancy and how it affected all women, I calculated my new salary.

And beamed.

20

Ally

The sperm donor catalog at Womanlyhood, a reproductive services center in Midtown, was much like the profiles on FindAMate.com. I could choose everything I wanted in a donor, from height to hair color to weight to eye color to profession. Graduate students were there aplenty. Sarah, who sat on my left rubbing her foot with one hand and flipping through a catalog with the other, was partial to a six-foot-two Scandinavian chemical engineering student with gray-blue eyes, blond hair. Zoe, on my right, was still marveling about how many poets donated sperm.

"Too bad you can't mix the soul of the poet with the responsibility of the engineering student," Sarah said, flipping through the donor book.

"Actually, they both sound great," Zoe said. "They all sound great. How does anyone choose?"

"Pretty much that way," said Womanlyhood's director. She leaned forward in her swivel chair behind her desk. "If you're very short, you can pick a very tall donor. If you're very left-brained, you can choose someone very right-brained. But all this is really the final step. Right now, it sounds like Ally here is exploring all her options."

And I was. At this point, I was at the researching stage. But I definitely had learned my lesson about choosing anyone based on looks or how he "sounded."

Rupert hadn't sounded like my type, and he was turning into one of the best friends—and lovers—I'd ever had. Me, with a man who went to journal-writing seminars on long weekends? Me, with a man who spent two hours in the kitchen cooking elaborate dinners—and for just the two of us? Me, with a man my family described as "incredibly nice"?

And he was. Between Thanksgiving night and now, which spanned a few weeks, the two of us had spent a lot of time together. We walked, we talked, we made love, we visited museums and city hot spots, we sat on cold benches in Central Park eating hot dogs. Emotionally, Rupert and I were in very similar places. It was like having my own personal support group.

I collected the literature from Womanlyhood, and my sisters and I headed to the elevator bank.

"Thanks for inviting us to come with you," Zoe said. "I don't mean to get all gooey and sappy, but I'm really happy to be a part of such a major decision and event in your life."

I slung an arm around her. "And I'm really happy you feel that way, kid, because I've already signed you up for future baby-sitting duty."

"Count me in," she said. "Wow, Ally. I can't believe how much your life has changed in such a short period of time."

Me either. A few days ago, I'd been practicing a few of the yoga positions Zoe had taught me (I'd gotten out of shape from avoiding gyms and Pilates instructors) when Sarah had come into the bedroom with my mail, which got forwarded from the house in Great Neck. I'd recognized the law firm Andrew used and slit open the envelope while in my pretzel pose, or whatever it was called, and breathing my breathing exercises, and the divorce papers inside had absolutely zero effect on me. I breathed in and out, my heartbeat didn't skip or jump. I simply was glad that he'd initiated so I wouldn't have to. He'd added a note which said he was willing to go no contest, a fifty-fifty split on the house, which we'd bought together, and a fifty-fifty split on the furniture, unless we both wanted the same thing, which was doubtful since we had completely different taste and he could have anything plaid or leather, which I'd always hated. I'd put the papers back into the envelope without breaking my position, wrote Send to My Lawyer on the envelope and hopped into a downward dog.

Speaking of My Lawyer, that was about to change too. Kristina and I were in talks to hang our own shingle, and as part of our benefits package, we were planning to include a day care center for our support staff's children. Funwell and Funwell could kiss my ass, in about two or three months, once Kristina and I worked out the details.

"What about getting pregnant the old-fashioned way?" Sarah asked, patting her five-month-pregnant belly as we stepped into the elevator. "Who knows what will happen between you and Rupert—you could be married and pregnant in six months."

"The key words are *who knows,* Sarah," I said. "I can't put my dream on hold for a man or for a maybe. I've done that. Things between Rupert and me are great, but I want a baby more than I want anything in the world, and I want to start the ball rolling."

"Even if it affects the relationship?" Zoe asked.

"If it does, then Rupert isn't the man for me, is he?" I said.

"Nope, he's not," Zoe said.

"No siree," added Sarah.

"I want a man to enhance my life, not *make* my life," I thirded. And it was true. I no longer needed a man, needed anyone to make me feel like a woman, like a person. And I didn't need a husband to give me a child. I only needed to *love.*

And I needed a house, a house of my own, which was also in the works. It was a stone cottage with three bedrooms, a lot of light and a view of the Hudson, and I would take possession on New Year's Day.

It would be the best New Year's of my life.

Zoe

As I headed toward Annie's restaurant, where I was meeting my mother and Daniel for New Year's Eve brunch, I saw two guys checking out a woman who was bent over, rummaging through her big toile bag on the bench in front. They were staring at her ass.

Oh God. It was my mother.

One of the guys whistled, and my mother turned around and smiled. Confusion crossed both guys' faces and they resumed walking.

"They like the package, but not the years," my mother said as I approached. "Their loss!" She enfolded me in a hug. "The Sally Jesse producers would be thrilled."

"Huh?" I asked as we sat down inside and ordered coffee and orange juice.

"Yesterday, a man and a woman who said they were from the show stopped me on the street and asked if I wanted to be on the show, if I had a daughter or son or husband who thought I looked and dressed too sexy."

Oh God. Was my mother going to be on the Sally Jesse Raphael show?

"And you said?"

My mother sipped her juice, leaving a pink rim on the white mug. "I said I did indeed have a daughter who thought I should look and dress my age, but that I liked my look just fine. I asked them why they thought anyone would have a problem with how I looked in the first place."

"And what did they say?" I asked.

"They said that when a person didn't look and dress the way they were supposedly supposed to look—" she made quote marks above her ears "—it made people uncomfortable. Unable to catalog, classify, put away as this or that."

"I guess that's true," I said. "I would like to catalog you as my fifty-year-old mother, in a wool tunic and flowing pants and sensible shoes."

"Why, Zoe?" she asked.

"Because…"

"Because why, honey?"

"I don't know." And I didn't, suddenly. "Well, actually, I guess because you went so overboard when Dad left. Yes, you always looked younger and dressed younger, but a year ago, you went crazy with it. Got Botox and little plastic surgeries. You turned fifty and stopped the clock."

"And that's a bad thing?" she asked.

Was it?

"So I'm supposed to accept that I'm fifty and age gracefully, whatever that means?" she continued. "I'm supposed to cut my hair and mute the makeup and not wear tight jeans, even though I have a great body? I'm supposed to look like how other people think I should look, instead of how I feel inside?"

"How do you feel inside?" I asked.

"I don't feel like a jilted woman, not anymore," she said. "Yeah, Zoe, I did. And yes, I went a little crazy with the dieting and exercising and Victoria's Secret catalog clothing when your father walked out on me. But so what? What does any woman do when she gets hurt? When her heart is broken? Some eat, some go on vacations, some lie under the covers for a few months. I decided to focus on the outside so that at least I could get some positive reinforcement."

"And did it help?" I asked.

"Yes, it absolutely did. Your father's leaving me for a woman half my age made me feel like total shit, Zoe. Like an old hag. I knew I wasn't. I knew I didn't look my age, but I needed to focus on it for myself. Not for him, not for anyone else. For me. And it worked. I was fine over the past three, four months."

"You came here to 'destroy his and that child's life' or don't you remember, Mom."

"Zoe, your father sent me an engagement announcement with a personalized note that said, 'See, I didn't leave you in vain.' Yes, I flipped for a little while. Gross insensitivity will do that to a person."

She was right. She was absolutely right. About everything.

I took her hand. "If we went on the Sally Jesse show, Mom, I would tell all of America that you look absolutely great and that everyone, including me, should mind their own business."

"Now, that's my girl," she said.

"I'm sorry I gave you such a hard time," I said. "It's taken me a while to see that people should be allowed to be who they are. No one should change for someone else."

"That's right, honey. No one should."

"All this time I thought you were changing to get Dad back, but I didn't realize you were changing for yourself. There's a fine line there."

"It must be like the dates you critique," she said. "Do people want to change their behavior or attitudes or how they come across because it's truly not working for them, or because it's not working for other people?"

"Exactly. It's hard to answer that, and I guess even the person doesn't really know at the time."

"Well, you know what they say about hindsight."

"Hindsight would have made Zoe say yes to me in junior high," Daniel said.

We both turned, and there Daniel was, looking absolutely irresistible in his sweater and jeans.

My mother beamed at him. "I always liked you, Danny Marx."

He beamed back at her. "If the waiter comes, will you order me the French toast?" he asked, then excused himself to the bathroom.

"I told you Charlie wasn't the one," my mother said. "A mother knows."

I laughed. "Maybe I'll start listening to you a little more."

The waiter did indeed come, and we ordered a brunch feast. "You'll have to do that from three thousand miles away," she said. "I'm going home tomorrow. It's one of the reasons why I wanted to see you today. To say goodbye—not that I saw you much while we were both here. I needed to come to grips with some things, Zoe. That's why I kept my distance. But I have come to grips and now I'm ready to go home."

"I'm so happy, Mom. I really am."

"I know," she said. "And I think one of those reasons has to do with the very cute guy coming this way."

Daniel put his hands on my shoulders, bent down to kiss me on the cheek with a pucker sound, then sat.

"Well, this amazing guy *and* school," I told her. "I'm applying to grad school programs for the spring. I'm finally going to get the master's I started four years ago."

"Good," she said. "I know that's important to you."

"And thanks to Sarah, I'll be paying for it by writing a monthly dating column for *Wow Woman*. Isn't that amazing?"

"*You're* amazing, Zoe. You're a great kid. I'm glad that you and your sisters got to spend this time together. If I could ever spend some time with them, I'd do a lot of apologizing. I wasn't exactly stepmother of the year. I wasn't even a nice person to them. And they were just kids. I'll always be ashamed about that."

"I don't know what I would have done without them these past few months," I said. "I'm not sure how I survived all these years without my sisters as my best friends. That's what they've become."

"Well, maybe when I come visit you," she said, "I can spend some time with them too. If they'll let me."

I smiled. Sarah and Ally had both changed so much over the past few months that I had a feeling they'd add forgiving my mother to their Why The Hell Not lists.

"You'll be okay in California without me?" I asked.

"Silly girl," she said, grabbing my hand and placing it flat over her heart. "You're always *here.* Distance means nothing."

I threw my arms around her. "I love you, Mom."

"I love you too, Zoe."

"Aw, shucks," Daniel said. "I love you guys too. Actually," he added, looking at me, "you, I just *like.* I don't love you at all. Not one bit. Not one single iota."

"I love you too, Daniel," I said.

His smile filled my heart. "Did you hear that, Mrs. Solomon?" Daniel said. "She loves me."

"I raised a smart girl," my mother said. "And you can call me Judith or *Ms. Gold* from now on. I'm taking back my maiden name."

My mouth dropped open. For my entire life, my mother's identity had been wrapped up in being Bartholomew Solomon's wife. Tonight, or tomorrow at the engagement party, I would make sure my father knew that I was done holding his love for Giselle over his head.

"I think Ms. Gold sounds sexy, don't you?" my mother asked.

Daniel and I both clapped.

22

Sarah

Sixty or seventy of my father's and Giselle's closest friends and relatives were packed into the apartment, celebrating the occasion of their engagement and New Year's Eve. Giselle looked amazing in a long, slinky ivory dress, her wild blond curls flowing down her shoulders, and my father, tanned and decked out in a tuxedo, was clinking champagne glasses and beaming from room to room.

Zoe and Daniel were holding hands and making out when they thought no one was looking, and Ally and Rupert were feeding each other cake and fingering dots of icing off the sides of each other's mouths and looking into each other's eyes and arguing the finer points of the Atkins diet versus the Zone.

"Speaking of the Zone, Sarah," my father said, taking my hand and leading me to a quiet corner by the window, "you're either way out of the Zone or pregnant. And I'll bank on pregnant."

"I guess it's pretty obvious now, huh?" I said.

He nodded. "I wasn't sure whether or not I should say

anything until you chose to tell me yourself, but it was getting obvious and you weren't telling me, so…"

"I'm sorry, Dad," I said. "I've been wanting to tell you, but I guess I felt funny."

"Funny? Why? It's great news, sweetheart."

"I guess because I didn't exactly plan it this way, to be pregnant and single, and…" I trailed off.

"And what, Sarah? What?"

He was looking at me, really looking at me, and waiting for an answer. I could either tell him the truth or I could just say I didn't know or that I was embarrassed or something, which wasn't true.

"I didn't tell you because I didn't think you'd respond the way I wanted you to."

He flinched. "And did I respond okay?"

"You responded the way I thought you would," I said. "By saying that it was great news."

"Okay, now I'm confused. What did you want me to say?"

All of a sudden, I realized how stupid what I was about to say was, how ridiculous it sounded. Did I really want my father to go ape on me about being pregnant and unable to take care of myself?

"I guess I wanted you to be scared for me," I said. "Instead of happy— Oh God, that's so backwards."

"Sarah, I'm not scared for you. I never would be. Because no matter what, I know you'll be fine. And I know that because you're a strong, smart person, and because you've got me as backup. How could you ever go wrong?"

"But, Dad—"

"But Dad what? Am I wrong?"

"Well, no, but—" He wasn't wrong, but—

But he was who he was. And I did have him as backup. And the pregnancy was great news.

"I'm due in mid-May," I said.

May. Four months away.

He pulled me into a hug. "Congratulations, sweetheart. May, huh?" he said, tipping my chin up to look at him. "Your mom was a May baby."

I smiled. "I know."

"That's just terrific, Sarah. Really terrific. Congratulations, honey."

"Thanks, Dad," I said.

"Your mom would be thrilled to know that you're expecting, Sarah. She always used to talk about you and Ally having children some day, all the grandchildren she would have. She liked to talk about sitting in a rocker on a porch and knitting while her grandchildren scampered around the yard."

"You don't think she'd feel funny about me not being married?" I asked.

He shook his head. "Your mom raised you and Ally to be strong, independent women. I think your mom would be overjoyed for you. And I think she would know that anything you needed, you'd only have to ask me for and you would have it. Anything, Sarah."

"I know, Dad."

"Do you?" he asked. "Do you, really?"

I looked at him, at this almost-stranger who was my father, and I realized that I did know. He wasn't there the way I wanted him to be, he never had been, but when I did have a need, it was fulfilled. He'd opened his home to me, no questions asked. Allowed me my privacy.

"You just need to ask, Sarah. If you need anything. I'm not the sharpest tool in the shed when it comes to anticipating needs. But I'm pretty good at giving."

"You are, Dad," I said, and I meant it. "Thank you.

Thank you very much. I've really appreciated living here for the past few months. I know I haven't told you so. I guess I don't know how you'd know if I didn't tell you."

"Fathers have a way of knowing, Sarah. You don't have to thank me for giving you what you need. That's my job."

I threw my arms around him. I was so in need of a hug, of strong arms around me.

"Just ask, sweetheart," he said. "That's all you need to do. And if you don't feel comfortable talking to me, you can always go to Giselle. You know that, don't you?"

That I did know. Since Thanksgiving, I'd gone to Giselle countless times, to ask questions about strange sensations in my body, to ask questions about the books I was reading, to ask how exactly you did suction a baby's nose, to ask, with tears streaming down my face, how you got over your baby's father not loving you. At that one, we went for a very long walk in Central Park, kicking up snowpiles, and when we arrived back at the penthouse, I'd felt a little better.

Just ask. I wished Just Asking worked on Griffen. We'd gotten together twice since our Baby Bonanza bomb, but things between us had been strained. We ordered in chicken burritos, we ordered in pizza, we made ice cream sundaes. We watched television. But there was no absentminded hair stroking. No hand on my belly. No talking, really. And no hugs. I'd made the mistake of kissing him, of really kissing him, and he'd freaked.

Or simply realized that that wasn't how he felt about me.

"Sarah."

I whirled around, and there was Griffen, in a suit and tie.

"Dad," I said, unable to take my eyes off him. "This is Griffen. Griffen, Dad."

"The proud father-to-be?" my dad asked.

Griffen smiled, tightly of course, and nodded.

"Can I announce it?" my father asked me, slinging an arm around me. "I want to share the great news with the entire world."

I laughed and nodded. "Go right ahead."

My father pulled his keys out of his pocket and clinked them against his glass. "Everyone, attention, please!" And everyone hushed up. "I have a very special announcement to make. I'm not only going to be a husband, I'm going to be a grandfather. My little girl is expecting in May!"

As everyone cheered and clapped, Griffen took my hand and squeezed it.

Maybe zapping at him with the registry gun had worked, after all.

That night, with a half hour left of the year, I decided to test the asking and registry zapping theories. Griffen and I were sitting on his sofa, watching Dick Clark and trying out the new heartbeat monitor he'd bought me as a New Year's gift.

"Isn't it great?" Griffen said. "The station taped a segment on baby products to air next week, and I ran out and got this for you. You can listen to the baby's heartbeat all you want, and then you can also use it after the baby is born. You put one monitor in the nursery and the other wherever you are, and you can hear every peep."

Ask. Ask. Ask.

"You know what I want to hear?" I said.

"What?"

"That you came tonight, to the engagement party, for a reason."

He glanced at me, then began fiddling with the heartbeat monitor. "I came because you asked me to. Because it was a special occasion for your family and I knew it was important to you that I meet your dad and his fiancée and your sisters."

"Oh."

"Sarah, I have no idea what you're getting at. It was important to you that I come, meet your family, so I came. End of story."

End of story. It couldn't be. This couldn't be it, what our relationship was going to be like.

"Griffen, what I need to hear from you is that this isn't enough for you, that you want more," I said. "You seem to go back and forth, but you seem to want to be here, to be with me. I need you to take that leap, Griffen."

"Sarah—"

Oh God. There it was again. The same *Sarah* in the same nervous tone with the same Lord, Help Me expression as in the restaurant on my birthday almost three months ago.

"I want more, Griffen," I said. "This nameless thing we're doing, it's not enough. The mixed signals are killing me. We sleep spooned together, but don't kiss. We hug, but not too tightly. We're seeing each other, but not dating. I want more. I *need* more."

"But—"

"No, Griffen. No buts. If you're going to commit to me, then commit to me. But I can't handle this limbo or whatever we're doing."

"This so-called limbo thing we're doing is working very well," he said. "Things are really nice just as they are."

"What does that mean?" I asked. "What kind of guy mumbo-jumbo is that? No, I take that back—I won't generalize. What kind of Griffen crap is that?"

"Crap? It's crap to say that I'm happy with things as they are? That our relationship is going well and let's just keep going?"

"Doesn't this remind you of another conversation we had back in October?"

He looked at me and shook his head. "What do you want? A marriage proposal?"

I stood up and walked to the window and played with the curtain. Was that what I wanted?

"I don't want you to propose to me because I'm pregnant, Griffen."

"So what do you want?" he asked. "What exactly are you asking me for?"

I want you to propose because you love me.

But I couldn't say it. I couldn't ask for that. Either he did or he didn't, but you didn't ask someone to love you. Did you?

"See, you don't even know," he said.

Oh God. Oh God. Oh God.

"I'm sorry, Griffen, but this whatever that we're doing, it's just not good enough."

And it wasn't. For me or for the baby. There was no such thing as a part-time father and I wouldn't let there be a part-time boyfriend.

"I'm going to go," I said, taking my coat.

"Sarah, c'mom," he said. "Can't we just—"

"Just what? Be friends who sometimes kiss? Be friends even though I'm in love with you?"

He bit his lip. "Sarah—"

"Goodbye, Griffen."

He froze. "What does *that* mean?"

"It means I'm leaving now," I said.

"But—"

"Ah, it's not so much fun to not know what someone means, huh?" I interrupted. "To not know where you stand."

"Sarah, things have been so nice," he said. "Can't we just keep on the way we've been going?"

"We could if I didn't want more than friendship," I said. "If I didn't love you. Do you hear me? I'm telling you I love you."

He took both my hands. "I hear you," he said. "And it means a lot—"

"If you say thank you, I'll punch you in the nose, Griffen, I swear I will."

"I wasn't going to say thank you. I just don't know what to say right now."

"You never do," I said. "And that's why I'm leaving. We can be friend*ly,* Griffen. But not *friends,* not like this. Not this buddyship where we fall asleep curled around each other. Where we spend practically every spare moment together. Where we spend hours discussing baby names. I can't handle it. I need what I need."

"Sarah, please."

"Goodbye, Griffen," I said. "I'll let you know when my thirty-week ultrasound appointment is."

I walked away, fast, and made myself not look back to see if he was still standing there, if he was about to say something, if he was going to come after me.

The moment I was outside I burst into tears. And in between sobs, I called Ally, but got her machine. Then I called Zoe and got her machine. Same for Lisa, Sabrina and even Giselle.

And then I called my father, who answered on the first ring with a cheerful "Solomon here!" as he always did.

★ ★ ★

The large two-bedroom apartment on E. Ninety-second Street was a tiny one-bedroom with a walk-in closet and a dead cockroach in the kitchen sink.

The spacious, airy loftlike apartment with high ceilings and "park views" was small and claustrophobic and had a view of a garbage-strewn tree plot.

The "must see" on E. Seventy-ninth was a fifth-floor walk-up, despite the words *elevator-building* in the ad.

I'd been apartment hunting with Lisa and Sabrina for the past three weekends, and every apartment I saw was either all wrong or perfect—except for the rent. And the fact that it would be only me and the Sweetpea moving in.

Griffen called every day, sometimes two or three times a day. And every time, despite how much I wanted that voice of his in my ear, I was polite, succinct, everything was fine, my prenatal appointment went well, no I don't need anything, you take care too.

And each time, Griffen would ask if he could come over, see me, listen to the baby's heartbeat at least, and every time I would say no. And then there would be silence, and then he'd say, okay, I guess I brought this on myself, and I would say I'm sorry, and then there would be silence and then we'd hang up, and I'd cry and wonder what he was doing.

I'd promised myself and the Sweetpea that we'd be in our new apartment by Valentine's Day. But at this rate, we'd be celebrating Mother's Day in the guest bedroom of my father's house. At least we'd have room to accommodate my getting-huge belly; Ally had moved into her new house a few weeks ago, and Giselle had helped Zoe find an apartment share via a Columbia University bulletin board with a student studying in the same psychology program to which Zoe was hoping to be admitted in September.

"I don't think you could fit in this kitchen," Lisa said, looking around the tiny narrow room. "Call the news stations—discrimination against pregnant women!"

"Just don't call Griffen's station," I said with a smile. And then his name did what it always did when I heard it: made me very sad.

"Hey, turn that frown upside down," Sabrina said, placing her two index fingers on opposite sides of my lips. "Sarah, you'll find a great place. We just have to keep looking."

"She's right, sweetie," Lisa said. "It took me and George two months to find our place."

I sighed and grabbed the *New York Times* Real Estate section. There was one circled ad left. "Okay, hand me my cell."

The moment Sabrina gave me my phone, it rang. The number of a real estate agency I was using but couldn't afford appeared on the tiny screen. There was no way I was asking my father to borrow money for the agency's fee, but perhaps I could talk the agent into a one month's rent fee instead of fifteen percent of the first year's rent. I was having zero luck on my own.

At my hello, someone who sounded exactly like Griffen said, "Don't hang up, Sarah. I'm standing in the nursery of the perfect apartment for you. I'm with a real estate agent from CitiHabitats. Can you come see it?"

"Griffen—"

"It's on Eighty-fifth and Third. Can you come?"

"I can find my own apartment, but thanks."

"According to your father," he said, "you've been apartment hunting for weeks."

"So now you're talking to my father?" I asked.

"I happened to catch him on the phone today when I called for you," he explained. "He said you won't accept any financial help from him or let his agent set you up and that he was afraid you'd take a walk-up."

A walk-up, even on my new salary, was about all I could afford. But at five months pregnant I couldn't manage one flight of stairs, let alone two or three or four. And there was no way I could lug the stroller I'd registered for up any flights of stairs, even when I got my old body back. *If* I got my old body back.

"Sarah, please come see this place," he said. "I have a feeling it's exactly what you're looking for."

After telling him no for a few more minutes, I wrote down the address he gave me.

"Just go see it," Lisa said. "Maybe it will be the one."

"Yeah, go," Sabrina said. "You have nothing to lose."

Yeah, nothing except standing in an empty apartment with Griffen and wishing we would be moving in together.

He was standing in front of the building when I arrived. A doorman in uniform with tassels gallantly opened the door, Griffen introduced me to the real estate agent, who'd been sitting on a black leather settee under a huge chandelier, and then we took the elevator to the twenty-second floor. A small health club was on the second floor, along with a playroom and a meeting room. A large laundry room was on the third. A pool was on the roof.

"Yeah, like I can afford this," I whispered to Griffen as the lights took us up and up. "What's the point of my seeing it?"

"Just see it," he said.

The second I walked into the apartment, I wanted to live there. The living room was huge, and there were two walls of windows, including a set of sliding glass doors to a good-sized terrace. The floors were shiny hardwood, parquet, and the long kitchen was shiny white with new appliances. The bathroom was marble and had Hollywood lights around the huge mirror.

The bedroom was huge. Too huge for one.

"This is where we could build the nursery," Griffen said, spreading out his arms in a corner of the bedroom. "Either a ten by ten in here, or we could do it in the living room. There's room either way."

"Griffen, I might be a well-paid senior editor now, but I still can't afford this place. I don't even need to know the rent to know that."

"It is pricey," he said. "But you'd only have to pay half the rent."

I raised an eyebrow. "I don't think the super is going to be interested in weekly pay-off sex with a pregnant woman," I joked.

He laughed. "No, Sarah, I meant you'd only have to pay half the rent because I'll be paying the other half."

"That's really generous of you," I said, "but how are you going to afford your place *and* half of this?"

"Silly, I'm planning to give up my place and live here, with you and the baby."

I slipped on my coat and headed to the front door. "Griffen, unless this is a feel-good movie or you're suddenly gay, living platonically with the father of my baby is a little too weird for me. And it's not good enough for me. It's not what I want. I explained this."

He ran after me and took my hand. "Sarah, calm down."

I yanked my hand away. "No, Griffen, I'm done calming down. And I'm getting really sick and tired of you suggesting things that you know I not only don't want, but hurt me to even hear."

"Sarah, I'm not talking about living here platonically."

I looked up at him.

He dropped down on one knee, reached into his pocket and held up a diamond ring.

Oh God. Oh God. Oh God.

"Will you marry me, Sarah?" he asked.

I gasped. Actually gasped. The man of my dreams, the man I loved, the father of my child was kneeling before me, offering me an engagement ring, asking me to marry him.

"No, Griffen," I said.

He paled. "No?"

"No," I repeated.

He dropped his other knee and sat up against the wall, wrapping his arms around his legs. "Well, then, I don't know what you want, Sarah."

"What I want is that ring on my finger when you can look into my eyes and tell me you love me, that you want to spend the rest of your life with me. That you want to marry me because of me. That's what I want."

"I—" He stared out the window.

"What?" I said. "Tell me how you feel."

He let out a deep breath. "All I really know is that I want to be with you. I want to be with you and the baby. I want us to live together. That's what I want."

I leaned against the wall and very slowly slid down next to Griffen. Our thighs touched.

"Being shut out these past few weeks has been hell, Sarah," he said. "I need to be with you. I need to be with the baby," he added, placing his hand on my stomach. "I want us to be together."

I put my hand on top of his.

"Sarah, if you'll have me, I think this place is plenty big enough for the three of us to grow together in. To be a family in. That is what I want."

"What do you think, Sweetpea?" I said to my belly. "Should we take him?"

The baby kicked.

Epilogue

Sarah

"Close your eyes," Griffen said as we arrived at our apartment door. "And no peeking until I say open."

"Close my eyes?" I repeated. "How am I going to see Liam?"

"You only have to close your eyes for ten seconds," Griffen said, "then you can open them again and make goo-goo eyes at the baby all you want."

I peered into the infant car seat that Griffen was so carefully holding. Our little son, Liam Maxwell, named for my mother, Leah, lay sleeping in his white cotton union suit and swaddled in a light blue blanket that Giselle had begun knitting for him on Thanksgiving evening.

It turned out that my father had thought Giselle was trying to tell him something by knitting the baby-blue blankie, and it turned out he was disappointed that she wasn't.

And now Giselle was expecting!

For some reason, my father was actually hoping for another girl. "I understand them just fine," he'd said.

Maybe he did, at that.

"Liam is so perfect," Griffen said, gently stroking his blue knit cap.

And he was. Six pounds, twelve ounces. Twenty inches long. Ten fingers, ten toes, and a fuzzing of dark hair, like mine. He had Griffen's nose.

I should have been exhausted, but I'd never been so wide-awake, so excited. Liam and I had been released from the hospital just an hour ago, and a moment from now, we would be welcoming him into his new home.

"C'mon, close your eyes," Griffen said again. "Do like Liam."

"Why?" I asked, shifting my hospital bag from one shoulder to the other.

"No reason," he said. "Just a little surprise."

I smiled and closed my eyes. The last few months had been full of little surprises. Like Griffen himself, for one. The first few weeks of living together had been an adjustment, since neither of us had ever lived with someone of the opposite sex, and he'd never lived with a pregnant woman to boot, and one with strange 2:00 a.m. cravings, which he cheerfully fulfilled by saying he might as well get used to being up at 2:00 a.m. anyway. We'd slowly furnished the apartment with exquisite hand-me-downs from Ally's old house and interesting antique pieces from drives up to Woodstock and Saugerties, and our apartment was now a home, a warm, comfortable, inviting home for a family. We'd built the nursery in our bedroom, and a corner of the huge living room was to be Liam's play area and filled with all the incredible shower goodies we'd indeed received, like a baby swing and an ultrasaucer and a high chair and a bouncy seat and more stuffed animals, toys, and children's books enough for six children.

"So we'll just have to have another baby in a couple of years," Griffen said.

Like I said, little surprises. We'd settled into a very happy space of excitement, of getting to know each other more and more, being happy in the moment, and anticipation for the baby and the future.

Griffen's parents had come over once a week for dinner or dessert that Mrs. Maxwell insisted on bringing herself. Comfort food meals of pot roasts and mashed potatoes and creamed spinach and carrots and layer cakes. She'd put in her bid for Harrison, her late father's name, for Liam's middle name, and she hugged me for the first time when I told her that Liam Harrison Maxwell was a grand name. Mr. Maxwell still tended to say *What?* quite often and asked just about every week when exactly the baby was due and if we knew if it was a boy or a girl, and each time we'd say May fifteenth and that we didn't know the sex.

"Sex is what got you into this jam!" Mr. Maxwell would then say and throw back his head laughing with a few hard slaps on his thigh.

"It's no jam, Dad," Griffen said every time. "Quite the opposite."

And his mother and I would both look at him with surprise.

The biggest surprise of all, though, was Liam's arrival itself. He decided to come into the world early, two weeks early, on May Day. I'd gone into labor on April 30th, in the morning, but Liam had taken his time appearing, as though he wanted to prove he was indeed a stubborn Taurus who'd insisted on waiting until the next day to be born so he could be a May baby like his grandmother and father.

"Are your eyes closed, Sarah?" Griffen asked. "They don't look closed to me."

"They're closed," I said, shutting them. Hmm, this felt good. Maybe I was more tired than I realized.

He unlocked the door. "Okay, now just walk right behind me into the bedroom, into the nursery. Okay, almost there. No peeking." He stopped, and then I heard a little whoosh and a little cry and then silence again. "Okay, open!"

In the three days I'd been gone, the nursery had been converted from a plain little room with the basics into a baby boy's dream world. A mural of the *Where the Wild Things Are* was painted on one of the walls, Max and the monster walking through the woods. The cashmere quilt Ally had bought on her honeymoon was hanging on another wall, on a quilt rod that apparently Mr. Maxwell had been carving in his garage for the past four months. Zoe had arranged all the books alphabetically on the bookshelves that Griffen had put up in my absence, and he'd hung huge colorful block letters that spelled out LIAM along the wall over his changing table.

I looked down into the crib and my heart almost burst. There lay our little Liam, looking exactly like both me and Griffen. One of his arms was up over his head, his little fist against his temple.

Liam opened his eyes and looked at me, and I picked him up and cradled him in my arms and kissed him on the forehead.

"Surprise!" came a group of hushed voices.

I turned around and found my father and Giselle, my sisters, Lisa and Sabrina and Danielle, holding her little Jessie (she'd won on the name), and Griffen's parents and brother in the living room. Mrs. Maxwell was already slicing pieces of the huge cake she'd brought over.

My sisters took a turn kissing Liam on the forehead. He opened his slate-blue eyes and stared at them and then up at me, yawned a huge yawn, and settled back asleep.

SHENENDEHOWA PUBLIC LIBRARY, NY
0 00 06 0243876 4